JUN 1 0 2023

D0481672

NO LONGER PROPERTY OF
SEATTLE PUBLIC LIBRARY

Künstlers
in
Paradise

Künstlers
in
Paradise

Cathleen Schine

HENRY HOLT AND COMPANY

NEW YORK

Henry Holt and Company
Publishers since 1866
120 Broadway
New York, New York 10271
www.henryholt.com

Henry Holt® and 🅗® are registered trademarks of Macmillan
Publishing Group, LLC.

Copyright © 2023 by Cathleen Schine
All rights reserved.
Distributed in Canada by Raincoast Book Distribution Limited

Library of Congress Cataloging-in-Publication Data

Names: Schine, Cathleen, author.
Title: Künstlers in paradise / Cathleen Schine.
Description: First edition. | New York : Henry Holt and Company,
    2023.
Identifiers: LCCN 2022052724 (print) | LCCN 2022052725
    (ebook) | ISBN 9781250805904 (hardcover) | ISBN
    9781250805911 (ebook)
Classification: LCC PS3569.C497 K86 2023 (print) | LCC PS3569.
    C497 (ebook) | DDC 813/.54—dc23
LC record available at https://lccn.loc.gov/2022052724
LC ebook record available at https://lccn.loc.gov/2022052725

Our books may be purchased in bulk for promotional, educational,
or business use. Please contact your local bookseller or the
Macmillan Corporate and Premium Sales Department at
(800) 221-7945, extension 5442, or by e-mail at
MacmillanSpecialMarkets@macmillan.com.

First Edition 2023

Designed by Meryl Sussman Levavi

Printed in the United States of America

1   3   5   7   9   10   8   6   4   2

This is a work of fiction. All of the characters, organizations, and
events portrayed in this novel either are products of the author's
imagination or are used fictitiously.

To Max, Tommy, Charlie, and Nick,
their grandmother's grandsons

Künstlers

in

Paradise

There was a time when the family Künstler lived in the fairy-tale city of Vienna. Circumstances transformed that fairy tale into a nightmare, and in 1939 the Künstlers found their way out of Vienna and into a new fairy tale: Los Angeles, California, United States of America.

Part One

1

⌒

THEY WERE TOLD LOS ANGELES WOULD BE LIKE THE MEDITERRANEAN. THE Mediterranean Sea was a sea of many tales: of Homer and his Cyclops and Sirens and heroes and sheep. Los Angeles had its myths, too, Hollywood myths, and like the villages and cities on the shores of the Mediterranean, it was blazing with bougainvillea and geraniums, with lemon trees and orange trees. But when they saw the sea itself, the Pacific Ocean, they thought it was as unlike the Mediterranean Sea they knew as the Alps were unlike the Sahara dunes. They could spot dolphins leaping and playing from the beaches of Los Angeles just as they could from the rocks of Capri, but the Pacific Ocean was a noisy, industrious sea, working day and night in the manufacture of huge swollen waves, delivering them, one after the other, crashing, to the shore. The water in the Pacific was bone-chilling, nothing like the soft, silent water in which they'd bathed on their Mediterranean holidays. And the sun—the sun was different, too. It was bigger, flatter, paler, brighter than a Mediterranean sun—a flat glaring disc in a sky that was enormous and bleached of color. It was not that the Künstlers were unhappy with their new home, so unlike European shores. No, they were not unhappy, not at all. They were stunned.

⁂

THEY arrived at the brand-new Union Station in Los Angeles. A driver collected them. He'd been sent by the movie studio that had made their escape from Austria possible. Of all the experiences of that long journey by ship and by rail, they would later recount, that first glimpse of Los Angeles from an automobile was what struck them as the strangest. The drive through the city might as well have been skippered by Odysseus, they said. It was that unexpected, that odd.

"Is it an exhibition?" Mr. Künstler asked. Otto Künstler. Some had heard of him. Some not.

"Is it an exhibition?"

Little houses like Swiss chalets, like cottages in the woods, like miniature castles, like Persian mosques, like cabins in Wild West movies.

"Novelty," said his wife, Ilse. "They like novelty here." She laughed then. "What have we done?" But she was excited. The only one who spoke even a bit of English, she asked the driver, "All is like this?"

"Like what?"

And they knew then that, yes, it was all like that: uneven, whimsical, nonsensical.

"I like it," their daughter said. She was eleven years old, named Salomea, known as Mamie. She sat in the backseat, leaning out the window, her mother beside her.

Ilse patted her shoulder. Brave girl, bucking us all up, said the pat.

But Mamie did like it. She had always had a tendency to brood; her father liked to say she was a Romantic, but her mother said no, she was too literal-minded. That was before Los Angeles, however. In Los Angeles, almost immediately, Mamie's brooding would become lighter, animated, transformed into something fanciful, into daydreaming, while her literal-mindedness revealed itself as something more subtle, something mischievous. Her grandfather, who understood her best, called it irony.

"I was born to be born in Los Angeles," she would say, all her life.

"Why are their cars so big and their houses so small?" she asked, leaning even farther out of the car window. There were orange groves and oil wells side by side. What could be more decadent? "I don't see a city. Do you? Where do they buy bread? They do eat bread, don't they? I have not seen one bakery. The trees have no branches, just hats on top."

"They're palm trees. Surely you've seen palm trees, Mamie," her father said.

"In paintings? Photographs? You must have," her mother said.

"I do not call these trees," her grandfather said. "They are potted plants. And they have outgrown their pots. Significantly."

Mamie stared out the window. "Golly," she said in English, a word she'd learned on the ship coming over.

Her father laughed. "This affectation of naivete is getting on my nerves a bit, darling daughter."

"The palm trees are quite gauche," she said to retaliate. She had no idea what *gauche* meant but she was sure it was apt.

Was her naivete an affectation? She would want you to think so, but in truth Mamie was wonderfully, liberatingly naïve. She wanted to clap her hands like a much younger child. She was delighted with the tall, skinny palm trees. She was fascinated by the landscape, dry and bright, the sky stretched thin, the oil wells lifting their prehistoric heads up and down. There were no shops on the streets, no people, no dogs or cats or cafés or museums or palaces. Just little troll houses, little troll lawns, overgrown potted-plant palm trees and smaller trees flowering above garish troll gardens. It was like a puppet show with no puppets.

✦

THE Künstlers left Vienna very late, 1939, almost too late. They were lucky to get out. So many of their friends and relatives did not, too dazed by disbelief and the comforts of just a year or two before. It was only with the Anschluss in 1938 that the Künstlers were shaken out of their own complacency. The family had lived in Vienna for a hundred years, prospered for the last fifty, and it took German Nazis invading, troops goose-stepping beneath their windows, to convince the men in the family there was no hope.

Before that, Grandfather Künstler had refused even to consider abandoning the city of his birth. Austria was not like Germany! Vienna was a city of music and love! Of beauty! Then the changes began in earnest. Mamie's school made her stand in the back of the classroom with no desk, then banned her from school altogether. Otto Künstler was relieved of his teaching duties at the conservatory. He was forbidden to perform in any concert hall. His compositions were banned.

The family left their house as little as possible that year. Mamie missed her long strolls through the city with Grandfather, though she did not argue. One day after the arrival of the Germans, she and her grandfather had been walking along when they saw a crowd of people jeering and laughing. The crowd—a mob, Mamie called it, years later—had circled around an old Jewish woman, forced her down on her hands and knees and made her scrub the filthy pavement. She was breathing hard, her face impassive, bent over the scrub brush. Two-handed. Back and forth. The dirty water stained the skirt of her dress. Back and forth. The sharp outline of her knees showed through the wet cotton. Back and forth went the scrub brush. And all around the old woman on the ground the gentiles— our neighbors! Mamie realized—mocked her. Old Jew whore, they said. Old Jew whore in the dirt where you belong. Scrub scrub. Back and forth. Then a woman kicked her. Then another woman kicked her. Then a man. Old Jew whore.

Mamie was pulled away by her grandfather. They walked home as fast as they could. Neither of them left the house after that day.

To stave off Mamie's boredom and fear, her grandfather told her stories, which served also to stave off his own boredom and fear. They developed an unspoken, perhaps unconscious, understanding during those months: they would look after each other. And during that time they became friends, even better friends.

The outside world was gone, locked out, but there were also more visitors to the big house than was usual. Men slipping in the back, men in the kitchen where men never went, men in the parlor with Otto and Ilse bent over documents and envelopes, the room heavy with whispers. Mamie watched them come and go, but they barely noticed her.

And then one night, all the rustling papers and hoarse whispers stopped. Mamie was told to pack a bag with what she thought essential. Helga, the cook and bosomy friend whenever Mamie needed comfort, hugged her one last time, both of them crying, only the cook understanding why.

And the Künstler family left the city of Vienna.

They took the train, uneventfully in Mamie's memory, to the Swiss border. Not for a minute did she believe she would never see her house again. She was frightened when soldiers or train officials boarded the train each time they stopped at a station. She was terrified of men in uniform; but men in uniform had been terrifying in Vienna, too. As soon as the train began again to chug and move rhythmically forward, Mamie dismissed the blustering men in uniform from consciousness. That instant and placid amnesia was not a feeling available to the adults, but Mamie noticed nothing of their feelings. She was on a fast-moving train. There were hills and mountains and pastures full of cows. She could hear the hollow clang of their bells.

When they reached the border, the family got out and presented various papers to various officials. Mamie sat on her little case and ate a roll her mother gave her, waiting. She didn't mind waiting. The station was busy, and from her low vantage point she watched shoes of all kinds pass by. Stockings with ladders, men's darned socks. There was such variety. Socks with clocks, argyle patterns; wool stockings, cotton stockings, now and then even silk stockings.

Hours later—Mamie had to be woken up—they were waved through a gate and Mamie saw her mother cry for the first time. Then her father cried, a shocking sight. She turned away and pretended, even to herself, that she had not seen anything of the sort.

They stayed in Switzerland with a family for three months. There were children in the family, but they spoke only French. Mamie slept in a room with her grandfather and played with the children during the day. It was summer and the children were out of school. The boy, Antoine, was a year older than Mamie. The girl, Yvette, was three years younger. Antoine taught her to play football and Mamie developed a thrilling crush on him. She watched his cheeks get red with exertion, admired his shorts with so many pockets, his tan legs. Mamie and Antoine were always together, Antoine leading the way on rock climbs, Yvette following Mamie like a puppy. And after a month or so, Mamie realized she was speaking to the children in French.

"You're like Heidi," her mother said when the three returned from a morning hike. "Brown and healthy."

"Heidi was always healthy, Mother. You're thinking of Clara," Mamie said in French.

Ilse, whose French was perfect, answered in German, "Yes, of course," and silently hoped Mamie would not turn out to be a show-off and a prig, then thought, Just let her be safe, prig or no.

Just when Mamie felt she was settling in, her family packed its bags again and took a train to Paris. Yvette cried at the station, Antoine took Mamie behind a pillar and kissed her on the lips.

"Why can't we stay?" she asked her parents.

"No place in Europe is safe for us, Mamie. There is only one place for us now," Otto said.

"America," said Ilse.

Mamie's grandfather said, "I do not like this." But he went along with the rest of them.

On the train to Paris, Mamie liked looking out the train window at fields of hay piled high into domes. Telephone poles flashed by and manicured trees lined one-lane roads. Were her parents frightened they would be questioned, their papers examined and rejected? They never said so, but looking back years later Mamie realized what they must have been going through. At the time, nothing seemed real to her. Not leaving Vienna, not the sunny months in Switzerland kicking a ball, not Antoine and the kiss, not his little sister trailing after her. Everything since she left Vienna had a dreamlike quality—off-kilter but thick with detail, all of it unexpected, all of it without explanation.

The Künstlers stayed with a Jewish musician and his family in Paris for just a week. The train they took from Paris to Le Havre left early in the morning, and Ilse and Otto stared nervously at everyone and everything. At first Mamie thought they were excited about going on an ocean liner. She certainly was. But she soon sensed their tension. Grandfather held her on his lap, tighter than usual. His beard was pungent with the smell of cigar, almost unbearable against her cheek.

When they got to Le Havre, Ilse and Otto were surprised by the crowds of American students boarding the ship.

"They must be running home," Ilse said.

"And we are running from home," said Otto.

Now, looking at the enormous ocean liner, Mamie began to take in the truth. They were leaving their world. She cried because she missed her best friend, Frieda, and Helga the cook and Muschi the kitchen cat in Vienna; she cried for Antoine and even Yvette. At the same time, even as she cried, she could not help being excited. There were four hundred extra passengers, the steward told them. Four hundred American students who would be sleeping on cots in one of the dining rooms, in the library, anywhere they could find space.

The *Île de France* was a beautiful ocean liner, even crowded with pink, rowdy American university students and gray, silent refugees. When they boarded, and found their cramped staterooms, Mamie was thrilled to see the bunk beds.

"Oh! I want the top bunk!"

"For you," Grandfather said, "I will make the sacrifice."

Back on deck, they waited for the ship to pull out of the harbor.

"Bound for New York," Otto said, now openly excited. "New York is unlike any city you have ever seen."

Mamie looked at all the people on the dock who did not have to go to New York.

"Do we really have to leave?"

"We're lucky to have the chance," Ilse said.

"Refugees," Grandfather said bitterly.

"We are lucky to be refugees," Otto said angrily.

"Oh, yes. We lucky, lucky Jews."

Grandfather took her hand and led her through the other passengers on the deck to the rail.

"When the ship moves, you wave my handkerchief," he said. "That is how it's done. And people on the dock shout, 'Bon voyage!'"

Mamie was crying again, but her grandfather diplomatically said nothing, just handed her his enormous white handkerchief that smelled, like everything he owned, of tobacco. The vigil began. They waited hours for the ship to sail. They went to their cabins and waited all night until, in the morning, the ship just where it had been the night before, they had a lifeboat drill.

"At this pace, we will get to New York faster in one of these," Grandfather said.

He continued to hold Mamie's hand, and she continued to hold the white handkerchief.

Ilse and Otto knew several of the other passengers who would be in their lifeboat if a lifeboat was really needed.

"I think your father would be pleased as can be if we ended up in that lifeboat in the middle of the Atlantic," Ilse said.

"To be in a boat with Piatigorsky, the finest cellist in the world? And as if that were not blessing enough, my friend Nathan Mulstein playing the violin? Yes, I would happily drown to such music."

"If only they could fit a piano for you, Otto. We would drown faster, but what music!"

Mamie found their hilarity offensive and said so. In French.

"Oh dear," Ilse said.

"Don't worry, little Mamie mouse. We will not need the lifeboats. We're safe here," Otto said.

"They joke to cover worry," Grandfather whispered. "Let them be."

✳

THEY did not actually sail until ten that night, when engines finally began to heave, smoke puffed from the three smokestacks, and the Künstlers watched France recede into darkness.

No one shouted "bon voyage" from the dock.

By then they knew that Germany had invaded Poland.

By the time they reached Southampton to pick up even more fleeing passengers, both England and France had declared war on Germany.

Mamie still worried about the lifeboats and the darkness each night when every light had to be extinguished to protect them from enemy ships. But watching the milky churning wake of the ocean liner, knowing that with each day they were getting closer to New York, she began to enjoy herself. The Americans called *die Schaumkronen* "whitecaps," the few English passengers called them "white horses." Mamie watched the white-topped waves from the deck and imagined they were Apollo's horses pulling their chariot westward to America.

New York City was so large and so busy she remembered it only as a blur of gray sound. They stayed overnight in a hotel, Grandfather and Mamie sharing a room, as they had on the ship. His snoring was famous in their family, but even his loud snoring could not drown out the rumble of city sound.

Then they piled onto another train for days of sky and plains rolling away together in every direction. They gaped and stared and shrank into their Viennese selves with weary awe.

An eleven-year-old girl was just young enough, as Mamie had discovered in Switzerland, to learn a new language quickly and without an accent, and she looked forward to learning English; her parents were just old enough to mourn the loss of their entire world and to be grateful for this vast new one, and her grandfather was so old and cranky that no world would do, old or new, big or small, least of all the next one. Westward they went, the Künstlers, once cultured, well-to-do citizens of enchanted Mitteleuropa, on their way to life as Jewish refugees in Lotusland.

Hot, disheveled, frightened, and fascinated, they straggled out of the train into Los Angeles's new station.

"New? This is something to brag about?" Grandfather said.

"Do you know how many Union Stations there are in the United States?" Otto asked Mamie.

Of course she didn't know. How would she know such a thing, a little girl from Vienna with nothing but a suitcase? "How could I know that?" she asked.

"It was a rhetorical question, Salomea."

"Well, how could I know *that*?"

"You're baiting me, Salomea," Otto said. Everyone called Mamie by her nickname, except her father when he wanted to get under her skin. Or she got under his. "But I will tell you anyway, Salomea. There is one in every northern state of the United Sates. Because of the American Civil

War. They are named after the Union Army. In the southern states of the United States, they have different names for railroad stations because they did not want to honor the Union Army."

Mamie remembered this conversation years later on a train that pulled into Union Station in Atlanta, Georgia, surely a southern state of the United States. Because, of course, the reason so many stations were called Union Station had nothing to do with the Civil War or the Union Army. Union Stations were hubs, that was all—stations at which trains from different lines converged. But her father, newly arrived in the United States, was an immediate patriot, and an imaginative one.

A car was waiting for the family at the new Union Station in Los Angeles. A young man who spoke no German had been sent to gather them up.

"You are employed by the European Film Fund?" Ilse asked in her stiff, formal, guttural English.

"I'm from the studio," the man said.

"Studio," she translated for her family, though the word was the same in German.

"God bless the studio," Otto said in German.

"God bless the European Film Fund. Without them, the studio would not have given us a second glance."

"God bless you, Ilse, for being in the theater so the European Film Fund could give us a second glance and talk the studio into giving you a job."

The two of them went on like this for a few minutes as the family settled in the car, Grandfather in the front seat with the driver, the rest in back.

"One hundred dollars a week, Otto."

"To write scenarios."

"And I hardly speak English!"

"Truly the land of milk and honey."

"And dollars."

"And better than any riches, we are safe."

The word, *unverletzt*, lingered beautifully in the car. They were safe, unharmed. They were together. They were alive.

"A job, and papers, a letter of employment for the government," Ilse said to the driver in English. "We are very lucky, are we not?"

"You make your own luck in this town," the driver said.

"What did he say?" Mamie asked.

"Something wise and inscrutable that I cannot quite understand."

Otto looked up the words he'd caught in his pocket English-German travel dictionary.

"*Glück*," he read. "*Stadt*. Luck City. Yes. It is Luck City for the Künstlers."

The driver took them down a winding road they would later learn to call Sunset Boulevard, and the light was what they would learn to recognize as winter light. The deep afternoon sun was low in the sky, floating red over the ocean, illuminating the ocean like fire, then dropping, all at once, behind the water, and the sky breathed and inhaled, and the fire shrank to a pink line and then even the pink line was gone, and the day was gray and steely night. They watched that happen, saw it from the American car as it glided along, saw the golden American day turn to American dark, felt the sun disappear and the desert cold rush in.

The beauty, the palms silhouetted black against the light, the sun so majestic and then—so absent. Imagine, for a moment, imagine that drop of the sun behind a large, dark sea, viewed by four refugees in a smooth, big car. The drama of Vienna had been a civilized drama—a drama of civilization at any rate, eventually of civilization turning on itself, devouring itself until there was only darkness. The drama the Künstlers saw at the bottom of the sloping road had nothing to do with civilization. They felt that this darkness, as much as the Los Angeles light, welcomed them.

They were taken to a house at the top of a small hill. Three bottles of milk were tucked into an icebox, as if they were any American family. Mamie half expected Muschi the cat to appear and wrap himself around her legs like an old friend. There was bread—a loaf of white bread.

"It tastes like a cloud," Mamie said when her mother buttered a piece and gave it to her with a glass of milk.

"If clouds have no taste," her grandfather said, "then yes, I agree."

But he ate his own slice. And drank some tea.

Someone had even left a stew in a pot on the stove, a beef stew in a land full of cows and cowboys. It was all so exotic. Everything had been done for the refugees to make them feel at home, all of it so foreign their heads were spinning. They bathed in hot water and slept in soft beds, dazed, exhausted by their train ride, by the crowded ship before that, by the shrinking of their world, slowly and painfully, the banishment from their friends, their house, their city, their country. They'd been squeezed and flattened, then released, like baffled birds, into this expansive place with its sky and sunset and sea.

In the morning, they could see nothing of the sky and sea, however. They could see nothing past the trunk of the palm tree in front of the house. The fog had settled in, a light comfortable fog that held them apart from everything and everyone, but also held them together, the four of them: Ilse, pointing to objects in the house and, consulting her little travel dictionary, trying to name them in English; Otto, smiling his brave refugee smile; Grandfather rummaging through drawers in the incoherent hope he might find a discarded cigar.

It was September 13, 1939. It was Mamie's twelfth birthday.

Her true birthday present was the house by the sea in America, she knew that. And so she was surprised that her parents had somehow found time in New York to buy her another present—a pencil case with a picture of Felix the Cat playing the violin on the cover and a ruler and pencils and six crayons inside. She used it for many years, even in college.

"Look at this," Grandfather said in the kitchen, "what is this contraption?"

"It opens cans, I think," Otto said.

"With electricity? Preposterous."

There was a phone call then. They all crowded around Ilse as she spoke to one of the women representing the European Film Fund. Mamie later learned that the European Film Fund was started in 1938, the year before they arrived, by Ernst Lubitsch and the agent Paul Kohner, two distinguished Hollywood Jews who knew which way the wind was blowing and found a way to help. They raised money and arranged for Americans, and the studios in Hollywood, to provide the necessary and desperately sought-after papers the U.S. consulate required to allow Jewish refugees into the country—signed, notarized papers guaranteeing financial support, proof that they would not be a burden to the citizens and the nation that took them in. Otto's musician friends had helped the Künstlers contact the right people, but it was somehow Ilse, suddenly metamorphosed from actress to playwright, who got the affidavit guaranteeing her a one-hundred-dollar-a-week salary at Metro-Goldwyn-Mayer Studios.

The person who called them that first morning in Santa Monica was the wife of a movie executive, and though it was his name on all the forms, it was she who seemed to run the show. She asked if they had settled in, and when Ilse said how much they loved the house, so near the sea, she was instantly reassured that it was only a temporary arrangement.

"Please, you musn't worry, we'll find a place farther inland very soon."

"No, please, we are so nice here near the sea."

"Oh dear, no, the air is just terrible there. Very unhealthy."

"Oh, but we are liking sea air," Ilse said.

Perhaps the helpful person on the other end of the phone line could also hear what Mamie heard: panic. Another move? No, please god not another move. And it was also true that yes, they were liking sea air. Who does not like sea air? they wondered.

"It's quite unhealthy, Mrs. Künstler. You have just arrived, so you don't realize the dangers."

"But many of important people of importance live in houses here. Our driver told us this."

"Oh, Mrs. Künstler, that is a different story. They can keep their windows closed. They have air-conditioning."

"Air-condition! In a private house!" Ilse marveled at America and its prosperity, but she convinced the woman from the EFF that the family be allowed to stay in the little house in the wonderfully fresh and bracing sea air that was, in America, unhealthy.

⁂

THEY drifted from room to room and back again, marveling that they were safe, that this modest house so close to the sea was where they were safe. Mamie had read every Karl May book about Winnetou, a wise Apache chief, twice, and she expressed surprise that there were no Indians around.

"You're trying to upset me, Salomea," her father said. "But I am too disoriented to respond."

They were grateful and fearful. They were full of thanks and resentment. They had lost so much. The house was a sanctuary, and it was so . . . "petit bourgeois," said Grandfather.

"Humble," Ilse corrected him.

"As are we," Otto said.

"Darling, you're such an optimist. Well, I suppose that is our only choice. Optimism! How absurd it is! Optimism."

Grandfather snorted and said, "Optimist? That's another word for masochist."

Mamie was the one who first found the orange tree. She took her mother's hand and pulled her outside to see it, to share her excitement at encountering an orange tree right there, in the fog in the small backyard on the small hill. Her father followed them out.

"There is something hopeful about oranges," Ilse said. "Their color, and that lovely smell—so bright."

"Now who's the optimist?" Otto reached up to twist an orange off its stem. "We are in Versailles!" he said, laughing. "Our own orangerie."

"Out of the question," Grandfather said.

No one paid any attention to him.

"Citrus," Grandfather said, pulling his bearded chin back against his old, flabby neck in disgust. He could not digest acidic foods. He would get pains in his chest and cry out that he was having a heart attack until reminded that he had absentmindedly downed a glass of lemonade.

In that odd, shining fog, the rest of them peeled oranges and ate them, acid and all, as charmed as Adam and Eve, though unlike poor Adam and poor Eve, they felt no shame and were not cast out of their garden. These oranges were not forbidden. They were ripe and sweet. After running, escaping, losing everything, they had found oranges. They had landed in Paradise, a place with oranges for everyone.

"We have been expelled from the garden," Ilse said, "into . . . the garden!"

There was a piano in the house, an upright piano of middling tone, but Otto did not complain. "On it, I will give lessons to American children of middling talent."

And when the fog lifted, the four of them walked down the hill through a sort of canyon and then a tunnel and there was a wide beach, the widest beach any of them had ever seen. That first afternoon, when the fog had given up and the sun had reasserted itself, Grandfather parked himself on a bench, but the rest of them walked along the sand to the waterline. They marveled at the expanse of it, so different from the narrow, cold beaches of the Baltic or the rocky crescents of France. This beach opened its arms to them. Not to embrace them. It was far too grand to enfold them in an embrace. No, it opened its ocean arms to welcome them endlessly. They took off their shoes and stockings and socks and Otto rolled up his trouser legs and they let the icy water of the Pacific touch their pale European feet. They felt small and America felt big. They welcomed the distances and the foam of the sea that meant they were so far from the horror of their homeland.

Otto did wipe his eyes with his handkerchief. He missed his lost city, he said, so far away, the fairy tale with a dark ending. But Mamie ran along the beach, following the tracks of shorebirds. The gulls had gathered in groups on the wet sand, and as she ran they scattered. But she wanted to stand on the beach with them, among them, and she ran on to the next gathering until those too flew off in irritable flutters.

After a while she gave up and stood still, staring out at the gray waves of the Pacific Ocean. They were enormous, crashing waves, frightening, really, but also soothing in their regularity.

"Looking for whales?" Otto asked.

No. She was looking for home.

"Ah," he said. He turned her around to face east. "Home is that way."

Her mother said, "No, Otto. Home is here now."

2

Mamie's grandson, Julian, was expected any minute. Carefully applying her lipstick, Mamie brought her face so close to the mirror she steamed it with her breath. She drew a face in the condensation. A clown face? She sometimes suspected she looked like a clown. Her hair was a much brighter red than nature could have provided. Bozo red? She wondered if anyone knew who Bozo was anymore. Well! Bozo or no, she was ninety-three years old, and she might as well go out with flair! Surely, after all these years sanely navigating an insane world, she was entitled to a little eccentric fun.

She peered down at her sweater. Dog hairs, yes; stains, no. She was ready. She could not afford to appear either insane or pitiful: she did not want Julian to feel he had to put her in a home or, perish the thought, take her back with him to his parents. And what if he decided to stay forever? She and Agatha had made their peace with the other's "little ways." What little ways would her twenty-four-year-old grandson have? Would the house smell of reefer the way her apartment had when she was married so long ago? Would he leave the television on a high volume the way Agatha did? Would he carefully wipe his feet on the doormat, straighten the pictures on the wall, order the dog off the couch? None of it sounded appealing. But he was a sweet fellow. Indulged by his parents, yes, but a good little heart beat inside that spoiled little boy.

She waited at the front door until she heard his suitcase bump up her front steps. She pulled at the door, but it stuck in the beach humidity.

"Agatha!" she screamed, for Agatha was deaf.

"Your Majesty," Agatha said softly into her ear.

The woman was right behind her! Mamie pointed, and Agatha extended a lean, sinewy arm to yank the door open.

Julian stood before them, a tall, skinny person, not a little boy at all as Mamie ought to have remembered. But it was a shock, this young man who reminded her of her father.

"Oh, Julian! You are all grown up!" she cried.

When he hugged her, Mamie was surprised at how much she had missed being embraced. He kissed her cheek, then grabbed Agatha for a hug, then dropped to his knees to greet the dog. Too much movement, Mamie thought. Too much jumping. She was not used to it and felt dizzy. She wanted to sit down. But Julian was up on his feet again lifting her off the floor in another hug. He had always been her favorite. She wondered if he knew that?

"Put down," Agatha said sternly. "Not gymnasium."

And they entered the house, the old Saint Bernard leading the way, Julian chattering about the palm trees, how cool it was to see them every time he came to Los Angeles, like, why should he be surprised, they had always been there, but it was two years, wasn't it, since he'd been here?

The house was the same. Outside, the shingles painted a color you might call brown or orange or maybe plum. The trim was baby blue, as was the door, as were the cement steps and their metal banister and the rusting lopsided swing that hung on the porch. Only very small children were allowed (or wanted) to sit there. Two outsize pillars narrowed as they reached the roof above the porch. When Julian got inside, he saw that everything in the house was just as he remembered it, too. The small living room had a big fireplace flanked by two cracked leather armchairs facing a couch. One wall was taken up by shelves, floor to ceiling, holding LPs, a thousand of them, surely, as well as a turntable, an old tube amplifier, and two enormous loudspeakers. In the middle of the room facing the speakers at a precise distance that must never be altered was a faded blue armchair in which only Mamie was allowed to sit.

She had gotten the house decades ago, before Julian was born, when

Venice was rough and cheap. She liked the price and she liked what she insisted on calling the "ambiance."

"You mean the gunshots?" her son, Frank, had said.

Well, she did like being in a place scruffy enough and unfashionable enough for artists and musicians and old-time residents and harmless riff-raff to afford.

"And in which category would you put yourself?" Frank asked. "Harmless riffraff?"

And she liked the orange tree in the back.

"I can't believe you're here," Mamie said now to Julian, squeezing his hand, partly out of affection, partly to steady herself.

"Ha! Neither can I!"

And that was true. Two weeks ago, he had been living in Bed-Stuy with no plans ever to leave.

Julian Künstler, twenty-four years old, was what his mother called a luftmensch. A woolgatherer, his father said. But a woolgatherer gathers wool, his mother responded, and where, may I ask, is the wool? She worried. They both worried.

Though not exactly a thorn in their sides, Julian also caused his parents to remark, only to each other but more than once, that every rose, no matter how beautiful, no matter how fragrant, has its thorns. Roberta and Frank Künstler were easygoing parents, and they thought easygoing was what all parents, all people really, should be. But that did not mean they had no expectations for their obviously intelligent and even more obviously intellectually wayward son.

"He's not superficial, I'll give him that," Frank said. "He goes deep."

"But he goes deep into such odd subjects. And then moves on to the next."

"Perhaps that's for the best. We wouldn't really want him to choose, say, medieval paleography, as a career."

"Or ska."

"Or the battle formations of Napoleon."

"That was the worst," Roberta said. She was a pacifist.

For years after learning to read, if not understand, Hebrew for his bar mitzvah, Julian studied and mastered alphabets. First the Greek alphabet, then the Russian alphabet. Devanagari, Arabic—both so beautiful. He learned as much pronunciation as he could, reading out loud without comprehending, then, satisfied with his accomplishment, moving on. Japanese, which he had recently tackled, was especially challenging. He had to give up on Kanji.

"Each letter is a whole word," he explained to his parents. "Each character is a word, not a sound. There are thousands of them. But Hiragana, now that's something I can sink my teeth into. It's phonetic."

He continued with a mini lecture that included insights into the Japanese alphabet used specifically for foreign, borrowed words.

"Do you want to be a linguist?" his parents asked him, their attitude somewhere between hope and horror. Academia was hell. There was the CIA, of course, for linguists, but that was several circles below hell. The United Nations, perhaps? Julian was in college by that time, majoring in Gaelic poetry and Film.

"A linguist? No, no. I just like alphabets."

"A graphic artist, then," they said. Not an easy career, but a career nonetheless.

Julian did not want to become a graphic artist, however. Julian was content to follow his intellectual inclinations wherever they inclined.

Thorns, his parents thought. But blossoms, too. While pursuing each of his useless hobbies, as Frank and Roberta saw them, he was as persistent and passionate as anyone could have hoped, even easygoing parents secretly ambitious for their beloved son.

"You're so smart." People had said this to Julian from an early age. "If only you would focus on . . ." whatever those people thought was important. Biology, said the biology teacher. And so Julian would buckle down and work hard and soon enough become distracted by taxonomy in biology class and soon after that begin his phase as an amateur taxidermist, his bedroom adorned with the stuffed pelt of a dead rat he'd found in Riverside Park. Or in his math class, while studiously mastering algebraic formulae, he became fascinated with Muhammed ibn Musa al Khwarizmi, the Persian mathematician who, he learned, had essentially invented algebra; then Julian looked into the word itself, *al-jabr*, which means *bonesetter*, which led him to a study first of etymology and then of anatomy. And another rat, just the skeleton this time, on his bookshelf.

He was a learned amateur in many subjects, but his interest always strayed after a while. Like a lover with a roving eye, he would spot a new, good-looking, tantalizing idea on the horizon. A flirtation would begin almost without his realizing it. Julian existed in an exciting, satisfying serial monogamy of intellectual pursuits.

His most recent temptress was screenwriting. He had happened upon screenwriting after a year of watching Japanese film, a pursuit ignited by six months of intense immersion in the video game *Shogun II* after his years of wrestling with the elusive Japanese alphabets.

"I'm copying out the screenplays of Kurosawa," he told his parents when they asked what he was doing with his life. "Word for word. To learn."

"In which alphabet?" his sister said when she heard. She was his older sister, a lawyer, married, and a mother. Her tone was sarcastic, but Julian had long ago learned to ignore her tone.

"All three."

"What an asinine waste of time."

"Gotcha!" he said happily. He rarely could fool Anabella. "I'm doing them in English in the good old Roman alphabet."

"What an asinine waste of time."

Julian's roommate was his best friend, Eli, whom he'd known since pre-K. They sat up late discussing the future, drinking too much, worrying about their lives, but not worrying too much. There would be plenty of time to worry seriously in that future about which they were worrying now with so little urgency. Julian's girlfriend, Juliet, often joined them in these late-night sessions. Someday they would do something meaningful, they were certain. Until then, Julian's part-time job at a children's bookstore and his vocation of copying the words of Akira Kurosawa were as fulfilling as any recent graduate of a liberal arts college had any right to expect.

And then, within a week, Julian's life as he knew it disappeared. Right out from under him.

First Juliet announced she was breaking up with him. Then the children's bookstore announced it was closing down. Then Eli announced he was moving out to go to law school.

So what was I supposed to do? he thought, now holding his grandmother's hand, the carry-on bag his parents had lent him dragging behind on its clattery wheels.

"What am I supposed to do?" he had asked his parents after Eli's announcement.

He had invited himself to their apartment for dinner, an unusual request, and they were wary. They sat on the couch, the cat between them, all three facing him with an eerie stillness.

"What am I supposed to do?"

He had hoped they'd say, Don't worry, Julian, we will see you through this until you finish your screenplay! We will pay your rent and continue the allowance we give you, even though you are twenty-four years old and don't actually do anything all day but of course you can't force the work when you're a writer, we do understand that.

He had hoped they would say this immediately, blurt it out in their eagerness to help him, talking over each other as they usually did, his mother finally taking over completely the stream of loving parental sounds.

His parents shifted on the couch. But they said nothing.

"How am I going to pay the rent?" he said. Hurting, deserted by friend, lover, and even Kurosawa—for the exercise had not yet yielded the inspiration for which he had hoped—he stood in the apartment he'd grown up in and panicked. "How? How?"

Still his parents did not speak. Julian could hear his father's breathing, heavy with cat allergies. But even the cat, pampered and obese, who Frank would rather have restricting his breathing than be turned out of the apartment, seemed uncomfortable with their stillness. She slid off the couch and left the room.

"Mom? Dad?"

His parents looked at each other, then emitted a synchronized sigh, and Julian knew things were not going well.

"Julian, you're just going to have to work this out yourself, son."

Son? His father the lefty lawyer never called him "son."

"These are things that happen to everyone, sweetheart. We know you will be able to weather this," his mother said. "You will pull yourself up by your bootstraps. I have faith in you."

Bootstraps? Faith? What were they talking about?

"What are you talking about?" he said. "I have to pay the rent!"

"You'll find new roommates," his mother said soothingly.

"Who? Where? Everyone I know is in law school or med school or grad school or they work for Google and can afford to live on their own in a Park Slope co-op."

"What does that tell you, Julian?"

"It tells me you want me to live with strangers! I can't live with strangers! Mom! Dad!"

They did their synchronized parental shrug.

"It's not my fault Eli suddenly decides to go off to law school!"

"It's your fault *you* are not going to law school," his father said.

"Oh my god. Not this again."

"Your sister hasn't done too badly."

"Your father and I haven't done too badly," his mother said. "Nothing wrong with the law, Julian. And why not get a writing job at least?"

They spoke so quietly. It made Julian even louder.

"At *least*?"

"Those new radio shows, maybe. Podcasts? Is that right?"

"Are you *kidding*?"

Couldn't they see? He was desperate. He was sinking. He was asking for their help. He was their son! There were no more real jobs, hadn't they heard? Writing jobs? Were they joking? Podcasts? Yeah, him and Rachel Maddow. There were no more magazines to work for, no more newspapers, publishers were merging and letting people go, bookstores were going under. Why did they think everyone decided to go to graduate school? Because there were no jobs!

"If you 'haven't done too badly,' why can't you help me? If I were rich, I would help you. When you get old and your money runs out and you're living on Social Security that won't cover the old-age home, I'll help you!"

"Thank you," his mother said. "I'll keep that in mind."

Then the lecture came. He had been prepared for the lecture but had expected it earlier, before he explained how dire the situation was. That it was delivered after he had explained his disastrous Dickensian circumstances was bad, very bad.

The lecture. It was, as always, about responsibility and independence.

"But I want to be independent, don't you see? That's why I need my own apartment. So I can be independent."

His mother said, "Oh god."

"You probably think I should come back and stay here in my old room."

"God forbid," his father said.

Julian was pacing now. His father was up and pacing, too. His mother shaded her eyes with her hands. Their pacing had always made her slightly seasick.

"You want me to come back and stay in my old room which you turned into an office anyway although why you need an office here I don't know since you have offices at your offices. You want me to move home!" He meant it as a taunt, because of course they wanted him home and he would rather live on the street. Well, not the street. But they didn't need to know that. "You want me to move back here!"

"Don't be absurd," his mother said.

"You act like I'm so entitled, but my computer's two years old, my phone is cracked . . ."

"How dare you talk about entitlement," Roberta said. "Do you have any idea how privileged you are, Julian?"

"For all the good it does me."

"My god. You are embarrassing yourself now, kiddo."

Uh-oh. Once the "kiddos" started he knew his mother was implacable. And why *had* he said that? Of course he was fucking privileged.

"Yes, I'm white and I'm male and I don't have student loans, I am privileged!"

His mother nodded rather vigorously.

"But who made me that way?" he added. "You did!"

Now she put her fingers in her ears. "I did not hear that."

"This is all beside the point! The point is my girlfriend dumped me, my best friend dumped me, my apartment is about to dump me, and now my parents are dumping me. Why can't I make you understand?"

"Julian, come on, calm down, this is not the end of the world," his father said. "It's tough, it's bad timing, but it's not the end of the world."

"Just the end of the gravy train? Is that what you're thinking? What is a gravy train, anyway? You always say shit like that. And, I mean, you act like I'm a drug addict. I just want to pay my rent!"

The argument continued. His parents said they were at the end of their rope. He had to grow up a little. For his own sake. They were worried about him sitting in that apartment day and night doing nothing. It was unhealthy. This was an opportunity, they said. To find a real job, to make new friends, to support himself and stand on his own two feet. Of course they would always be there, they loved him so much, this argument was ridiculous, of course he would find a job and a roommate . . .

Julian paced and occasionally kicked a chair leg. He knew he sounded pathetic. He knew he was pathetic. But couldn't they understand how he felt? Maybe it was good they didn't. He had never felt quite as lost as he did now. He was lost and he was as sick of himself as his parents were sick of him. And he was scared. And if they knew how frightened he was, how lost he felt, they would send him to a shrink. Not even a Freudian shrink, who would conveniently blame them. But some kind of Cognitive Behavioral Therapist who would say exactly what they were saying. Because they were right. He knew that and hated them for it.

His mother must have sensed that he was about to burst into tears. She often sensed things like that, always had. She reached and took his hand in hers and pulled him back to the table, into his chair, then stroked his face.

"You'll be okay," she said softly.

Why did her hand, her gentle touch, which he had craved the entire time he'd been there, her confidence in him, why did it enrage him? Because he was about to say: Yes, you're right; and start crying like a baby.

"You know what? Fuck you! Fuck you both!"

He successfully fought off the tears, but nothing could stop the parental explosion brought on by those *fuck you*s.

"Enough!" his father bellowed. "Enough, enough! You will find a roommate and you will find a job. That is that. Finished."

"You're infantilizing me!" Julian yelled.

His father slammed his fist on the table, making the dishes jump, and his mother yelled, "You're impossible, Julian," and Julian threw his napkin at his mother, and his father yelled, "Apologize to your mother this minute," and Julian said "Fuck off" and his mother rose from her chair with such violence that it fell backward and said "Don't you ever fucking talk to either of us that way" and sprang at him like some sort of wild jungle animal and his father grabbed her arm and Julian jumped back and tripped on his father's armchair and fell back into it and, embraced by cushions and yellow legal pads and pencils and an appalled and spitting cat, yelled, "You're so bourgeois! You're so bourgeois!" and his mother and father, together, stopped, still as statues, and stared at him with pity.

Then, in their special, slow, deep voice of liberal disgust, a chorus and echo of their hero Senator Joe Walsh, his mother said, "Have you no shame?" and his father, a stickler for exact quotes, said, "Have you left no sense of decency?"

It was at that moment that the phone rang. It was at that moment that Julian's immediate future was determined. It was at that moment that Grandma Mamie called from Venice, California.

The phone, a landline that announced callers in a shrill robotic voice, said, "Call from (pause) Salomea Künstler. Call from (pause) Salomea Künstler . . ."

It startled them back to themselves. There was quiet except for the telephone mispronouncing Salomea Künstler. Salami Cunt-sir. It had always made them laugh. Even now, they could not help smiling.

Grandma Mamie made her offer like a fairy godmother. Or was it a Faustian bargain? Julian wondered about that in the months to come.

"Julian! I want you to stay with me for a few weeks," she said. "We will fatten you up."

"Like Hansel and Gretel?"

She laughed, the phone was on speaker, and the three of them smiled again. Julian remembered how much he liked her laugh, a startling burst of sound.

"Perfect," his parents said in unison before he could respond. "That settles that."

"Cheers!" His father poured him a glass of scotch, the good stuff.

"Off to seek your fortune," his mother said. She had said that to him when he decided to run away when he was four and he asked her to help him tie a handkerchief to a stick. "You were so cute," his mother added, not bothering to mention that incident.

"I'm not four."

"Exactly," she said, smiling, raising her own glass to toast his new adventure.

Julian's grandmother was not four, either. She was ninety-three and feeling her age, she said in that fateful phone call.

"My wrist is not completely broken," Mamie said. "But—"

"You fell? My god, are you all right?"

"It's just a hairline fracture, Frank. Don't get excited. Jesus, you people are so excitable. Wait until you're my age. A hairline fracture, Frank dear. Nothing, really. But they have encased it in a plastic torture device on top of these godawful Ace bandages, and it's getting to be a bit much for Agatha. You remember Agatha, don't you, Julian? You met her when you were a little boy. My assistant, housekeeper, companion, and general dogsbody?"

"Don't call her that," Frank said.

"After you two have been together for so many years," Roberta said. "Really, Mamie."

"It's Shakespearean," Mamie said. "Well, maybe not. But it ought to be. Shakespeare invented the word *puppy*. That I'm sure of."

"I love dog," they heard Agatha say in the background.

"I was there two years ago, Grandma. Of course I remember Agatha." Agatha, he did not add, was unforgettable, a person of indeterminate age and indeterminate nationality whose job description was both indeterminate and, as far as Julian could tell, all-encompassing.

"And poor Agatha has had to stop driving after a teeny-weeny fender bender, didn't you, dear?"

"Points," they heard Agatha say.

"Oy," Frank said.

"But I wrap wrist so goody," Agatha was heard to declare. "Tight, tight."

"Oy," Frank said again. Agatha, a terrible driver, was also an impeccably medically misinformed caregiver.

For months Roberta had been warning her husband about his mother's frailty. She gave him a look now. The look said:

I told you she was getting old, Frank! She's ninety-three! I told you we should have moved her back here with us. Not with us in the same apartment, naturally, she wouldn't be comfortable, but in a place close by.

And he gave her a look right back that said:

Have you met my mother?

Her look replied: Here we go.

His: You've known her for forty years!

Hers: Yeah, yeah, yeah. Thirty but who's counting?

His: She will never leave her house!

Hers: Yeah, yeah, yeah. She will never leave her orange tree! Well now she won't have to!

His: Exactly!

They smiled at each other.

"All this fussing," Mamie was saying. "But it *has* gotten a bit inconvenient here."

In the background, Agatha could be heard repeating "tight, tight," with greater and greater insistence.

"Mamie's house is so charming," Roberta said to Julian when they'd hung up. "A tad run-down, at least it was when we last visited, but charming, really charming. Craftsman, you know."

"A craftsman? Really? Buried under the porch?" he said. There was no response except a chuckle from his father.

The bungalow was built in 1929, just a year after Mamie was born. It stood on a quiet street in the Los Angeles neighborhood of Venice, once a pleasure city, then, when Mamie moved in, a neighborhood nicknamed the Slum by the Sea, a magnet for impoverished artists. Now that the tech companies had arrived the real estate agents had elevated it to Silicon Beach.

The house stood behind a low white fence and a sliver of front yard covered in orange nasturtium. The fence needed painting.

"It always needs painting," Mamie would say when this was pointed out to her. "Sea air is very destructive. And unhealthy! I have it on good authority."

Perhaps, Julian's parents suggested, Julian could take care of the fence while he was there.

Julian, who had never seen his father or mother touch a paintbrush or a hammer, who knew they relied exclusively on the building's talented and taciturn super who trailed a thick scent of cologne, had not bothered to reply.

That night after he'd slunk back to Brooklyn, Julian's parents marveled at this almost miraculous phone call. It addressed two separate problems—Julian and Mamie—and solved them both. Removing their son from the disarray of his life and depositing him into Mamie's disarray—the perfect solution! Mamie would look after Julian. He could find a job in the movie business! And Julian could look out for his grandmother. And live rent-free. As for Agatha and the car, well, Julian was such a good driver, in spite of growing up in Manhattan and not learning to drive until his senior year of college.

"He's a good boy," Roberta said that night as they got ready for bed.

"I said it would all work out."

"Divine intervention," Roberta said. "It's almost spooky."

"I always told you my mother was an angel and a witch."

They laughed and turned out the lights and slept the gentle, nourishing sleep of the virtuous.

3

JULIAN PUT ON HIS SUIT. HE'D GOTTEN IT A FEW YEARS AGO FOR HIS MATERNAL grandfather's funeral. This was the first time he'd worn it since then. First, and last, suit since his bar mitzvah. It still fit. The bar mitzvah suit, on the other hand, had never been quite right. His father took him to a local tailor to have it altered, and neither of them had noticed that one sleeve became several inches shorter than the other. His mother had not been pleased.

Julian's mother and father were not religious Jews, but they had a soft spot for ritual. They saw the bar mitzvah as something akin to, say, Mongolian throat singing. They were "tickled," they said, that Julian had chosen to go through with it.

They said the same thing now when he called from Los Angeles to say he'd gotten his first interview. The *fuck yous* and thrown napkins were long forgiven and forgotten.

"We're just tickled, Julian."

"It's just an interview."

"Hollywood!" they said.

"Assistant," he said, "to an assistant."

But he was tickled, too. Here he was in Los Angeles, in a suit and tie, about to step into a vintage convertible. Maybe my life will start, right here, right now, he thought.

The car in which he hoped he would be driving into his future belonged to his grandmother, who had climbed in beside him the first day he arrived to teach him to use a stick shift. It had been a humbling experience for Julian, but so many were these days.

"Happy motoring," she'd said after hours of jolting and screeching gears. She thumped his arm in congratulations with the formidable wrist brace. "There's always so much traffic you won't have to shift out of second, anyway."

Julian found her in the garden now. "I'm off to the interview."

She threw him a kiss with her good hand. "Remember, they are as scared of you as you are of them."

Julian, telling himself she probably meant well though you couldn't always tell with her, waved without comment.

He found Agatha in the kitchen. "Goodbye, Agatha. Thank you for ironing my shirt."

"Tide," she said.

He smiled and nodded. "Tide." Whatever that meant. Time and tide wait for no man?

"You buy," she said. "Pod, no powder."

He drove off wrapped in the smooth reassurance of the Google Map Lady's soothing voice interrupted only intermittently by the grinding of gears. Zipping along Palms Boulevard, he felt like a young man in a movie. Grace Kelly might have been beside him. Or Juliet.

Julian and Juliet. It was practically Shakespearean, one of his grandmother's favorite words. Their breakup had been more Seinfeldian, though: Juliet would not lend Julian her umbrella.

"But it's pouring."

"I don't know you well enough to know if you are a reliable umbrella returner."

"You've known me for two years! We've been together for two years!"

"And that's the problem."

It had devolved from there. As the rain came down in sheets outside her apartment in Crown Heights, Juliet told Julian he was passive and indecisive and solipsistic and he was always late and he was getting boring.

"Boring? Did you really just tell me I'm boring?"

"Two years of listening to you, but I still don't know you? You're emotionally withholding, but you never stop talking about your emotions. I'm tired of it. You're a good person, you're sweet, but I'm worn out."

"Boring?"

Boring? He might indeed be passive or indecisive, he could not quite remember what *solipsistic* meant, and *emotionally withholding* seemed to have been tacked on as an afterthought, but *boring?*

He said, "I am not boring."

"Okay, well, I don't know what to say, Julian. I'm just sick of you worrying about what you're doing with your life and then doing nothing with your life and then talking endlessly about how you're doing nothing with your life. When you're not watching gory Japanese movies. And quoting them. 'Gilgamesh's sperm'? Really? It's tiresome, Julian."

"Lone Wolf and Cub? They're classics."

But he was even more shocked by that old-fashioned word *tiresome*. It was a word for a doddering, querulous old auntie. He felt the warmth of what he told himself was rage but knew was embarrassment. It had never occurred to him that he might be tiresome. And *boring?*

"Let's take some time apart, okay?" she had said after hours of him tiresomely explaining why he couldn't possibly be boring, that it must be her, that she must have found someone else, that she was depressed, that her therapist was giving her bad advice.

"I don't go to a therapist," she said.

"Well, you should!"

And on that unfortunate note, the relationship had, not surprisingly, ended, and Julian Künstler drove his grandmother's convertible to Beverly Hills with neither Grace Kelly nor Juliet Seager beside him. He parked in a parking structure that required him to grind the gears more than he would have liked as he made the sharp curves in the serpentine lane leading up to more curves. He arrived at his interview on time. The assistant who showed him in to the small production company was not wearing a suit, he noticed. He was young and slender like Julian and handed him a bottle of water. Julian followed him to an office where the CEO, who had gone to college with the father of Julian's best friend, Eli, was seated behind a large desk, the hills and sky of California framed in the window behind him. He asked how Eli's father was. Julian saw he was not wearing a suit either. They shook hands, and the assistant led him to a smaller office where Julian spoke of how much he loved answering phones and filing, how starting at the bottom and working his way up was his dream, how his part-time job at a children's bookstore had prepared him for the alphabetical requirements of this exciting new position.

"I told you only agents wear suits," Eli said when Julian called from the parking garage.

"I forget where I parked. There are so many levels."

They talked for the thirty minutes it took Julian to find the little dark-green convertible.

"Hey, you'll get the job, and if you don't, you'll get something else. You worry too much."

"I need two hands for this car," Julian said. And they hung up.

On his way back to his grandmother's, the helpful Google Map Lady suddenly grew silent. Julian's phone battery had died.

Julian cursed the vintage car, which had no place to recharge a cell phone, then thanked the universe that had allowed the day to progress to late afternoon when the sun was setting so he could follow it west. Venice was west of Beverly Hills, he knew that much. Or was it south?

Two hours later, when he found his grandmother's house, he was as relieved as if he had found the Northwest Passage.

"I'm home!" he said.

Later, he thought how prophetic that was.

4

Mamie began to rely on Julian almost immediately. Not just to drive her, with her fractured wrist, and Agatha, with her speeding tickets and suspended license. Although that was such fun, her grandson so proud each time he shifted a gear. But Mamie also began to turn to him for company. She had not realized she missed having company. There was Agatha, after all, underfoot, by her side, behind her, hovering overhead, too, it sometimes seemed. Agatha was human companionship, there was no doubt. They had come to be close friends over the years, squabbling and joking. They understood each other perfectly. But an actual conversation with Agatha was a journey into another dimension. There was the dog, and he was a true companion, warm and loyal and in agreement with all she said. But Julian was different.

It wasn't that he did much. He drove where he was asked to drive, certainly. He carried groceries and changed light bulbs. When asked. But he was primarily recumbent, checking his phone for messages that never seemed to come. Girlfriend? Job interview? She could remember those days of waiting for her life to begin, just.

Did his presence make her look back on those days when she, too, waited for beaus and jobs? Yes. And of the days before.

"Julian, you are so young."

"And feckless," he said complacently.

"Who told you that?"

"You did. Yesterday."

"Ah. Well, your fascination with your telephone sometimes provokes me to . . ."

To what? she thought. Jealousy!

"Jealousy."

Julian turned away from the little screen and looked at her with genuine surprise.

"I want your attention," Mamie said. "I mean, here you are."

She reminded herself of an awful old woman in some novel she'd once read who would not let her "companion" have a minute's peace. And never lit the fire until November.

"Are you cold?" she asked.

Now Julian looked concerned. "It's, um, seventy-eight degrees."

"Well, good, then."

"Grandma, you want me to pay more attention to you? I thought I was just annoying."

"You are annoying, Julian. You have a habit of wiggling your foot when you're sitting, and you pace in small spaces, and you chuckle and snort when listening to things with those earpieces in your ears."

Julian laughed. "You are not the first person to point these behaviors out to me."

"But I don't want to squander this time we have together. Time is so easily squandered. Time comes and goes too easily. If you don't pay attention, ninety years have passed by and left you behind."

"I think it's the other way around, Grandma. You leave the years behind."

She shook her head. No. Emphatically no.

Julian pondered what his grandmother's ninety-three years might have held. Mamie had been ejected from her home, just as he had. Although the comparison was obscene, since she had been ejected by Nazis and he had been ejected by loving, if misguided, parents. But other than that, he had only a vague sense of his grandmother's past. He knew she had escaped Austria with her parents and grandfather when she was eleven years old. And she'd told him stories when he was little that were probably made up of scraps of her life.

"You know, Grandma, I don't know much about the years that left you behind."

But she did not choose to enlighten him that day. She wanted to walk the dog with him and see how her neighbor's renovation was coming along.

"Then we'll relax with a martini."

Julian hated martinis. But he had plenty of weed.

"Do you ever smoke weed?" he asked, half joking.

"Not for seventy years."

"Grandma! Really?"

"I grew to prefer the grain and the grape."

And they walked down the bumpy sidewalk side by side, Mamie leaning comfortably on her grandson's steady arm.

5

Then came the virus. Like a storm, it drifted west from New York City until even Los Angeles felt its force. And the lockdown began.

So this is quarantine, Julian thought. This uncertainty, this quiet, this fear.

In New York City, terror. In Los Angeles, guilt.

"That's the problem with safety," Mamie said.

"Guilt?"

She nodded.

Julian and his grandmother were stretched out in two chaise longues, side by side like an old couple by a Miami pool. The sun was shining, the sky was a deep, rich blue. The rasp of the colorful propeller planes from Santa Monica Airport, the muffled roar of the LAX jets—gone. Julian said, "It's so quiet it's . . ."

"Deafening," Mamie said.

Yes. Mamie often came up with the right word.

Julian stared at the bright sky. My mind is empty, he thought. In a churning, opaque way. It's like a tornado of dust.

Why couldn't he concentrate? On something? Anything? But all he had learned seemed as useless as his parents said it was. Alphabets? Ridiculous without their languages. Kurosawa's screenplays? Kurosawa had already written them.

"I'm terrified, pissed off, and bored," Julian said.

"That is a perfect description of my childhood, Julian. Uncanny." But you're not a child, Julian, she thought. "Buck up, kid," she said. She reached over and punched his arm.

The sun came through the new leaves of the little red maple, lighting them up, it seemed, from within. And the smells, the beautiful smells. Julian tried to focus on the beauty of this little garden. When he'd arrived in February, the city was full of jasmine. The jasmine choked the air with its beauty. But he'd been here for two months now, and the jasmine was dead, hanging grimly on the fence, all its beauty, all its fragrance dried up and gone.

Now there were new flower smells.

"What's that smell, Grandma?"

"I smell? Dear god. I do my best but . . ."

"Not you, Grandma. The flowers."

"Well, you might have said so in the first place." She sat up. "Privet. That's privet. Much undervalued in my opinion. So airy and fresh." She breathed in. "Wonderful."

Imagine having an opinion on privet. But his grandmother had an opinion on so many things. "It sounds so old-fashioned," he said. "Privet."

"Well, why shouldn't it? I'm old-fashioned."

Actually, you're just old, he thought.

"The other smell is honeysuckle." She pointed to a vine climbing up the towering hedge of privet. Some of the honeysuckle's blossoms were deep yellow, others creamy white, each one bigger, more lush, than any East Coast honeysuckle flower he'd ever seen. The privet flowers looked weedy beside them.

Julian stood and picked a yellow honeysuckle flower and pulled the stamen out with his lips. No honey. No taste. He flopped back on the chaise, disappointed, and wondered what day it was. The few jobs he'd interviewed for had vanished, of course. There were no interviews now. There were no jobs to interview for. No production, no assistants to assist. The offices were closed. The city was closed.

"I don't know what day it is."

"Saturday," his grandmother said. "What difference does it make?"

None.

"Nothing makes any difference anymore, I guess," he said.

"Do you feel sorry for yourself, Julian dear?"

"Yes. I know that's petty. I mean compared to what other people are suffering and everything."

"Well, humans are petty, and you *are* about as human as they come."

I am the sacrificial son, Julian thought, not sure if that was a biblical reference or not, but sure that it ought to be. When your grandmother breaks her wrist and her dogsbody has lost her driver's license for speeding, the sacrificial son is sent from his home to drive the old ladies around while he looks for a job and an apartment when, all of a sudden, a plague strikes and there is no place to which to drive the two old ladies who, like the sacrificial son, must not leave the house, and a few well-meant weeks in this meteorological paradise become an endless desert of hours and days and nights and meals and alcoholic beverages stretching forever to the horizon while thousands of people are dying in the plagued land reluctantly left behind. Surely that was in the Bible somewhere.

"How are you sleeping?" he asked Mamie. "Because—"

"We don't sleep," she said. "The old."

"Well, I can't sleep either. That bird outside my window, for one thing."

"The mockingbird! Nighttime crooner. So beautifully, so many different songs. Do you remember your first night in your new apartment? I think you were three. You moved from the back apartment across the hall to the bigger place in front. Your new room faced the street. All night, you thought the taxis were driving right into your room." She shot him one of her grandmother looks, You were so cute, it said, but I won't embarrass you by saying that out loud. Then she smiled and could not hold back. "You were so cute."

"Thank you. But that bird sings so loud, all night. So, when a mockingbird mimics another bird, like a sparrow or whatever, how come the sparrow doesn't wake up and think, 'Oh! A sparrow calls to me!' Why is it singing anyway? Nothing to sing about in this world. Is it looking for a mate? I don't have a mate and you don't catch me singing all night. I would like to kill the mockingbird, Atticus be damned."

"He'll stop soon. It's spring, Julian. Give the bird a break."

"You know what I wish? I wish I was numb."

"Wise words from one so young," Mamie said. "Now pick an orange from the tree. It will cheer you up."

An orange fresh from a tree was nice, the smell did lift his spirits for a moment. But he soon sank back into whatever this mood could be called, it was new to him, new to Julian who knew his way around lethargy, depression, anxiety, the blues, fear, and sullen withdrawal. But this?

"Up, up!" Agatha said. She came through the kitchen door carrying a large, tarnished silver tray on which rattled a martini shaker, a frosted martini glass, a jar of green olives, and a frosted glass of beer.

"Ah, the jingling tray! Thank you, Agatha."

Julian checked his phone. "It's only four o'clock."

"Quarantine hours," Mamie said.

"Should I write a sci-fi screenplay about a virus that takes over the world and everyone is stuck inside together and they all kill each other, like the cats in that children's book you gave me, *Millions of Cats*, and the virus doesn't even have to infect anyone to take over the planet?" As soon as he said it, he regretted the words. Virus, virus, virus. He hated the word.

"I'm sure you can do better than that, dear," his grandmother was saying. "Sci-fi seems so mundane right at the moment."

Before the lockdown, Julian had ferried his grandmother to the dentist, the dermatologist, the optometrist, the cardiologist, the rheumatologist, the orthopedist for her wrist, the podiatrist, and, early each morning, the beach. He would walk with her and Agatha and Prince Jan up and back on the Venice pier. Grandma Mamie stopped to pet every dog, to chat with young runners stretching their calf muscles and with wizened men fishing for polluted dinners. She pointed out different types of gulls. She breathed the air with relish, wet misty air or clear air from a blue sky.

"The sign says no dogs," Julian said the first time. "Will we get a ticket?"

No dogs. Since seeing that sign that said NO JEWS at the swimming pool in Vienna all those years ago, Mamie felt a deep solidarity with dogs. She stopped her small, careful steps. She shook her fist and its plastic cast at him. "Where will it end?"

Then: "Let them try to ticket this broken-down old dame. Let them try!"

Julian had never lived near a beach. Senior citizens could park there for free on weekdays, and they were waved into the parking lot by a smiling attendant. Julian felt like a VIP at a club. He loved driving the convertible. He shifted gears effortlessly now. Traffic did not faze him, hills did not faze him, his grandmother's chiffon scarf flowing in the wind did not faze him, the sight of Agatha in the rearview mirror, always grim-faced Agatha beside the bulk of Prince Jan Saint Bernard in the backseat, did not faze him.

But now the doctors' offices were closed. The beach was closed. Only the grocery stores and pharmacies were open, and none of the Künstler household, not Mamie, not Agatha, certainly not Prince Jan, and not even Julian, were allowed to go inside either store. By order of Dr. John Jay Robertson, Julian's brother-in-law, husband of Annabella Künstler, older bossy sister.

"We don't know much," Jay told Julian. "But we do know how contagious it is and we do know how deadly it is and we do know how vulnerable the elderly are, and if Mamie isn't elderly, I don't know who is. Not to mention Agatha. How old do you think she is, anyway?"

"Agatha? Like, how old was Methuselah?"

Jay laughed, then said in his most serious doctor voice, "This is no joke, okay? If you go out and visit a friend or go to Trader Joe's you could pick up the virus, and even if it didn't kill you, you would pass it on to Mamie and it would kill her, Julian. Don't let those two old bats out of the house for any reason. And wear a mask when you walk the dog."

Annabella came on the phone then and said, "Don't fuck this up, Julian."

"Thank you for your confidence."

"You're welcome."

Julian listened to the background of sirens in Chicago, where Jay and Annabella lived. He listened to the silence in Los Angeles. He listened to his sister, Generalissimo Annabellissima as she was known in the family, tell him about the terror and death in Chicago and New York, the rising cases in California, and the frailty of Mamie no matter how tough she pretended to be. He listened to it all: what was sweeping toward him and his grandmother and Agatha and all of California was lethal and unstoppable.

The only safety was to hide in your house or behind a mask, to cross the street if you saw someone coming in your direction when you walked the dog. Walking the dog or pacing up and down in the living room, as he was now, Julian felt restless and caged. His grandmother walked in circles around her garden for exercise, like a prisoner in the prison yard.

"I like slang," she said on one of these circuits. "Teach me some new slang, Julian."

Julian thought. Slang? "You mean like GOAT?"

"I don't know, Julian. That's why I'm asking. What is goat?"

"Greatest of all time."

"That's pathetic. Unpoetic and imbecilic."

"Do you like 'doomscrolling'? That's what I do on my phone: reading about how terrible everything is."

"Yes, that's a good one. Yes, yes. I like that. Very colorful. I used to keep a slang notebook. You know, I was the translator for the whole family. I'd say, 'Gee-whiz.' And they'd answer, 'Gee-viz!' Or I'd say, 'Don't make me laugh,' sarcastically, when I'd been told something I disagreed with, and they would look at me, puzzled, and say, 'But you like to laugh, do you not?' Then I'd say, 'Nuts!' when the lead of my pencil broke or some such annoyance. And my father would pass me a bowl of walnuts!"

"I like 'Nuts!' Sounds like a Humphrey Bogart movie."

They continued their walk, round and round the garden.

"I'm getting dizzy," Mamie said. "Or as Agatha says, 'Diz.'"

Julian felt a little diz himself and they went inside, away from the glare of the sun, and sat down at the kitchen table.

"Have you spoken to your parents today?"

Julian shook his head. "I am a little homesick, though."

Mamie launched into an impression of Frank and Roberta, capturing not only their voices but their gestures as well:

"'Frank, I'd like a glass of water.'

"'There is a drought! The aquifer is disappearing!'

"'I'm thirsty, for god's sake. What is wrong with you? Get me a glass of water.'

"'Have you seen what's happening to the fjords? To the Arctic?'

"'Get. Me. A. Glass. Of. Water.'

"'Here. And why couldn't you get it yourself?'

"'The cat's on my lap, that's why! Hey, this is half empty.'

"'I prefer to think of it as half full.'

"'This glass will have to be washed, a glass that was not utilized to its fullest potential. What a waste of water, Frank.'"

Mamie went on for a good fifteen minutes. "You forgot what a good mimic I am, didn't you? Whenever you get homesick, Julian, dear, you come straight to Mamie."

6

~

During these early days of the lockdown, Julian was sometimes frightened in a new global way, and sometimes merely angry. On the angry days, he would wake up angry, the way you wake up with a headache, anger banging at his skull, so angry that his anger seared away everything in front of him, everything he saw, everything he heard. So angry that he hated the houses he walked past with Prince Jan. Hated the houses with well-tended gardens and midcentury house numbers, where did they think they were anyway, Palm Springs? Hated the houses with rusting refrigerators in the yard, hadn't they heard Venice was gentrified now? Hated the palm trees, ridiculous things invented by Dr. Seuss, not even real trees, not even native to L.A., just somehow "iconic." Hated the roses, white plump roses everywhere, huge and scentless. Hated the phlox, this was not England, there was no water to waste on fucking phlox. Hated the virtue-signaling succulents. Really? Your solar panels not enough? Hated the absurd little green lawns and hated the gravel laid down to substitute for lawns during the last drought. Hated the huge Range Rovers, hated the stubby Minis and Smart cars, the phalanxes of Teslas. Hated the crows and the hummingbirds, the fat reclining cats, the yapping dogs at every gate, the bicyclists, the electric scooters abandoned and blocking the way, the little libraries, the eucalyptus roots pushing up the heaving sidewalks. Hated the man wearing a mask, hated the woman not wearing a mask more. Hated the brutally sunny side of the street and the chilled shady side of the street. Hated the silence, hated the roar of a sudden helicopter. Little old man, shriveled and stooped over his cane walking a three-legged chihuahua? Hate.

Julian bent to pick up Prince Jan's shit with a biodegradable bag decorated with pastel hearts. The biodegradable bag? Hate. Prince Jan's shit? Hate.

He had trouble hating Prince Jan.

"But I'll get the hang of it," he told the dog.

They trudged along Abbot Kinney, a sad street lined with boarded-up international luxury-brand stores for quarantined international tourists.

"I want to go home," he told the dog.

Prince Jan gazed into his eyes.

"They banished me," Julian continued. "How would you feel if Mamie and Agatha banished you?"

They walked west toward the closed beach.

"The whole fucking world is banished," he said to the dog.

Prince Jan ignored him. Perhaps he could not hear Julian through Julian's mask. Perhaps he could no longer hear at all. But Prince Jan ignored so much, it was hard to tell. He ignored the blue sky. He ignored the man wearing a bulky down parka, shorts, and flip-flops. He lived only for dirty tissues in the gutter, for the occasional twisted cast-off surgical mask.

"But I bet you study yoga," Julian said. He was bringing out all the clichés in his rage.

And then there was Jupiter. Every night, in the lucid darkness, there was Jupiter, bright and clear, an enormous speck, unblinking among the stars. He hated Jupiter. For one night. Two, three nights. And then, there was Jupiter again, Jupiter, faithful Jupiter, right where Jupiter was supposed to be. Julian had an app that reassured him that it really was Jupiter. Night after night after night. And Julian began to love Jupiter and to look for Jupiter as soon as he stepped into the darkness.

"Look, dog. There's our friend Jupiter. Right where we left him."

No wonder people had once navigated by the stars, he thought. Stars were reliable. They knew where they were supposed to be and when.

"But we're not navigating, are we, dog? We're not going anywhere."

7

MAMIE WATCHED HER GRANDSON ASLEEP ON THE CHAISE, SO INNOCENT, OR perhaps disoriented was a better description; no, he was innocent, a child in a world run by aged children straight out of *Lord of the Flies*. And here he was with her, in her garden, protected by hedges of flowers. No one could hurt him here, or her. They were safe and suffocating. How different it had been when she first came to Los Angeles. She hoped he would feel that expansive relief someday. She wondered if she ever would again.

There were already so many other émigrés here when she and her family got off the train and drove toward the ocean. People her mother knew from the theater, people her father knew from the world of classical music. Writers, directors, composers, actors, conductors, musicians. Why did they call themselves émigrés instead of immigrants? she wondered. Or refugees. To distinguish themselves from the ordinary folk, from the ones who took jobs as maids and chauffeurs? Surely, they all felt the same anger and confusion thumping in their ears. As well as relief. Don't ever forget the relief, Mamie.

Julian's hair had grown since he arrived. He had let his beard grow. He looks unkempt, Mamie thought. But who should he be kempt for? Me? Hardly. Agatha? One does not even know if Agatha can see anymore. She never wears her glasses. Where was Agatha anyway? Mamie listened carefully. Was she resting? She certainly deserves to rest, looking after me all day. She had known Agatha a long time. But you can know someone and not know them at all. Agatha had been an acquaintance, someone she met while walking on the beach, someone she said hello to every day for years. But Agatha had too many black eyes for someone who walked on the beach and was not a prizefighter. Mamie never asked her a thing about the black eyes, just one day, without planning to, offered the back house, rent free, in exchange for light housekeeping. Well, the house-keeping isn't light anymore, is it, Agatha, my friend?

Frank had been shocked when she'd invited a stranger to live with her. But Frank had not grown up when she had. Frank had not been sponsored by people he never met, by organizations made up of strangers trying to help, to do anything they could to get other Jews out of Europe.

And into Hollywood, Beverly Hills, and Pacific Palisades we came. Looking for jobs, looking for jobs for others, making up jobs at the studios. No one was happy here at first, Mamie thought. But neither were we dead.

She looked at her sleeping grandson and recalled how hard she had worked to empty her mind of tragedy. It was difficult to imagine that she had first encountered tragedy with a mind as blessedly blank as Julian's. And so much younger. She hoped he could keep his wits just that way. Why shouldn't he turn away from the world as it was? Why shouldn't he dull his senses with sleep and video games? There would be plenty of personal horrors in his life, there always are, why should he have to watch the world now as it sickened and died? Better to plan battles in sixteenth-century Japan on a computer screen. But the world was sickening and was dying now, and there is only so far you can turn. Julian would never shake off the memory of this time, no matter how many video games he played; she knew that. She had never been able to shake off her own memories no matter how hard she tried. The minute she heard the ghastly presidential candidate attack immigrants, it all came back, though it had never left. The war, the rounding up and murder of Jews. The Holocaust. When had she first heard that word? Long after she knew what it meant. She had pushed those days and years away, tried valiantly to make it all as distant and unreal as possible, a mythical event far from her life, like the sacking of Troy. It didn't work. Of course it didn't.

But she had tried. Her grandfather pretended Vienna and Europe were still the same, the home he left behind, intact and waiting for his return. She knew that was impossible. Instead of looking back, she had carefully arranged her thoughts. Tidy away the friends you left behind, the house as it was, the streets, the crows, a color different from the crows here. And out altogether with the camps.

But what hard work. Denial was a constant activity. You had to keep at it. No wonder people said you daydreamed, Mamie. Daydreaming was your own little kingdom. Your bolt-hole kingdom.

Dear old Al, you once told me that all that denial I had trained myself to live with made me distant and cold. "Well worth it," I said, didn't I? It was not something you ever really understood, but, Al, believe me, day-dreaming has never been a luxury for me.

I'm daydreaming now, aren't I? Well, well. What else should I do? Knit?

Ha ha! said her arthritic hands.

Oh, Al, you don't mind me talking to you this way, do you? You were never much of a listener. But you're dead now, so you don't have much choice.

Look at your grandson's wavy hair sparkling in that beam of sunlight, Al. How pretty. I like having him around. Like a Prince Jan who can talk. Even Agatha likes him.

Maybe it's time I started to remember instead of this heavy labor of forgetting. Maybe you're right, Al. I'm getting tired of forgetting.

But, Al, six million.

And my neighbors, Al. They spat on my uncle, the banker. They made an old woman scrub the sidewalk. I saw it.

I'm sorry, Al, but how can I live with these memories?

Yes, I know. I have no choice. I knew that even then.

So I listened. Another kind of protection. Forewarned is forearmed. I listened to everything any adult had to say, about the war, about whether the United States would declare war, about Finland and Stalin, about terri-fying letters from friends still trying to escape. My parents tried to protect me from the news from Europe. I can still see them, head to head, discussing the war in fearful, anxious whispers when they thought I was not listening. My mother never spoke of all they'd lost because she didn't want to think about all she'd lost, but sometimes my father could not help himself. Then my mother would say, "No, Otto. Turn away from all that. It has certainly turned away from us."

There was only Grandfather to tell me about the past.

"Julian," she cried out. "Wake up!" She banged her cane on the floor. "I want to tell you about your roots."

Julian lifted his head, looked at her blankly.

"Wake up, I say."

"Are you okay?" He jumped up now, alarmed.

"I've been thinking," she said. And talking to my dead husband, she thought. "And I have to speak to you. It's very important. It's about my family, which is to say your family."

Oh god, who was sick? Oh no no no. Who had gotten sick?

"I want to share more of your heritage with you."

"Is that all?" he said, furious. "I thought someone was sick. Or dead."

"Well, yes, they are all dead. My grandfather told me about them. They were dead before even my time."

"Are you fucking kidding me? I can't fucking believe you."

"Oh, yes, it's all true. As far as I know."

Now she was teasing him, he could see. No wonder she drove his mother crazy. Roberta did not have much of a sense of humor. Then again, this was not funny.

"Not funny," he said.

"I'm going to fill in some gaps for you Julian. I've heard that some grandchildren record the wisdom of their grandparents on videotape for posterity. Well, school projects, really, I imagine. *Posterity* is such a grand word. But videotaping will not be necessary here. You may just listen. Or takes notes, yes, that's fine. You know, my parents never spoke about their pasts. It was my grandfather who did."

"My parents don't have pasts."

"Well, I do, which means you do. So we will begin with my mother. She came from a small town in Galicia."

Mamie moved inside into the cool shade of the living room. Prince Jan and Julian dutifully followed.

"The Jews in my mother's town did not wear black hats and tunics," Mamie said. "They were westernized German-speaking Jews, something of which I should be proud, my grandfather made very clear. The snobbishness of our family toward less assimilated Eastern European Jews cannot be exaggerated, Julian."

"I will never minimize our snobbishness, Grandma. I promise."

"Julian, dear, you look tired. Go wash your face and perk yourself up a bit. Go on. I'll be here when you get back."

I'm sure you will be, Julian thought. But he was pleased she was telling him about his family. He would write it up later and use it for his screenplay, *Exiles in Space*. A working title, he quickly reassured himself.

He was also curious. His parents' histories seemed to go back only as far as the 1960s, no further, and no further forward, as far as he could see. He went and splashed water on his face in the bathroom, trying not to notice the white and aluminum seat in the shower, the various old-people pads.

"Okay," he said. He took a small notebook out of his pocket with a ballpoint pen that had leaked and left a small blue circle on his jeans pocket. He settled himself on the floor, facing his grandmother. "Go."

"You used to sit like that when you were a child."

"I know."

"You're not a child."

"I know."

"So sit on the couch, pal."

Julian groaned, but he got up and sat back on the couch. "Okay?"

"Much more suitable."

Then she told him that her maternal grandfather, who died when she was a baby, was a lawyer and for a few years was even the mayor of the town. They lived in a large house with a courtyard and had an orchard of apple trees.

"On Fridays, the beggars came. Like office workers showing up to a job, they came the same time every Friday."

Mamie's mother was terrified of them. She was just a little girl, and as the gate to the courtyard was opened, she would run and hide. The beggars would enter the courtyard, a ragged swarm, and Mamie's grandmother would hand out coins and smile.

"And then the beggars would flutter away, gray as moths, to the next house."

Julian nodded. He liked that image. Wait, no he didn't. Those poor gray beggars. They were people, not insects.

"My father grew up in a very different atmosphere," Mamie was saying. "He was born in Vienna when it was still the imperial city. When he was little, he would see the kaiser riding by in his carriage. He could see him, see his face—that beard, you know? The fluffed-out white side-whiskers and mustache. Just for a moment as the carriage rumbled by. The kaiser held a place in my father's family and heart that it's so hard to understand. Franz Joseph! He was absolutely central to everyone's consciousness. His presence so . . . present! Intimate, really, yet so grand. I suppose he was like a revered, beloved uncle, if that uncle had all the family money and land. Now here's an example, Julian. The kaiser was known to travel in his carriage everywhere. He was never seen on foot. There was only one place he had to go on his own feet, people said: the toilet. So that's what they used to call the toilet: 'where the kaiser walks on foot.' Not the john or the WC, but 'where the kaiser walks on foot'!"

Julian was clearly delighted. Mamie tried to remember some other droll detail.

"Ah! Got it. The kaiser was known to take cold baths. So taking cold baths was considered a patriotic act. Guess who had to take cold baths, summer and winter? Poor little Otto Künstler. My poor father! A little Jewish boy growing up in a wealthy household. And if my father complained about cold or discomfort? The reply would be, 'If it's good enough for the kaiser, it's good enough for you.'"

This was rather nice, telling stories her grandfather had told her. The good stories. Julian was scribbling in his notebook. He understood her words, something she was never sure of with Agatha. At this rate, she thought happily, I shall be spurred to eloquence. Or close enough.

"The kaiser was a fixture," she continued. "August uniforms and homely cold baths, both. My grandfather repeated all these stories to me once we got to America. He'd say, 'It was better then.' For him, a cold bath was an obvious sign of respect due Franz Joseph, Emperor of Austria, Apostolic King of Hungary, King of Croatia, King of Galicia and Lodomeria, and Grand Duke of Krakow."

Julian said, "How do you spell Lodomeria? What *is* Lodomeria?"

"Is my name Google, Julian? Grandma Google? Look it up, boy. Now. To continue. In Santa Monica in our small, homey, lovely house near the ocean my grandfather would sometimes say sadly, 'We have no kaiser here.'

"And I'd say, 'We have a president, Grandfather. It's much better, you know.'

"And he'd say, 'So they tell me.'

"He mourned a culture of music and philosophy and cold baths. He was what the immigrants called a *beiunser*. It means, literally, 'at our.' But you get it: the people always saying, 'Back home it was better.' Like Grandfather. I did notice, though, that his baths in our new house in the New World were always piping hot."

Mamie smiled at the memory. Her grandfather, growling and puffing, his wide body bent and crooked, his gray hair, the color of steel, growing in every direction, the bits of tobacco on his lips.

"Grandfather and I used to walk together everywhere. In Vienna. Across the Atlantic Ocean on the ocean liner's deck all the way to America, and then: Los Angeles."

"And here we are," Julian said. "Not allowed to walk anywhere."

"Such a shame. Use it or lose it, the orthopedist says."

"Was it quiet then, the way it is now?" Julian asked. The eerie pandemic quiet, all the bored cars stuck at home in lockdown with their drivers. "The freeways hadn't been built yet, right?"

Agatha stood directly in front of Mamie between her and Julian.

"Yes?" said Mamie.

"I wait."

Mamie craned her head around Agatha and said, "Is it still quiet here now? I'm so deaf I don't always notice. Not as deaf as Agatha. No one is as deaf as Agatha."

Agatha helped her stand up and they began to move slowly toward the bedroom. The dog heaved his bulk up from the floor and followed. A parade.

8

In one of several rigid household rituals that did not change during the days of quarantine, Agatha rang the cowbell attached to the wall outside the kitchen door every night at six o'clock.

"Schedule for olds," she said. "Very important."

Important for youngs, too, Julian thought. Youngs have lost their bearings. Youngs are drifting in their helplessness. The idea that punctuality still mattered in these days that both dragged and rushed forward—it reminded him that time still existed. He loved the clang of that cowbell.

"Six o'clock!" he would call out, as if to reassure himself.

Agatha, a ropey, terrifying person to a child, was still terrifying. She had lived in the back cottage, the guest house, for years. Her job was sometimes described as caretaker (of the garden and house and back cottage, never of Mamie), sometimes as assistant, and of course sometimes (most accurately) as dogsbody. She was no spring chicken and had grown quite deaf. Her English, never altogether distinct, had withered into a scratchy, lurching dialect that might or might not have resembled her native language. She had moved, against Mamie's will, into the main house when Mamie fell and fractured her wrist. She was devoted to Mamie, who had hired her when she was down-and-out in some way that no one really could discover. She cleaned with the intensity and frequency of the truly compulsive. And she was an excellent cook.

"The lap of luxury," he said as he sat down with the two old women. "Thank you, lovely ladies, for inviting me to this tantalizing dinner."

"Someone is in a good mood," Mamie said.

"It's so beautiful here, it's hard to maintain gloom for too long, even for me."

Then, no warning, in a perverse show of power, Gloom returned, and Julian was unable to stifle a desolate sigh. Here he was, eating a well-cooked meal, sleeping comfortably in his converted garage "cottage," which was considerably nicer than his Brooklyn apartment had been, not a roach to be seen, still thinking about Juliet, who he knew was safe at home with her parents, who happened to live in Sherman Oaks, not that far from Venice, but who would not even answer his texts, which to be fair were both numerous and lengthy. And here he was, safe if lonely and unproductive, beneath the palm trees.

Okay, but were his parents safe? What if they got sick? Or his sister or Jay, who had to go to work at the hospital every day, or their two little boys? And Julian's parents were not young, though they did not seem to realize that, and not always sensible. Just yesterday, his father called him while standing on line waiting to go into the Verizon store because he needed the cable box fixed.

"You don't need a cable box," Julian said. "You have the internet."

But his father said, "Oh, you and your internet," and stayed put.

His mother, meanwhile, insisted on going to Barney Greengrass every Sunday to get lox.

"I thought you were vegan."

"We thought a little fish would be nice. Under the circumstances."

"You can order and have it delivered," he said.

"Oh, I can use the exercise," she said.

They were insane, he'd always thought that. But it never occurred to him that they were careless. That was his prerogative as a young person. They should stay in their own lane.

"I wish my parents would stay home. They don't seem to understand what a quarantine is."

"And you understand all too well."

He sighed again.

"You sound just like your father," Mamie said. "That sigh." It reminded her of her own father's sigh, too. Mamie had trained herself not to think of her father's sighs, to remember him instead smiling and embracing "America." But there he was, suddenly blown into her thoughts on the sound of Julian's sigh. She looked at her grandson with concern.

He sounded like her father, but with that beard he was beginning to look like her grandfather, albeit a younger, more groomed and fresher version. And did she detect that weighty émigré look of disillusion in his young face?

Mamie took Julian's hand gently in hers. Then: "Oh!"

She stared, horrified. "Oh! Look at that old claw on his young, beautiful hand."

Julian did not seem to hear or notice the claw. He sighed again, then said, "It's just . . ."

"Yes," she said. "It's 'just'. . . But remember this, too, Julian: it's *un*just. I'm so old it doesn't matter. I'm not going anywhere anyway. But you . . ."

"Me what?" he said. "Where am I going? Nowhere, just like before."

He had spent the mournful night listening to Matt Berninger and Billie Holiday and sometimes even Taylor Swift and thinking about Juliet.

How petulant he is, Mamie thought. And he is obviously not listening to my comforting advice and wise words. Offended, she withdrew her hand. Yes, you are old and dried-up, she said silently to the hand. But you meant well, caressing the hand of the ungrateful grandchild. And you are mine, Hand. I will not abandon you. She placed the hand affectionately against her cheek, resisting the urge to give it a kiss of consolation.

Then she turned her attention to her grown grandson, tall, skinny, brown hair sticking out every which way, but good-looking in his reddish pandemic beard, a grown-up grandson who was not grown at all. Well, none of them were, these big entitled American children. If the war had not interrupted her childhood, would she have grown up into an entitled Viennese child? Perhaps, but she would also have been married and had two children of her own by the time she was Julian's age. Julian was sweet, tender, a dear and darling boy, but he was not a man. How long until he became a man? What did that mean, to be a man? To be responsible, she supposed. But her husband, Al, had been a man and as irresponsible as they come. She didn't miss him, not after all these years, a lifetime without him, but she still loved him. He had made her an American. She'd gotten her citizenship already when they met, she'd had no trace of an accent, she knew how to dress like a girl her age, how an American college girl should dress. But she always knew she was different. It was Al, a white man playing jazz trumpet, who taught her that everyone knows they're different and everyone is right, which makes us all the same.

She examined her hand again for a moment. She and her hand and all the rest of her had been through a great deal together.

"You know what, my friend?" she said turning to Julian. "*You* need to grow up."

"Oh, here we go," said Julian. "Here we go . . ."

"Now you sound like your mother. Honestly, Julian, can't you pull yourself together long enough to let an old lady wax poetical for one minute?"

Julian wanted to continue arguing, he really did, but he could never figure out how to get past a certain point with his grandmother or Agatha. They kept changing sides. Better to give in now.

"Okay, okay. I get pissed off. So what?"

"Slam," Agatha said. "Slam door, so many door."

"You have no manners, that is true," Mamie said. "But you're absolutely right to be angry. That's what I'm trying to tell you, but of course you're too angry to listen. Anger doesn't help, as we all know. But it's the right frame of mind for a young man in this moment. Good for you, Julian!"

"Goody!" Agatha said. "Goody job."

How do you deal with people like these two? How? Julian put his head in his hands. His anger, his gloom, his reason, were not up to this task. Sometimes the wine helped. It flowed freely here, he had discovered. He had never had so much wine in his life.

"I, on the other hand, was properly brought up. My anger has always been mannerly." She smiled in a mannerly fashion. "You see?"

Julian started laughing. He couldn't help it.

"Good," Mamie said. "Because, frankly, dear boy, I am tired of your endless puling."

9

JULIAN DID NOT REALLY LOOK LIKE HER GRANDFATHER, MAMIE KNEW. THE
beard, it was the beard, she supposed. Because Julian was young and handsome and tall and slender. Her grandfather had been squat and bent like a
tired apple tree. And he shuffled so when he walked. But he was old, she
reminded herself. So old.

"Julian!"

He came rushing into living room from the garden.

"What? What's wrong?"

"Do you think seventy is old?"

"Jesus Christ."

"Because my grandfather was seventy when we got to L.A., and we all
thought he was ancient."

"Age is a state of mind."

"Well that is a crock of shit if I ever heard one."

"What does a crock of shit actually sound like, I wonder?"

"We thought Grandfather was an old, old man. When I was seventy I
was touring, for heaven's sake."

"And beating Dad at tennis."

"Oh, please, I could beat your father now. He has a weak serve, poor
dear."

"Did your grandfather play tennis?"

Mamie laughed. "What a thought."

She tapped her cane abstractedly, soundlessly on the carpet.

"You call?" Agatha said, appearing from nowhere. She often seemed to hear the cane tapping even before it tapped.

"Did I? I was telling Julian about my grandfather."

Agatha retreated.

"He liked to work," Mamie said, "smoke his cigar, complain about his meals, and take long walks. No tennis."

Sounded like an oddball profile on a dating site, Julian thought. But he did not interrupt. Mamie was in full flow now. He settled on the couch and took out his notebook and pen.

"Grandfather's family had lived in Vienna for a hundred years," Mamie said. "My family. Your family."

He had one son: Otto, Mamie's father. Otto Künstler was a relatively respected, relatively well-known composer who, like the old man, was decidedly comfortable in his hometown. Such a grand hometown! Who wouldn't be proud to live in the land of Mahler and Mozart? Cozy, cosmopolitan, a utopia of culture, safe as houses.

"Of course, houses are not particularly safe, are they, Julian? We know that now."

Mamie's mother, Ilse, on the other hand, had grown up in the far reaches of the Austro-Hungarian Empire. Pogroms were within living memory. She harbored a small, hereditary pool of fear that her Viennese husband and father-in-law did not. From the time Hitler came to power in Germany in 1933, Ilse had been restless and wary. Otto and his father thought she was naïve; she knew they were.

"My mother tried to make them see that the sprawling Austro-Hungarian empire was over. Jews had been just one oddity among so many oddities in the empire. Hungarians, Poles, Italians! There was room even for us Jews. But that was over."

"End of World War I. Battle of Vittorio Veneto."

She looked at him in surprise. Then said, "Oh, yes, your military history phase."

"And the empire broke up until Austria was just little Austria with a big capital."

"Vienna," Mamie said softly. "Small parochial states are never good news for Jews, Julian," she added. "Always remember that."

Mamie could hear her mother saying, "We live in Austria now. Not the empire. *Austria*."

She had not understood why her mother was ferocious about this distinction.

"Look around you," her mother had said to Grandfather and Father.

But when they looked around them, they recognized their past, not their future.

"Look next door," Ilse had said.

They looked, but they saw only the Prussians. Prussians! Pah! A crude people not worth thinking about.

"I didn't know what she was making such a fuss about, or care," Mamie told Julian. "I was still a child, and that is time-consuming, if you recall."

She remembered hikes into the Vienna Woods, walks to the Schönbrunn Palace, through the gardens, to the zoo there to look at the elephants with their sad, intelligent eyes. She remembered swimming in the Alte Donau. They went to the Prater, sometimes, too. She would remember those jaunts all her life.

"But did I notice when the Nuremberg Laws were put in place in Germany? In 1935? I was eight years old, Julian! How could I? Did I hear my parents discussing the Aryanization of Jewish businesses? If I did, I did not understand them. I had no idea then that my mother was desperate to convince my father and grandfather to sell Künstler's."

"What's Künstler's?"

"The beautiful department store my great-grandfather started. Well, it was a small textile store when it began. Then, well, you know how it is . . ."

Julian nodded noncommittally.

"The sale did us no good in the end," Mamie said. "Everything was confiscated before we could leave. Our money, our paintings, my father's piano, and later our house—the house we lived in, Julian. All taken away."

He nodded again. What was there to say?

"Now, I know this all sounds a little familiar. Not because we've discussed it. But because you've seen so many TV shows and movies and read about it all in books. It's one reason I don't like to talk about it. Not because I'm traumatized, as your mother is constantly insisting. But because one's trauma becomes banal when its trotted out too many times. It wasn't banal, though, Julian. Oh, it was anything but banal. No matter how many times it happened, and still happens, to no matter how many people, confiscating a life and a history is never commonplace. It is hellish. This is the story of so many people, I know that. Palestinians among them, I know, so please don't start in on me. But it's my story, too. My own. And so I will tell it to you."

"Did you ever tell my father?"

"God, no."

"Why not?"

Maybe Roberta is right, Mamie thought. Maybe I *am* traumatized. Or was it just a mother's protective instinct?

"Oh, who knows?"

Then she told Julian how, the day of the Anschluss, they parted the curtains and saw soldiers marching, a perfection of parallel rows that gave off a whiff of inhumanity. But there were plenty of humans, too, gathered messily, frantically on the sidewalks, all shouting Heil Hitler. The swimming pool they had gone to now faced them with a sign that said NO JEWS. Those signs were all over the beautiful city.

"I knew that we were being thrown out of our country by those awful, mechanical soldiers because we were Jews. What I was less sure about was what a Jew actually was. The Jews I'd seen, the ones I knew were Jews, wore black kaftans and long beards and fur hats and were as alien to me as polar bears. They existed, but they had nothing to do with me. The only thing I knew about religion was that my father sometimes composed music for church services, and I would go with my mother to hear him play in a church. Christianity struck me as morbid and absurd and frightening: that poor bloody, emaciated corpse hanging everywhere in Vienna. I knew I was Jewish. But that was like saying I was Mamie Künstler. It was a name. My name, no more, no less."

"I understand that," Julian said.

"Maybe. You had a bar mitzvah, though."

"Well, partly because all my friends did."

"Well, all my friends didn't. And I wish I could say that I began to learn about my religion at this time, to understand its value, to feel its power. But I didn't. It wasn't until much later that I learned anything about Judaism. Because even when it's got you tight in its grip, history can pass you by. Especially when you're a child. When I asked my grandfather what a Jew was, he said, 'Someone who is chased from country to country.' And, under the circumstances, that seemed quite sufficient."

They brought only one small overnight bag each. Mamie's was made of red leather lined with black-and-white-checked cotton, another minor detail she never forgot. There was a little pocket inside in which she carefully tucked the Steiff terrier she slept with. His name was Franz.

"Franz is my son's name, your father's name, although he calls himself Frank. One cannot blame him. One celebrates it, really. A true American."

Franz the terrier, who expressed no qualms about his Germanic name, accompanied the family on their train ride from Switzerland to France, a week in Paris with Otto's musician friends hugging Mamie and offering her pastries and unrecognizable bread. There was a large, long-haired tabby cat named Teetee who purred and drooled and slept curled beside Franz and her. Then at last they took a train to Le Havre and boarded the ship and Mamie's mother said, "Now we are safe." This would be the last crossing the *Île de France* made as a civilian ship. All day long, all night long, the beautiful, art deco ship rolled up each gray swollen mountain, then crashed into the watery gray valley below. The spray was indistinguishable from the wet fog and rain.

"Maybe that's when I fell in love with fog."

The passengers wrapped themselves in scarves and blankets, lying damp and sickened by the sea on deck chairs. Mamie, blissfully immune to seasickness, wandered the boat freely, scouting, up and down metal stairs as narrow as ladders. "We were on our way from the slow, sad, perilous annihilation of our lives and careers and friendships and studies. From what we could hardly believe our world had become. But we were off to a land of make-believe!"

One of the other passengers, a shapely young woman from Berlin, had a small Pomeranian dog she let Mamie walk for her. The young woman was headed to Hollywood not to write pictures like Ilse, but to act in them.

"The child should have a dog in America," Mamie's grandfather said.

"We are not in America," Mamie's mother said.

"The lady does not even speak English," Mamie said. "How can she be in American pictures if she can speak no English?"

"How can one write American pictures if one speaks no English?" her mother said.

Mamie's father put his arm around his wife. "Everything is possible in Los Angeles."

10

~

AGATHA OPENED A BOTTLE OF WHITE WINE, THE GLASS MISTED WITH COLD. The pop of the cork was greeted with a "Brava!" from Mamie.

"No for you," Agatha said.

"Oh, yes, for me," Mamie replied. "Yes, indeed."

Agatha shrugged and poured her employer a glass, poured it to the brim.

"No spill on wrap. I just wrap wrap."

"Agatha, didn't we just get you some hearing aids? Before this virus? I think it might help your English."

Agatha did not hear.

"Or she's pretending not to hear," Mamie said to Julian.

Then Mamie was silent again. It was a dinner of long silences and chicken cooked with oranges from the tree in back and crisp warm bread Agatha had defiantly baked because Julian told her there was a shortage of flour because everyone in America suddenly wanted to bake bread.

When they had finished, the three of them sat outside, Julian and Mamie still drinking wine, Agatha sipping tea, her pocketbook, as always, hanging from her wrist.

"That was delicious," Julian said. His parents' menus leaned toward bulgur wheat.

"Fresh oranges," Mamie said. She looked up at the tree proudly. "My orange tree."

"You tree, but I pick," Agatha said. "I cook."

"And I eat," Julian said.

They sat and listened to the quiet.

"You taught me that, Grandma. To listen to the quiet."

"Yes," she said, and put her finger to her lips.

Julian's mother had always said that Grandma Mamie was *saturnine*. That was the word she always used, though Mamie was so emphatically cheerful. Frank would tell Roberta it was because saturnine sounded like Satan and that was what she really meant.

"Anyway," Julian said after a while, the quiet losing its charm, "I'm sorry." He always felt sorry these days. For being safe. But what was he apologizing for right now, he wondered. For being passive and indecisive and solipsistic and boring? That sounded right. Even the boring part. Even he was getting bored with himself these days.

"*Non, je ne regrette rien,*" Mamie said. "No regrets. That's on Edith Piaf's tombstone."

Julian was already googling it. "No, actually it's not."

"No? Well, it should be."

"Yeah. No regrets! That's a good one. I should get that tattooed on my arm."

His grandmother gave him a horrified look, accompanied by a shudder. Oh god. He remembered now. The tattoos from concentration camps. On the inside of people's arms. "Oh Grandma, sorry, shit, sorry. I wasn't thinking."

She shrugged and, as she sometimes did, closed down. Agatha glared at him.

"Well, so, I do regret *that*. That's for sure. So, no 'No regrets.'"

"No," Mamie said.

Julian almost asked her what she wanted on her gravestone. Which of course he would also regret, so shut up, Julian.

"I think I will put 'Shut up, Julian' on my gravestone," he said.

"Perhaps I should put it on mine," Mamie said dryly. And dinner was over.

11

Looking back on that time, Julian could not remember the exact date or even the month that Mamie told him to get off the floor and listen to her stories. The months of fear and confusion, the delicious dinners, the glasses and glasses of good wine, the spats and misunderstandings, the long slow walks with Prince Jan—none of it exactly separated itself into a calendar's squares. Everything just continued in a world where everything had stopped, like a wave, a wave that never really ended, never retreated back into the sea, just rolled and rolled in place. He did know Mamie began to tell the stories in the spring, but spring began so early here, what did that mean? It was after the jasmine time, during the weeks of privet, just before the jacaranda. It was when the pandemic was in full force in New York and his parents watched Governor Cuomo every day at one o'clock. It was when they banged pots and pans out the window at seven o'clock in the evening and everyone in Italy sang "Bella Ciao" on their balconies. It was when Los Angeles was scared. Or was it when Orange County was angry and refusing to wear masks? Maybe it was later. Or before. How could he remember? The stories had wafted into the stillness of his life like the dry California air.

He and Mamie would sit outside in the dark on those quiet nights, just a few stars visible. He would aim his phone with the astronomy app at the sky. And they would talk. And he would listen.

"Do you think I'm morose?" he said one evening, expecting a hearty denial.

"Indeed I do."

"Oh. Are you morose?"

"Hardly."

"You do get lost in thought sometimes. Maybe I'm just lost in thought."

"It is a nice way to phrase it. Lost in thought."

"Don't get too lost in the thoughts," Agatha said. She tapped her head.

"Yes, well, it does sound a little like dementia." Mamie spread her fingers into what Julian thought of as the Vulcan greeting and made a ritualized mock spit: "Pooh, pooh."

"Pooh, pooh," Agatha said, doing the same.

Even as a little boy, Julian had noticed the way his grandmother would sometimes stare into space. *Stare* was almost too strong a word. Her gaze drifted, sightless. He would try to imagine what she was thinking about. The thoughts of a grandmother were intriguing, especially a grandmother who was usually so vibrant suddenly looking at nothing and saying nothing, suspended. He finally decided she was thinking of him.

Maybe Mamie was daydreaming about him right now, he thought on that starry night. Perhaps she was gazing at the stars, divining what he should do with his life. Maybe she would make up a story about him and it would come true.

He wondered if those stories she'd told him when he was little were stories of her own childhood in Vienna, though the stories had never been children's stories. There were children in them, a child who resembled Mamie first and foremost, but the stories followed the child through an adult world. Adult conversations were overheard from the silent child lying immobile beneath the sofa, adults in the story telling their own stories: clandestine meetings beneath towering trees in the Vienna Woods, a young man and young lady throwing themselves down in the cushions of wildflowers or jumping into carriages and sneaking off on secret trips together to exotic places. People whispered in cafés, their faces almost touching; they caught the last train, its engine belching smoke; they boarded luxurious boats and waved white handkerchiefs, calling, "Bon voyage!" No one in the stories behaved the way you'd expect an adult to behave. They ran away from home, grown-up adult people leaving "without a by-your-leave"—Julian remembered that phrase. Grown men and grown women jumped into the lake with their clothes on, or without any clothes at all. They wore top hats while they slid gaily, like dancers, on the icy Viennese sidewalks. Every decision by every adult made no sense to a child, not the child in the story, not to Julian the child.

In one story, a man named Herman decided his best friend, Fritz, needed a wife. He put an ad in the paper seeking a pretty widow, not too old, with (essential) a decent dowry. Julian—was he four years old, five?—had marveled at the idea of a dowry. Would he someday have a dowry?

"I don't see why not," his grandmother said. She was a feminist, she added.

Of the dozens of letters and photographs Herman received from prospective brides, he chose one sent by a young woman of great beauty and acceptable wealth whose name was Rose. Herman, wanting to make sure she was worthy of Fritz, arranged to meet Rose at a café. Rose brought along a chaperone, a plain, flat-chested, scrawny friend. Herman himself, unlike the handsome friend to whom he was devoted, perhaps a little too devoted his mother sometimes thought, was bowlegged, slightly cross-eyed, and his collar was speckled with dandruff.

Julian recognized a fairy tale when he heard one, and he had leaned against his grandmother's leg from his seat on the floor and waited for the beautiful lady to fall in love with the ugly but kindhearted Herman instead of Herman's handsome friend Fritz; for Herman's friend Fritz to then fall in love with the plain chaperone. Or for Herman and the plain chaperone to be transformed by a kiss or a potion into a handsome prince and beautiful princess.

But in Mamie's story, the beautiful lady named Rose saw the ugly Herman and mistook him for the man she was supposed to meet and marry, and she motioned with disgust to her plain chaperone, and they rose to leave. When Herman saw what was happening, he realized the mix-up and quickly approached Rose to show her the photographs he'd brought of his good-looking and accomplished friend. Rose agreed never to mention the ad in the paper, a meeting was set up, and Rose and Herman's handsome friend Fritz were wed. As for Herman? He married a woman who went insane and had to be institutionalized, he beat his daughter, and soon went bankrupt. The plain chaperone lived with her parents until she died of tuberculosis some years later.

"But, Grandma Mamie," little Julian had said, his voice trembling, "that's so sad."

"Rose was happy," she replied. "As was Handsome Husband Fritz."

"But the others . . ."

"There are always others," she'd said, and she had risen from her chair and gone for a long walk.

"Mamie, what a horrible story to tell a child," Roberta said after Julian, a little teary, ran to tell her the sad tale of Herman and Fritz.

"My grandfather told me that story," Mamie said. "He had a handsome brother named Fritz, you know. Fritz died in the First World War."

The little boy suddenly felt proud of having been told what he now realized was an adult story, and he rose to his grandmother's defense. "It's just a story, Mommy." He patted Roberta's hand with his own small hand to comfort her. "It's just a story."

"You told me some crazy stories when I was a kid," Julian said now, looking over at Mamie, wondering if she was cold. "Do you want a sweater? Blanket?" He zipped up his sweatshirt. But Mamie shook her head. She was acclimated to the desert cold nights, that's what she always said. Like a cactus.

"That's what Grandfather and I did to amuse each other," Mamie said. "We told stories when we were stuck in the house."

"In Vienna?"

"Yes. The year before we came to America. We couldn't leave the house that year."

"Like now."

Mamie seemed to think about this.

"Well, maybe not," Julian said, suddenly self-conscious. Was this another tattoo faux pas? Was the virus to be compared to the Nazis? Was that in the worst possible taste? An insult to his grandmother? An insult, even, to the virus?

"Nothing is like anything else," Mamie said at last. "Yet we keep going around in circles."

The stars had begun going around in circles, and Julian realized he must have had too much wine.

"Julian, why don't you tell me a story tonight?" she said after a while.

"Me? I don't have any. And I'm pretty drunk."

"That's disgraceful."

"Well, Agatha keeps topping me up."

"Not the wine, you imbecile."

"Oh."

"No stories? It's sad."

He nodded. He certainly would not tell her about *Exiles in Space*. Maybe he should call it *Émigrés in Space*.

"How can you be a writer if you have no stories? What have you been doing all these years?"

"Daydreaming."

"That's a start," Mamie said. "Won't take you far, though."

Julian looked at his phone. Woozy. He'd really had too much wine. With difficulty he scanned his emails and texts. Something from Juliet? No, nothing.

"Julian, you have to do something besides staring at your phone," Mamie said. "It's obscene."

Julian thought, My god, did she see me watching porn?

"A young fellow like you. Read a book, Julian."

"I can't concentrate."

"Any book. Read the phone book."

"We don't have phone books anymore."

"Really? What do children sit on at restaurants? Did you know Prince Jan Saint Bernard is named after a book?"

"He is? What book?"

"*Prince Jan St. Bernard.*"

Julian laughed.

"The Saint Bernard in the book is trained to rescue people in Switzerland but ends up in sunny California."

She patted the old dog, then said, "I have lots and lots of stories. Don't I, Agatha?"

"Not paid to have opinion."

"Oh, someone is cranky."

"I know all you stories."

Agatha brought Mamie her after-dinner coffee, a ritual Julian could not understand.

"Doesn't coffee keep you awake?"

"I told you, the old do not sleep."

"She don't sleep," Agatha said.

"Maybe that's why? The coffee?"

"Nonsense. The story I will tell tonight is about daydreaming. And a very, very famous actress."

"Who?" Julian asked.

"Oh, they're all dead. Everyone is dead."

And she began.

12

⌒

"Once upon a time," Mamie said. She smiled, raised her eyebrows, which, carefully tended to by Agatha, were the same clown color as her hair. "Once upon a time! Oh, I love to say that. Once upon a time in an exotic land not at all far away called Santa Monica, a little girl who had just turned twelve was walking on the beach. She wore no shoes, and her bare feet left faint prints in the hard cold sand that was wet with early morning fog. What a wonderful fog, the little girl thought. Fresh with the smell of the sea. The little girl and her family had arrived in Los Angeles only a few weeks before after a long and perilous journey through many lands and over a wide sea. She was alone in the fog, a powerful feeling for a child who also, at long last, feels safe, and the little girl listened to the waves she could not see, the fog was that thick. This is like a dream, the girl thought, a lovely dream. I am floating in the New World, the girl thought. Someday, perhaps, when the country she had been forced to flee was returned to its proper rulers, she would be swept back there on the back of a white bull, a god disguised as a beautiful white bull. She remembered with sadness the land she had left, but she reveled in the sound of the sea, in the chill of the sand, in the soft fog that hid her and kept her safe.

"She walked and walked and saw no one. She walked more, cold but exhilarated. She had been imprisoned in the land she left, you see, and this freedom to walk alone, unseen, was glorious to her.

"But then! In front of her she saw a shape. She came closer. The shape was a bird, a huge bird, a gull, the biggest gull the girl had ever seen, its face and neck glittering white, its back the deepest black.

"Oh! thought the girl. This is a mother gull sitting on her eggs.

"She watched the gull spread its wings, leaning on them like crutches. The magnificent bird was not sitting on its eggs. It was trying to get to its feet. It was injured! It couldn't get up, it couldn't stand, it couldn't fly. The little girl felt sorry for the big, injured bird that struggled and struggled on the misty beach. She would never forget that bird, never forget its futile struggle. She took off her jacket. She would try to help the bird, wrap it in her jacket and carry it to safety. She did not know what safety for an injured bird was, but she knew she had to try.

"Just as she was about to spread her jacket over the struggling gull, suddenly, very suddenly, the big bird stopped struggling. It was still. Very still.

"The gull was dead. Just like that, the life went out of it. The big black-and-white bird was the first creature the girl had ever seen die."

Mamie took a breath. She closed her eyes.

Then Agatha said, "Eh, dirty birds."

Mamie opened her eyes, shook her head sadly. "She was standing right beside me then," she said.

Julian glanced at Agatha.

"Not Agatha, good lord, Julian. It was the most beautiful woman in the world. *She* was standing beside me as the gull gave up and life left it behind. And she said, in that voice of hers, that deep voice, '*The Seagull*. Have you seen it?'"

"Wow," Julian said softly.

"You think it profound?"

"Well kind of, yes."

"Chekhov? The poor bird was still warm!" She lifted her chin and gave him a fierce stare. "I call that bad taste."

13

THE NEXT STORY CAME A FEW DAYS LATER. IT WAS, MAMIE SAID, A SEQUEL.

"She was wearing sunglasses of course. In my memory, no one wore sunglasses in Vienna. Perhaps there was no sun. I cried when I got home the day we saw the seagull die. People were dying in Europe, Jews, friends, all the aunts and uncles and cousins, and I cried over a bird? But it was so awful watching death, watching it happen, as if it were an action, something taking place, when it is quite the opposite."

"She becoming morbid," Agatha said.

"Becoming?" Julian said.

"And why not?" said Mamie.

Yes, why not? Julian thought.

He knew he was lucky being in such a beautiful place during such a monstrous, perilous time in New York, and he felt a deep, empty guilt he had never known before. Was that morbid? He almost longed to be back in the city, stuck inside his apartment, afraid to touch the doorknob. His parents were recklessly buying lox, and his friends were locked in their lonely, dark studios with their dirty laundry. Terror, isolation, the wail of sirens carrying the sick to their deaths. And here was Julian, lounging by the bougainvillea. It was wrong to be here safe in a garden. It was wrong that everyone else wasn't safe in their own gardens.

"By the time we got to America," Mamie was saying, "as we in the Künstler family called Los Angeles, there were already ten thousand German-speaking refugees here. Ten thousand! It seemed like one hundred thousand and it seemed like twenty lost souls, it seemed like everyone and it seemed like the same twenty people—the twenty people you would meet at teas and parties and dinners. There were famous people like the Manns and Franz Werfel and the unavoidable Alma Mahler; Bert Brecht—"

She called him Bert? It was like calling Hemingway Ernie. Bert and Ernie. "You knew Brecht?"

"Everybody dead," Agatha said.

"Everyone knew everyone. And everyone came here like you, Julian."

"Because their parents didn't want to pay their rent in Brooklyn?"

"Refugees from a world gone mad. They all thought they could find work in Hollywood. Not so different, really, from the pretty girls and boys escaping the terrors of Kansas or Idaho, the ones who came hoping to be discovered, to become movie stars. It was just the terrors that were different."

And now we have a new terror, she thought. I'm so tired of terror. I was tired of terror the first moment I felt it, that young Gestapo officer with his pink cheeks banging on our door. He wanted to make sure we'd sewn on our yellow stars. How thoughtful of him. Just the sound of the knock—how did I know to be afraid? I wet my pants. Humiliation and terror, how easily the two fit together.

And then, somehow, there they all were in the land of oil wells and pelicans.

"Terror brought us all here and dumped us down on the beach together. But what a pile of people! The Feuchtwangers and Alfred Doeblin, the Viertels, Bruno Walter, Otto Klemperer, and Schoenberg and Stravinsky, who did not like each other at all, by the way. Lubitsch. Oh, I could go on and on."

"She go on and on," Agatha agreed.

"Do you know the famous story of Otto Preminger? Well, he's at a roulette table in L.A., and everyone is speaking Hungarian, Ukrainian, every Eastern European language, and he says, 'God damnit guys, we're in America. Speak German!'"

Mamie read all this later, she said. She read that they had a Weimar sensibility. They drank strong coffee and schnapps. She read they were called the Colony.

"That's what the books say. A colony of close-knit German-speaking refugees, feuding and spatting and eating Sacher torte—it sounds right. But we didn't live in history books, for heaven's sake. We lived in Santa Monica. And I lived in my head, as much as possible. That's where my memories are, in my head, but they're also from my head, if you get my drift."

Like Zeus, she thought, picturing a classical, bearded head, her memories flying out of it, little Athenas. An owl on their shoulders, each bearing a shield that could turn their enemies to stone.

"Drift, indeed," she said aloud.

Agatha waved her hand in front of Mamie's eyes. "You there?"

"For heaven's sake," Mamie said, slapping the hand away. "Now, remember I turned twelve just when we arrived in Los Angeles. And remember that I spent the year before cooped up in a big, stuffy house full of fear. Quiet, dignified fear on the surface, but you could feel the terror. Not unlike the way we feel now, I suppose, but the brutality! Well, that came from human beings, not this invisible germ. And then, voilà! The relief I felt the minute we arrived at the house in Santa Monica—it's hard to describe. Here I was, free and safe, even outside."

Mamie lifted her arms to the sky, her face turned up, as if toward a god. "Outside!" she cried.

"Nature lady," Agatha said, eyebrows raised skeptically.

"All I wanted was to stay outside. The sheer joy of it! The sky! The banana trees! The beach! All the oranges! My only memories of the first week was walking, practically skipping and dancing, in the Los Angeles sunshine, the Los Angeles fog."

Mamie could be so dramatic. It made Julian a little uncomfortable. He did not want her to become gaga on his watch. Even the dog seemed disturbed by her outburst and put his head on her knee. But stuck inside for a year? How awful for a kid. And then landing here and not speaking English? No wonder she was tough. And odd. "Did you have any friends here?" Julian asked.

"My grandfather."

"No American friends your age? Sounds lonely."

"You're projecting, Julian, my little captive. But, yes, I was lonely, at first, and angry, too. At the same time, everything was so new and exciting. A new land, and what a land!

"I was amazed, enchanted! I was like Odysseus on Calypso's island!"

She could suddenly, vividly remember the joy of receiving Edith Hamilton's *Mythology* for her fourteenth birthday—Pegasus flying away on the cover. She'd read it with the feeling that she, like Odysseus, was on an enchanted island. That she, like Pegasus, could fly. Fanciful, she thought again. Be careful, old girl. Fanciful can lead to delusional. Calm down, before they cart you off to that dreaded Home away from home.

"Lonely?" She shook her cane at Julian for emphasis. "I could walk out of my house—by myself! That trumps company, my dear."

She glared at him.

"Now, back to business, without further interruption one hopes. The next time we meet the beautiful movie star, it is Thanksgiving. We, the newcomers, are invited to join a typical American family for this echt American holiday. We are picked up by a chauffeur in a lovely big car and deposited in front of a house so whimsical, its roof like a Turkish mosque, with a smaller Turkish mosque over its garage, that we think we must be on a movie set. Then a tiny woman in colorful clothes swings open a heavy, Tudor front door and greets us in a piercing voice that immediately brings a peacock and peahen racing toward us, both of whom also begin shrieking.

"'God in heaven!' my mother says. 'That is no turkey.'

"'Would you like to see my bathroom?' the lady of the house shrieks. An amiable shriek, mind you, but the greenhorns are alarmed! Peacocks, domes, and now this deafening invitation to the bathroom?

"'Is she drunk?' I whispered to Grandfather in German.

"'Insane,' he whispered back somberly.

"'She used to be an actress in silent film,' my mother whispered to my father.

"'She has not adjusted well to the sound era,' he whispered back.

"'Would you like to see my bathroom?' Mrs. Movie Mogul cried out.

"That's what I called her in my mind. And forever after.

"'What does the woman say?' Grandfather asked. 'What is the costume she's wearing? Is this a fancy dress party?'

"Our terrifying hostess was dressed in what I assumed was a costume from a movie—red gaucho pants, a white silk pirate sort of blouse, laced up the front, and a bright orange sash across her chest. I actually thought at first she must be an entertainer hired for the evening, or even an American ambassadress, who could tell? Her lipstick was a wonderfully startling red. She was tiny, no taller than I was.

"She spoke with an exuberance and volume I did not yet recognize as American good manners.

"'No one told me it was fancy dress,' Grandfather was muttering. 'But isn't the poor foolish American lady cold? All skin and bones. With so much American food, all skin and bones and not even a sweater. Do they have no coal? With all their food, there is no coal?'

"All of us Künstlers were freezing cold; wet, too. Soggy shoes, clammy clothes, damp hair. The rains had started, and water swept down the street, rivers of it, rushing rivers. Worse than that, the residents of Los Angeles did not appear to heat their houses or even insulate them. Franz Joseph would have been quite at home in the chill of that Hollywood living room. California—always sunny and warm. Californians seemed to believe that even when it was cold and damp.

"Shivering, we followed Mrs. Movie Mogul into the sprawling mosque-roofed, Tudor-doored hacienda and gawped at the other guests. While my father and grandfather were swathed in Austrian wool suits, Austrian wool sweaters, and thick wool socks, to which Grandfather had added a knitted wool shawl, the other men wore light suits and silk shirts. The women, lovely women with smooth hairdos, wore sleeveless silk and satin dresses, high-heeled shoes—certainly no sweaters. My mother, in contrast, was wearing her good wool suit and warm wool stockings. I wore a wool dress, but my legs were bare and chilled above my socks. Imagine how dowdy and foreign we looked. All that wool! We were like wet sheep. Sheepish wet sheep."

Mamie could almost smell the damp wool now. She had felt both humiliated and defiantly superior upon walking into that room. Silly Americans, she'd thought; if only I could be like them, she'd thought. The story of the immigrant, she thought now.

"So imagine these glamorous Hollywood people, twenty or so, maybe more, with their cocktails and elegant shoes and all around them, on every wall of the living room, a mural of the Moguls—wife, husband, two daughters, one son, even the dog—life-size, each dressed and adorned in elaborate medieval garb—even, as I said, the dog. Armor, curled pointy shoes, floppy velvet caps. It was creepy—those unromantic, well-fed American faces on the bodies of knights and damsels. It was as if we'd walked into a poorly told fairy tale.

"My parents introduced themselves and me and then my grandfather. Grandfather's lapels were sprinkled with cigar ash. He smelled like an old, wet cigar. He was ugly, too. Bowlegged. Hairs in his ears. Many would have found him, quite justifiably, a repulsive old man. I adored him.

"My mother and father ignored Grandfather as much as they were able. He embarrassed them. But they embarrassed me, so it all evened out, and I reveled in his outlandish old-man presence. We had become close friends during the previous year, best friends, confidants, allies. It was Grandfather who harangued my parents about a dog. I wanted a dog, my own dog who would follow me from room to room and sleep beside my bed, and Grandfather took up my cause. Even before we arrived on American soil, on the ship coming over, Grandfather demanded that I have a dog.

"He coached me on how to convince my parents. The health benefits of walking a dog, the lessons in responsibility, in kindness and nurturing. I suppose he himself also wanted a dog but was too stubborn to say so. I plagued my parents about the dog, every day, at his urging. We enjoyed ourselves, Grandfather and I.

"That Thanksgiving party was not a great success, I must add. The immigrants were clearly uncomfortable and so not sufficiently full of thanks. With the exception of my mother, we could not join in the conversation unless the other German-speaking exiles also spoke German, which would have made the host and hostess and American guests feel left out. And the bounty of the meal—the heaps and heaps of strange food. It was impossible to see all that food and not think of the scarcity we'd left behind. How could we possibly indulge in the mounds of sweet potatoes and turkey and gravy and stuffing and Indian pudding with the enthusiasm expected of us? We tried. We ate. But I think we must have looked miserable. No hostess likes miserable guests, Julian. Remember that.

"'Do you have turkey in Vienna?' Mrs. Movie Mogul asked.

"'We have nothing in Vienna,' my mother said. Then, in German, 'We had everything in Vienna. Turkeys? We had turkeys, delicious turkeys. Until we had no turkeys, no food, no nothing. What difference does it make now?' Then in English again, 'How delicious is your simple American method of cooking turkey. I must learn now that we are here.'

"'The Indians invited the Pilgrims to join them in a feast,' said Mrs. Movie Mogul.

"'Their first mistake,' my mother muttered in German.

"'The child needs a dog,' Grandfather said.

"'My father does not speak English,' my mother said. 'I apologize for him.'

"'A dog, I say.'

"'He thinks it would be beneficial if my daughter had a pet dog. It has become his rocking horse.'

"'Hobbyhorse,' said the hostess. She had not liked being told her turkey recipe was simple.

"There was talk of the war, which the United States had not yet entered. And of course talk of film and actors and actresses. Great excitement at the prospect of *Gone With the Wind*, which was about to come out. I couldn't follow most of the conversations. But there was one beautiful blond lady in a fabulous dress, what a color, I can still see it, not gold, not bronze, something between, as if there were a more precious metal, oh it was gorgeous, and she had big blue eyes like a baby, although her hands looked rather old. When she spoke, I could perfectly understand everything she said because all she kept saying was, 'Well, I'll be goddamned.'"

"A movie star?" Julian asked.

"Constance Bennett. You've never heard of her, have you? The young are barbarous. And then there was an ancient English woman, a famous stage actress who'd moved to Hollywood now that she was old and forgotten. When I think back on it, the poor dear was probably fifty. She fought with everyone who tried to help her, that's what I heard later. I can well believe it. When we were leaving that interminable dinner, we were waiting just behind her to sign the guest book."

"They had a guest book at Thanksgiving? I thought that was for funerals."

"Well, the party was a bit funereal, really. Dull, awkward, endless. She must have thought so, too. She signed her name then wrote: 'Quoth the raven . . .'"

Mamie was enjoying herself now. "'Quoth the raven'! Oh, I knew that much English. My parents read that poem aloud to me even in Vienna. Oh, and there was a very distinguished Englishman talking to my parents about some new method to regain your eyesight, though he seemed squinty and half blind to me. My mother introduced him as Aldous Huxley and his wife, Maria. I didn't know who he was. He was just another adult. And then my grandfather interrupted him to complain about the cold; my mother turned pink with embarrassment but translated. Huxley called over a gregarious woman with stylish short hair as she walked by and said, 'Fraulein Loos has just the thing for Europeans who suffer from the cold, don't you, Fraulein Loos?'

"'You mean the Peter Heater?' the lady said. 'Yes, I knitted one and sent it to Adele Astaire to cheer her up.'

"She had signed the enclosed card: 'Knitted by an old maid—from memory.' Grandfather and I were clueless, even when another émigré translated, but my parents were overcome with laughter. Oh, it was good to see them laughing. I never saw Anita Loos again, but I've always thought fondly of her. A Peter Heater. You have no idea who these people are, do you, Julian?"

"Aldous Huxley? Of course I do."

"The others?"

He shook his head.

"It's all wasted if you don't know who anyone is. We will have an intermission while you google."

Mamie watched Julian tap at his phone, then write in the notebook he slipped out of his pocket.

"Still taking notes? Good. This is your history."

"Gossip," Agatha said.

"Exactly."

The story resumed. They were back at the Thanksgiving party. Glamour everywhere. Excess everywhere. Absurdity everywhere.

"It was like being at the zoo," Mamie said. "I studied them all. Easy to do for a little girl. I could stand beside them and turn my hand with an imaginary cigarette just so. I could repeat their words to myself until I got them just right. 'Well, I'll be goddamned! Knitted by an old maid from memory!'

"But there was one guest I stayed away from. I was aware of her all evening, but I tried not to look at her. Sometimes I could not help myself. The woman from the beach. The one who stood above the dead seagull and thought of Chekhov.

"She seemed almost violently out of context. That mural of the medieval movie mogul family. The men with tanned faces, the women in dresses that sparkled. On the beach she had been wrapped in an old camel hair coat, the collar turned up, and wearing a hat low over her face. Hatless now and wearing indoor clothes—not a shimmering dress, but a dark suit, very simple. She was out of context, yet unmistakable.

"And she was so beautiful my heart pounded each time I caught a glimpse of her. She didn't recognize me from the beach, for which I was grateful. That strange, serious, preposterous encounter was not something to share at a party of Glittering Americans.

"When she brushed past me, the slightest touch of elbow against my arm, I felt off-kilter.

"The room was full of beautiful women and beautiful men. But none of them compared to her. I could not altogether keep myself from looking, staring probably, as surreptitiously as possible, but staring. I have never seen beauty like hers, before or since. Luminous. It was a kind of sublimity, her beauty. Quiet. Reserved. Unapproachable. Incomparable. And magnetic. Yes, as if she were a magnet pulling your gaze. When she threw back her head and laughed, the room seemed to fade away, and there was just her.

"And me."

Mamie put a hand over her eyes the way Julian's mother did when he paced. But she was smiling, a small almost secret smile.

"Then I heard my grandfather's voice," she continued, lowering her hand, looking again at Julian. "That gruff petulant voice, and I saw that he was standing beside her. '*Hund*,' Grandfather was saying in German. 'It is not a home without a *Hund*.'

"'*Ein grand Hund* for your grand-*Tochter*,' she said in a mixture of English and German that made the others laugh."

Mamie paused, then:

"Oh," she said, dreamily. "Oh, it began then and there."

"What did?"

"Why, the beginning, Julian. As I just said."

Julian wrote: The Beginning.

"A few days later," Mamie said, "a big, cream-colored automobile pulled into our driveway. A chauffeur in livery got out and stood formally by the back door of the car.

"My family gathered in the driveway to see what important person would step out. A studio executive? A representative of the European Film Fund? A government official to send us away? My father smiled, but I could feel his concern. My mother did not even bother to smile. Grandfather grumbled about his lunch, when was he to have his lunch, would this visitor interrupt his lunch? Unacceptable! Who called on people at lunchtime? The Americans lacked all courtesy.

"'A gift from a friend,' the chauffeur said.

"As my mother translated, the chauffeur pulled open the car door.

"The important visitor stepped out. I should say leaped out, for the important visitor, the gift from a friend, was a puppy! And not a dachshund, the only type of dog my parents had considered under the grandfather-granddaughter barrage. No. This was a big, foolish puppy with big foolish feet who blundered down from the backseat and tumbled onto the driveway.

"A Saint Bernard! And she had a small wooden cask attached to her collar.

"Grandfather removed the cask and sniffed it contents and said, 'Excellent brandy.' Then he said, 'This is a dog for a new life.'

"'*Ein grand Hund* for your grand-*Tochter*,' my father said. Because obviously the puppy was from her."

Mamie felt a quiver of heat at the memory. That moment. That woman. Now, now, Mamie, you old harpy. Now, now.

"That puppy really was a dog for a new life. Full of joy and utterly at home. She was a vision of what America could be like. Did you know, Julian, that Schoenberg had a Saint Bernard?"

No, he did not know that Schoenberg had a Saint Bernard.

"Well, now you do."

But even Schoenberg didn't receive his dog as a gift from *her*, Mamie thought.

"Anyway," she said, "I got mine first."

"I will make a note of that."

There was another intermission as Agatha went inside to fix the jingling tray. Mamie wondered if Julian had ever been in love. Passionately in love. It seemed unlikely. The boy was so unformed. When does form come along and show you what you are? When does it embrace you, shape you, and reveal you to yourself? Constantly, she supposed. When would that happen to Julian? Soon, she decided. She would see to it. A late bloomer still must bloom!

Agatha returned with their drinks on the tarnished silver tray, her pocketbook, as always, swinging from her wrist. Like the queen, Mamie once remarked. Or that awful Mrs. Thatcher.

"Agatha, you watered my gin," Mamie said now. She pursed her lips at the glass, now stained with her pink lipstick.

"You too old for gin," Agatha said.

"I am too old to be without gin." She put her glass back on the tray. "You may water the geraniums with *that*. Julian, make me a proper martini."

Julian did as he was told, bringing the bottles of gin and vermouth outside so she could scrutinize his technique, her bleary old eyes trained like a bird of prey's. He had worked briefly as a bartender. Better at that than his short, sad stint as busboy when he'd spilled most of a pitcher of ice water on a man's lap. Bartending was far easier. Why didn't they start you out behind the bar, and then, when you were properly trained, send you off in charge of cascades of ice water aimed at awkwardly located glasses? Well, the restaurants and bars were all closed now, so no one had to worry about clumsy busboys. Now there was Agatha and her pocketbook and her tarnished tray. Feeling a sudden solidarity with servers everywhere, even the intimidating Agatha, he said, "Would you like me to polish that tray?"

Agatha launched into an enraged monologue of foreign (one assumed) words (one assumed).

"Okay, okay, mea fucking culpa."

"Don't you watch *Antiques Roadshow*?" Mamie said. "Patina, patina, patina. You have much to learn."

Once she had approved her drink, Mamie said, "Would you like to hear a joke?"

"Joke important for olds," Agatha said.

"Yes, thank you as always, Agatha. Now this was an émigré joke going around back then. Let's see. One sunny day, two German-speaking émigrés meet on the Santa Monica boardwalk and stop to chat. Each is walking a dachshund on a leash. As the men greet each other, the two dogs also greet each other politely. Then one dachshund says to the other dachshund, 'Tell me, were you also a Saint Bernard back home?'"

"Funny," Julian said, "but sad."

"The best jokes are."

"You must have liked the dog. Since you have another. Saint Bernard, I mean."

Prince Jan moved, iceberg-like, toward them now. He lay down at Mamie's feet with a great sigh.

"She was grand," Mamie said.

Julian had never had a dog. Growing up in New York City, his contact had been more with dog excrement on the street than with dogs themselves. He had no sentimental attachment to dogs and was just a little afraid of them. What was the point of a dog? People were starving. Cars lined up for miles waiting at food banks all over the country. Everyone searching for toilet paper. They might as well have been in the old country, whatever and wherever that was. Yet here was Mamie's dog being fed organic food, pumpkin and venison and duck. The dog had peanut butter cookies and freeze-dried liver snacks and salmon skin and dried sardines. The dog did not have to worry about picking up a deadly virus by touching the mailbox. The dog did not have to wear masks on walks.

"I think dogs are effete," he said.

"Effete!" said Mamie. "That's a good one." Yes, she would have to work on the boy, but there was definitely a spark there. "Now, my first Saint Bernard, that great big bouncing puppy, was a gift that came bearing a gift. A package wrapped and addressed to me. It was very exciting. I tore off the paper. It was a book. The title: *Prince Jan, St. Bernard*."

"You are a literary dog," Julian said to the dog, now sleeping by his grandmother's feet. "An effete literary dog."

"He drool, too," Agatha said. "Much much drool."

"The book was a novel about a Saint Bernard in Switzerland, trained by monks to rescue travelers in the Alps," Mamie said. "But he ended up in California. An exile."

"Like us."

"She wrote in the book, 'To Salomea and your many California adventures ahead.' She signed her initials."

"Who?"

"Greta Garbo. Are you listening to me at all? Am I wasting my elderly breath on you?"

At the word *breath*, Mamie was taken again by that faintest of shivers, a sweet cool breeze that catches your bare arm, unprepared. Stop it, Mamie, old thing. At once. "Pay attention," she said sharply. "She signed the book. *Prince Jan, St. Bernard* by Forrestine C. Hooker." Mamie suddenly broke into a smile again. "She signed it 'G.G.'"

"Woah. Do you still have it?" Julian wondered what that would be worth but knew enough to keep quiet.

"I read the book religiously. I treasured it. Of course I still have it. When that Saint Bernard puppy rolled out of that limousine, I knew what I had suspected the minute we arrived in California: this was indeed a land of myths and goddesses. One had only to make a wish out loud and the wish would come true."

She leaned over, and Prince Jan lifted his silky head for her kiss.

"Garbo's nickname in the press was La Divina," she said. "I took to thinking of her like that. A goddess. A distant divinity who waved her hand and conjured bouncing puppy dogs." Among other things.

14

How the hell many times had Mamie met Greta Garbo? On the beach, at Thanksgiving . . . Wasn't Garbo supposed to be a recluse? But why would anyone be a recluse on purpose? He, Julian, was a recluse, and he did not like it at all. Who would choose this life? Maybe he could be a recluse like Greta Garbo—walk on the beach, go to parties with movie stars. That might work. He would take it up with Jay.

His grandmother was napping. Beside her on the bed lay Prince Jan Saint Bernard, an enormous mound of white and chestnut brown, his big head heavy on the pillow next to hers. They were a pair, a sleeping couple. Agatha was probably napping, too. There was no one to talk to. Or listen to.

He took out his notebook and tried to record the improbable coalescence of vegetation Mamie called her garden. A towering palm tree. An arbor covered with wide-leafed grapevines on which grapes were never allowed to ripen because they attracted rats. Red geraniums in pots. A brilliant white rosebush against the house, bougainvillea beside it framing the kitchen door. One rusty lime hanging from a branch of a diseased lime tree with curled leaves that Agatha and Mamie discussed heatedly, daily, trying to determine what had gone wrong. Along one fence the jasmine and honeysuckle and privet tumbled and climbed together, each blossoming in its own time. There was lavender buzzing with bees beside a flourishing bush of rosemary beside a patch of bristling succulent spikes that looked like they belonged underwater. And of course, the orange tree.

"She knew Greta Garbo," he said out loud after a while, the plant inventory finished. "Unbelievable."

He said the same words to Mamie the next day.

"Oh, my dear child, you have no idea."

Julian was accompanying her on her afternoon constitutional, the slow circling of the garden. Round and round they went, ducking beneath the branches of the orange tree.

Mamie wondered if she wanted Julian to have an idea, or if she preferred to keep that part of her life in silent, shrouded privacy. The word *shrouded* disturbed her. Did it imply death? Of course it did. Death that would die again with her when she died. What a shame. A good story it was, too.

Agatha appeared with pocketbook and tray. "We sit."

"You knew a lot of people," Julian was saying.

"Yet here I am alone with my memories." She glanced at Prince Jan. "And my dog."

"Ahem."

"And my grandson."

Agatha stood up. "More icey."

"And Agatha, my Martha."

"She get like this after gin," Agatha said. "The yellow dog."

"The black dog, Agatha. How many times have I told you?"

Yellow dog. That reminded Julian of politics, and politics was its own black dog. They watched three hours of MSNBC a night like hollow-eyed drug addicts.

"*She* used to get visits from the black dog," Mamie said vaguely.

"Garbo?"

"I suppose we all did in those days."

Then she gave a mighty sneeze. Julian had never heard a sneeze as mighty as Mamie's. It didn't even sound like a sneeze it was so loud.

"Allergies," she reassured them.

"You sneeze as elephant," Agatha said. "Not dainty."

"My father used to throw his newspaper in the air when I sneezed. He'd say, 'Salomea, cease!' He made me laugh in those days. Before he became sad."

"Salomea doesn't sound like a Jewish name," Julian said.

"But 'Julian,' the name of a pagan Roman emperor, does? Salomea was beautiful and she danced. Among other things."

"Other things." Agatha pulled a finger across her throat. "Other things!"

"Yes, but didn't people have more traditional Jewish names in those days? Like, I don't know, Ruth? Or Miriam?"

"Not in Vienna, god no. Well, not until the Nazis made every Jew change their name to Sarah or Israel."

"I love your name," Julian said. He stared at the olives in her glass. Three green olives.

"Can I have your olives?"

"Certainly not."

"I make duck for dinner," Agatha said. She headed back to the kitchen. "Go good with oranges. So many oranges." She took the ice bucket and left them.

"My father bought a duck in a drugstore," Mamie said. "Its name was Dandy."

"They served duck at a drugstore soda counter?" Julian said. "Pretty fancy drugstore."

"Honestly, Julian. Not *duck*. A duck. A duckling, tiny waddling little fellow in a little blue harness made of ribbon. And a little straw hat."

Not sure how to respond—PETA outrage? An appreciative awwww?—Julian was silent.

"He liked to pay visits to the Mexican family who lived nearby. There were still so many Mexicans living in the canyon. The last of the families who'd gotten land grants. I can't remember their names now. No comment from you, Agatha," she yelled toward the kitchen. "Dandy loved that family. He visited them every day to play with the children. Then he would waddle back to us at five o'clock sharp. 'After a long day at work,' my father would say."

Julian, poultry on his mind, said, "You should call the Thanksgiving story 'Garbo Eats!' Because, you know, 'Garbo Talks!' And 'Garbo Laughs!'"

"Yes, dear, I get it. But she was always on such a strange diet. I'm not sure she did eat. Maybe some raw this and that. I'm surprised you know who Greta Garbo is, Julian."

"I am not a cinema illiterate," he said. "I majored in film." Gory cult samurai film, but still. And I watched *Ninotchka* on Turner Classic Movies, he did not add. With Juliet, he did not say. On her bed, he also did not say. After sex, he thought wistfully and definitely did not add.

Mamie called Prince Jan's name, and the dog woke and turned his head to look at her. "Do you know who Garbo is, too?" Prince Jan put his head on her bony knee. He closed his eyes.

"He don't care for Garbo," said Agatha, back with her bucket of icey.

Julian noticed there were now no olives in Mamie's glass. And just two pits. Where had the third one gone? He hoped she hadn't swallowed it.

15

~

After dinner, they sat outside in the long, faded evening light.

"Another beautiful night. You barely have any weather here," Julian said.

"Unless you count earthquakes and droughts and mudslides and wildfires," Mamie said.

Agatha searched the garden for stray glasses, a pebble perhaps, or a leaf or flower petal to sweep up. She was relentless.

"I saw a flock of parrots fly by today," Julian said. "Parrots!"

"Paris has virus, too," Agatha replied.

"Well, yes, Agatha, it does," said Mamie. She had been relieved of her bandage and cast at last after a tele-appointment with the doctor. She moved the hand up and down, a slow flapping that reminded Julian of Queen Elizabeth's wave, which he said.

"No, you're simply not paying attention to detail, Julian. She moves the arm from the elbow, like this, so she won't tire."

Julian tried it. Mamie was a gifted mimic—she constantly imitated politicians as she watched the endless bad news. Her voice, yes; her face, but also her body.

"Poor Queen Elizabeth," she said now in a Queen Elizabeth voice. "Even older than me. And still with that ghoulish scarecrow."

She nodded approval at his wave.

"Have you ever been to England?" he said.

Mamie looked at him with scorn. "Do you think because I never travel that I have never traveled? I hate it now, it's true. I traveled too early and for the wrong reasons. But I have gone almost everywhere. Do you know why? Because I could."

"Did you ever go back to Vienna?"

"Never."

"I guess that would be hard. You can't go home again, as they say."

"This is home, Julian. I do hope we don't have to run away again. I'm tired of being an immigrant. All my life, I have been an immigrant, even though I am home. What if I have to be an immigrant evicted from my immigration home? I hope you are registered to vote, young man."

"Money," said Agatha. "Immigrant come for money."

"Agatha, really."

"Immigrant come for money."

"People come because they're in danger or impoverished. Honestly, Agatha, what a thing to say."

"I come for money."

"Oh well, you. Did you find any?"

"You will leave me riches." Agatha laughed.

Mamie laughed.

Julian wondered if Mamie would have enough money to last out her life, much less leave Agatha a pile of riches. He had no idea. It was not something one could ask, he knew that. But that made him wonder what other things he had never thought to wonder about Mamie. How hard it must have been, to raise her son alone, for example—something he had never thought about before. The story in his house was always about how hard it was for his father, a story pushed by his mother and pushed away by his father with unconvincing denials. But what about Mamie? A single mother in a time when single mothers were not acceptable? A violinist supporting the two of them? That's a lotta sonatas.

"That's a lotta sonatas," he said, just to test how it sounded.

"I gave lessons, too," Mamie said, as if she'd heard his thoughts.

16

⌒

MAMIE'S STORIES DID NOT COME EVERY DAY, THEY DID NOT COME EVERY NIGHT. Grandma Mamie was not Scheherazade or Chaucer, she was not Boccaccio. She was a ninety-three-year-old violinist with severe arthritis in her hands and time on her hands. She might launch into a tale first thing in the morning or last thing at night. Julian never knew when a story was coming, so he kept his pen and small Moleskine notebook in his pocket at all times. The words were not his, but as he typed them into his laptop at night, they felt real, and in that moment they belonged to him. And if they ended up in his screenplay? What then? Because bits of his grandmother's stories were popping up in the outline—memories the space travelers were ordered to forget. If he mentioned any of this to his grandmother, that tenuous reality would disappear, disintegrate, dissipate. He typed those words, too, to keep them for himself. Disappear, disintegrate, dissipate.

Sometimes Mamie's stories were told in the first person, sometimes the third person, all about the same little girl, the eleven-year-old wrested from her home in the old country, a place of high civilization and low, ugly barbarism.

But she loved America, she told him. Right from the beginning.

"It was that first day on the beach, that first autumn day in America on the Santa Monica beach. My birthday. That was the day I will always associate with being an American. The immensity of the ocean, a new ocean, not the old, leaden Atlantic that I had crossed and left behind. And every day that first winter, as I walked along the beach while my grandfather sat on his bench, I knew my father was right—anything was possible in Los Angeles.

"Days were brighter here, more vivid than any days I had ever experienced. Fear did not cloud them. Hunger did not cloud them. Guilt and sadness blew off in the wind, scattered like foam. Birds hurried across smooth, wet sand, and the surfers appeared on top of waves like mythical creatures. Even when it rained, the birds and the men on their surfboards were still there.

"Sometimes, while we looked out at the ocean, Grandfather would tell me about the mythical Europa. Europa—the beautiful princess whisked away to Crete by a god disguised as a gentle bull. And there was also Europa the moon, circling the planet Jupiter. And of course, Europa the land the Künstlers had to leave. I used to stand on the beach in Santa Monica, the broad white beach, my feet in the icy water, and I would wait. For a gentle, mythical bull to carry me off through the waves, my tunic flowing, carry me off to . . . where? I never got that far in my daydreams.

"Grandfather carried a large black umbrella even on the sunniest days, and during a downpour just before Christmas, he and I easily fit beneath it. Just the way we had when we were back home in the Viennese rain.

"'So,' Grandfather said triumphantly on one of these wet walks, 'this is your paradise, little one? Wind, sand, a typhoon. For me, I prefer the Café Central.' He had to yell to be heard over the rain. He had a cigar in his mouth, as usual. It was sodden and drooped at the end. He'd come with me because he always did. He was a loyal and stubborn old man. I was a stubborn little girl, and even the rain seemed better to me than sitting inside. But now I looked at my grandfather stooped beneath the umbrella, his beard glistening with raindrops, and my own loyalty kicked in. I put my hands in his and the big umbrella rested on his shoulder like an immense black pinwheel and I turned us both around, as if we were dancing, and we both hummed 'The Emperor Waltz,' our secret, unsophisticated favorite, and made our way back to the house on top of the hill.

"'Very kind of you to give up your walk for your old grandfather. An old-fashioned courtesy I would not expect from one so young.'

"'As I am fond of saying,' I said, 'I may be stubborn, but I am not selfish.'

"It was the beginning of my epigrammatic phase. I began many sentences with 'As I am fond of saying . . .'

"'As I am fond of saying,' I said fondly on that rainy day, 'youth is not the same as modernity.'

"'You are neither young nor modern, little Salomea,' Grandfather replied. 'Even at twelve years, even in Los Angeles, California, United States of America. You are of the old country, like me.'

"And we sat in the living room, our wet clothes steaming in front of the fire, listening to Tommy Dorsey on the radio and smoking cigarettes."

It sounded romantic to Julian, full of adventure. The wide, empty beach, the clothes steaming before the fire, the cigarettes, the big band music on the old radio. What he wouldn't have given to have had that much freedom at twelve! Then he thought, Shut up, Julian. His new silent refrain. Romantic? She was twelve! She was only twelve and had to start a new life! At twelve it is frightening starting a new school, a new grade, even. When he was twelve, he was scared to tell anyone he watched *Teenage Mutant Ninja Turtles* in case they thought he was babyish. He was depressed by having to get his braces tightened and distraught when his face broke out. He had a crush on a girl in school named Emma that weighed heavily on him. And were his skinny jeans skinny enough?

What if he had been wrenched from this sheltered Upper West Side life, from begging for a bigger allowance so he could afford sushi for lunch, from his restless, mandatory pre–bar mitzvah Friday night attendance at the synagogue? What if he were brought to a new country with an entirely different way of life? Like, say, Saudi Arabia?

He looked around his grandmother's house, at the books and LPs and piles of sheet music and signed photographs of conductors and the violins in their cases lined up against one wall like soldiers guarding the past, keeping Mamie's reality in sight. She was heroic, his grandmother. He would have vanished in the Old World out of complacency, in the New out of petulance. She had done neither. She had flourished. She had planted herself beside her orange tree and flourished.

Is your hair that color, that orange red, because you eat oranges? he had wanted to ask her when he was younger. But now he thought it was because she had planted herself in her new world and was determined that people see her there. Her hair was celebratory: she had survived.

Perhaps that was why she'd begun telling him her stories now. Not just for his family history or to push away the boredom, not just to pass the time that clung to them like wet, heavy mud, but also to celebrate, to rejoice in what had been, and, just as important, more important, what had not been. Émigrés were escape artists, Mamie once said. "Not only because we escaped the evil of our homelands, but because we must continue to escape—we must escape daily from the eternal strangeness of our new world by making it our own."

When Mamie emitted her harsh morning smoker's cough and handed him her mug of black coffee to carry so she could walk out to the garden leaning on the silver-handled cane Julian feared would snap, it was so slender and elegant, he followed her with a new admiration. He had always loved her. She was different from anyone he knew—so rude, so kind, so quick, so easily amused, so easily disgruntled. But he was beginning to sense how much had gone before, how much she carried with her and within her, how this funny, eccentric grandma whom he'd always thought of as thinking primarily of him, her grandson, was a person of twists and turns and depths and heights and whole vistas of thoughts and ideas and desires and concerns he could only glimpse from afar.

He thought about that as he fell asleep. He thought about it again when he woke up.

"Julian!" his sister said when he told her his revelation. "I believe that is called . . ."

"Empathy?"

"I wouldn't go that far. You're just a beginner. The opposite of self-centered, stage one, amateur level, let's see, what would you call that? Fellow feeling 101! Let's start there."

"You're a deep well of empathy yourself, aren't you?" Julian said, his feelings hurt by her sarcasm, though he had expected exactly that. And even before they hung up he forgave her, as he always did.

"My coffee is cold," Mamie cried out from the garden.

Julian left his bed where he'd been talking to Annabella and offered to get Mamie some hot coffee.

"*I* do," said Agatha, appearing out of nowhere, with her silver tray and her pocketbook. She glared at Julian.

"I'm not trying to take your job, Agatha," he said.

"You say."

17

"We are exiles," Frank's voice declared from Julian's laptop, "wandering the desert—"

"Hardly wandering, Frank," said Roberta's voice. "I could go for some wandering right about now, even in a desert."

Julian settled his chattering laptop on a pile of books on the coffee table in the living room, then settled his grandmother against a pile of pillows on the sofa facing the coffee table.

"Why are we going crazy having a Seder on Zoom when half the time we don't celebrate Passover properly in real life?" said another voice from the screen. Julian's sister's forehead swooped in and out of a square, then her full face, frowning, flushed, her hair a surprise color: French's mustard.

"What did you do to yourself?" Roberta cried out from her Zoom tile.

"I made a mistake, okay? You try it. You try coloring your own hair, ordering the dye online, just try it."

"Mommy's a hot dog," one of Annabella's children cried out from Annabella's square. His face bobbed up in front of hers.

"Mustard, mustard, mustard," the other son began chanting.

"It's a festive color," Grandma Mamie said.

"The reason we are having a Seder is this: the world is shit! And when the world is shit, Jews have to pay attention," Julian's father was saying. "We will raise our four glasses of wine—"

"You've already had your four," Roberta said.

"Do you remember, there was a joke, but I can only remember the punch line: 'Mustard, custard and you, you big turd.'"

"Grandma said *turd*," the little boys cried in delight.

Julian googled the punch line. "Oh god, Grandma, it's a totally homophobic joke."

"I look at this beautiful family of ours, look at you out there in your squares, I mean this from my heart, deep in my deepest heart, and I just really have to say this, because even a pandemic and thousands of miles, I just want to say this, from my heart, to all of you, with all of you here but not here, oh how love will conquer this too, and this too shall pass, as we raise our glasses and curse the plagues and the horse they rode in on and Donald Trump cursèd be his name . . ."

Julian hated it when his father was drunk. It was deeply embarrassing, although Frank did nothing but become sloppily, aggressively sentimental.

"Look at us!" Frank was saying. "*Look* at the *love*!"

"I can see you, Daddy, but where is everyone else?" Annabella said.

"Grid," said Jay. His masked nose moved into Annabella's square. "Grid view, honey. There."

What must Mamie really make of all this? Julian wondered. Had she been expelled from Vienna, from Mother Austria, from the center of Middle European culture, her mother's family expelled from the house in Galicia with the apple orchards, for this? The "grid view"?

Agatha appeared in the living room with a plate of homemade matzoh. Oddly shaped, sprinkled with sea salt, delicious. Julian had already eaten two.

"Holiday Jew crackers. Julian tell me recipe from computer."

Mamie requested a better view of her great-grandchildren. Julian tried to remember how old his nephews were. Five and three maybe? They showed Mamie their clip-on ties. When it was time, Annabella read the four questions in English (not one of them could do it in Hebrew), and they repeated what she said, after each word, lisping with child charm.

"Oh my god, they are beautiful," Frank was shouting. "The beauty of the young and the ancient. Wise, the wise son, the other one, silent? So beautiful, such heritage, did you hear that? The foolish son!"

He had reached the stage of inebriation at which he spoke loudly, picking up the threads of conversation that had long been left behind.

"This is pandemonium," Annabella said.

"Pandemonium," Frank responded a few minutes later when the rest were singing "two zuzim." "We showed them," he added. "We showed them all."

Mamie heard them all say goodbye, but her eyes were closed. The flickering boxes, the screen leaping from person to person, then settling into a grid of faces at odd angles—it had been a little too much. That and the wine. That and Frank making a fool of himself, which somehow made her miss him more. That and the virus that kept them apart. That and, well, family. Pandemonium? Is that what Annabella said? Yes, indeed. All of them together, even on a screen, was pandemonium. Family was everything. Everything is a bit much.

18

~

It wasn't until the next day that Mamie told Julian the story of her own proto-Zoom. "We called it a family photo," she explained gently.

"Quaint."

"Our grid may have been more subtle visually, but the social lines were strictly drawn."

The men were arranged by status, their wives beside them, all radiating in order of importance from the regal center, two rickety elders on two rickety wooden chairs, a fanning out on the floor at their feet of small children cross-legged and itchy in their bows and crinoline and lace collars and woolen shorts. Aunts and uncles, mothers and fathers, the rich ones and the poor ones, four generations of Künstlers all dressed up. Uncle Gustav the Speculator was relegated to the outer boroughs, though he was well-off at that time and had brought presents from Paris for everyone. But whenever Uncle Gustav visited, he either handed out presents from Paris or asked for handouts. Always flush or broke, never in between, Uncle Gustav was not considered quite respectable. Uncle Erich the Banker, Uncle Friedrich the Lawyer, Uncle Hugo the Factory Owner, Mamie's grandfather the Merchant, they all took their places around their parents (who were addressed by all members of the family as Great-grandmother Künstler and Great-grandfather Künstler).

Mamie was one of the fidgety cousins on the shining floor.

"I remember the smell of wax, the herringbone design."

She grinned and began to wave her arms. The photographer, she said, waved his hands like a conductor: "You go there, no, there, stand up straighter, young man, straighten your head please, little girl, and everyone hold it, hold it, and there we were, all finally in our places, our very own grid—and then . . ."

Mamie widened her eyes, lifted her orange eyebrows, and whispered: "A scream."

It was a bloodcurdling scream.

"Pandemonium!" she said. "Everyone began moving at once, looking, turning their heads, which child, why, was someone hurt . . . The grid dissolved. The photographer waved his arms helplessly. Someone tried to comfort the screaming, wailing child, but, no, that child wasn't the screamer."

"Was I the crying child? Or was it my cousin Rose, Rose who perished at Dachau? I just don't recall."

She didn't skip a beat at the mention of Dachau, Julian noticed. Or of her cousin who perished there. What an intricate, convoluted bundle of emotional strands she must carry around inside that heart. He wrote that in his notebook: intricate, convoluted bundle of emotional strands inside her heart. Then he crossed it out. Then he wrote it again.

"Everyone was running hither and thither, grabbing children to comfort them. The screaming continued and it was not-quite-respectable Uncle Gustav who somehow got to the noisy culprit first. He gave the child a good smack, which caused the other adults to set up their own howl, an angry howl, and Aunt Mathilde, who was a singer, cried out in a voice accustomed to reaching the last seats in the balcony, and then two men were pulling off their jackets, holding out their fists to fight, and one of them was my father, and the other man was yelling, as loud as could be, and everyone could hear it . . ."

Now she paused for dramatic effect.

"Julian!" she said. "Julian! Uncle Gustav was yelling in . . . in Yiddish! The forbidden, vulgar language of the shtetl, of the Jewish slums. The disgraceful, buried secret of a language. Yiddish!"

Another dramatic pause.

"The room became silent. A horrified silence. We never spoke what we Viennese considered a mongrel language, the speech of the poor, of Eastern European Jews, unenlightened, practically medieval."

"Künstler snobbery," Julian said, nodding.

"Exactly. And then, in that sudden shocked silence, my father, out of the blue, boxed my ears! Embarrassment? The need to do something? Because I was there? It was a casual sort of blow. The poor photographer pretended nothing had happened, people drifted back to where they had been posing, and the photograph was taken.

"I know the photograph was taken because I saw it in an album later that year.

"The album is gone now. Along with the great-grandparents, the speculator, the singer, all the aunts and uncles and cousins. My father, mother. Even, I presume, the photographer."

Julian said nothing. What could you say in response to such a story?

"There you have it," Mamie said after a while. "Pandemonium. Grids. Families."

And Julian did come up with a response after all: "Oy gevalt."

Part Two

19

⁓

MAY ARRIVED, BILLOWING WITH ROSES. THE LOS ANGELES STREETS WERE quiet. The Los Angeles hospitals were full. And Julian met a girl.

As he walked old Prince Jan, Julian could not help admitting that Los Angeles really did have a spring. It went from January to May, from the earliest buds to this profusion of roses. There were roses everywhere. They climbed trees and utility poles, they cascaded over fences onto garbage cans in the alleys.

Perhaps it was inevitable, Julian thought, that after months of walking Prince Jan through the neighborhood's peaceful streets several times a day, he would begin to recognize the other people walking their dogs. He began to greet them with pleasure, almost excitement. Fellow man, woman, teenage boy. They all instinctively adhered to the dog-walking etiquette of admiring the dogs at the ends of other leashes. Hello, they each would say, nodding, their grinning faces pushing their masks up. Hello.

What was not inevitable, what took Julian completely by surprise on one of his walks, was this girl. A girl his own age! A charming and attractive girl!

This miracle was the result of his own bad temper and petulance, and he considered pointing out this happy irony to his detractors (his family), but he knew they would somehow twist the situation and continue detracting.

The wondrous encounter happened on a hot afternoon. Julian had been sitting in the garden, scratching a mosquito bite and bitching about the humidity and the mosquitoes, neither of which was supposed to exist in Los Angeles. What kind of paradise was this? Sweaty, itchy, tedious, the sun glaring.

"I mean, enough is enough," he said. "But the sun just goes on and on and on."

Mamie pointed to her eyes covered by dark sunglasses, pointed to her wide-brimmed sun hat, pointed to the door leading to the sunless inside of the house. Her look said, "You are an ass. Go away." But she said nothing.

"Okay, okay. I'm just in a lamenting mood, I guess."

"You are whining, Julian. Lamentations sound entirely different."

"I'm lamenting the state of the world. And the burning sun. And the humidity. Which are signs of climate change."

"I read the newspaper, Julian. But you don't hear me whining."

You're going to die soon no matter what happens, he thought.

"Huh," he said.

"I understand the world is going to hell in a handbasket," Mamie said. "But that is no reason to mope, young man."

"Yeah? Well, I think it is."

"Suit yourself, Julian. Suit yourself."

"Yeah? Well, I will," he said. "Not that I need your permission."

"Be my guest. Oh, wait. You *are* my guest."

Maybe it was the heat that had put them both on edge. Or the months of proximity. Or the fear. Or the humidity, plain and simple, Julian thought. Or, see above, Mamie—the fucking mosquitoes!

"I will walk *your* dog now," he said, standing up. "*And* I will mope."

"Multitasking?"

Julian snapped the leash onto Prince Jan's collar. Somehow that sound, the metallic click, snapped Julian's anger off like a light switch. He looked back at his grandmother in her pressed jeans and paisley shirt, her giant Italian sunglasses, her straw sun hat, her *New York Times* opened like a sail before her, and he felt a stab of love and admiration and pity. He wondered what she could possibly expect from life at this point in hers. What could you want from a life at that age? To go back to the life you were once able to live? Or to quietly exit the life you were now stuck with? Mamie did not complain in front of him, but he heard her sometimes talking to Agatha, protesting the diapers, the pain, the fatigue. Agatha showed no sympathy whatsoever, which, he reflected, was probably why Mamie felt comfortable talking to her.

"You old. What you expect? Old Woman. What you thinking?"

"Thinking? Thinking is all I have left, my dear."

"The world is sick from virus. Think that."

"Yes, Agatha, that is sure to cheer me up."

As he led Prince Jan away, Julian wondered how long this would last, this claustrophobic prison called California, this guilt.

"So many dead," Mamie murmured from behind the newspaper.

Julian said nothing. He was ordered by his parents to discuss Covid as little as possible with his grandmother. It was all anyone thought about, but his father in particular begged him to shield Mamie from the grim news. Mamie read two newspapers a day, newspapers made out of paper that were delivered by an unseen hand each morning. That, in addition to the hours of cable news. But Julian's father was still insistent.

"Don't frighten her," he said. "She's lived through so much."

And I've lived through nothing, Julian thought. And now I am living through this nothing, this void in this vapid place while New York is gasping for breath.

"I'm taking the dog out to walk him in the sunshine while New York crumbles," he said. "Which confuses and shames me, okay?"

"I know you feel guilty being here and not in your own city," Mamie said. She turned to look at him. "I do understand, Julian. It was the same during the war, all of us here beneath the palms while our old world burned to the ground." She put the newspaper down, removed the sunglasses, and looked at him seriously. "Until it happens to you," she said, "you cannot know what it is to be an exile, a perpetual stranger."

"Until it happens to you," Julian said, half to himself.

"I was bitterly ashamed that I was here, in safety."

Julian repeated the words.

"Thank you, Grandma Mamie." Their argument, or tiff as she might have put it, was over. He felt now as if some sort of pact had been made between them, as if they were comrades, comrades in emptiness, strangeness, and guilt.

"Now go take your walk and lament in peace," Mamie said.

They shared something, he and his difficult grandmother.

"Go on, go on. Why are you looking at me like that?"

"I'm bitterly ashamed that I'm here in safety, and you're the only one who understands that."

He dragged the sleepy old dog through the house and out the front door. Prince Jan began to flag after only a couple of blocks, for which Julian would later thank him profusely.

They turned around and ambled along the deserted street back toward Mamie's house, the dog sniffing the ground, Julian sniffing the musty smell of his mask. A crow stood beside some garbage cans making soft, irritable sounds.

"Come on." Julian pulled at the old dog's leash. "Come *on*, dog."

But now Prince Jan Saint Bernard had collapsed in contented, rebellious fatigue.

"Your dog's so sweet!" said a voice from across the street. "Like a big bear."

Julian was about to answer with a dismissive "Ha, right," when he noticed the speaker was young, his age, and female.

"He's very old," he said.

The girl, the young woman, the recognizably human creature who was not his grandmother or Agatha, was also walking a dog, a gangly brown puppy straining at its harness.

"She's a puppy," said the girl. She seemed to be apologizing. She was wearing a flowered cotton mask.

"Nice mask," he said.

Oh god. Nice mask?

He forced an embarrassed smile, realized it was covered by the mask, swore to himself, then noticed she was smiling, he could tell: her eyes.

She said, "Thanks!"

They walked on their separate sidewalks, the street between them, Julian pulling Prince Jan, the girl pulled by her puppy.

"What's its name?" Julian said, loudly. Yelling, actually. Across a street. At a girl whose face he couldn't see. Was she pretty? She was beautiful to him in that moment, that much he knew.

"Cindy," she said.

He stopped. "Really?"

She shrugged. "My little sister named her."

"You live here?"

"I do. On Marco. I mean, I was supposed to be off enjoying my last semester of college, but, yeah, here I am."

They walked on a bit on either side of the street, parallel, slowly, because of Prince Jan.

"This old giant is Prince Jan," he said after a while. "What's your name?"

"Sophie. My dog has an unfashionable girl's name and I have a fashionable dog's name."

"I love the name Sophie," he said.

"Yeah, thank you, me, too. Poor Cindy, though," she said to the puppy. "How about you?" she asked Julian. "Max! I bet you're a Max. All the boys from New York City are named Max. And all the dogs!"

"No. I'm a Julian."

"Huh. I don't know any dogs named Julian. Sorry."

"How'd you know I was from New York?"

She pointed to his Mets cap.

"Right. So I was supposed to come out here to help my grandmother for a month or so."

"But you got caught in the pandemic? Wow. That's bad."

He nodded.

"But try living with your *parents*."

"Yeah, I see your point." He shuddered. "Especially my parents. Especially now."

"Too much Fox News?"

"No. Too ostentatiously woke."

She looked puzzled.

"Trust me," he said. "Unbearable."

Then he stopped and said, a bit theatrically, perhaps, "An exile, a per-petual stranger." Pause. "I am bitterly ashamed that I am here"—pause—"in safety."

She laughed.

"What?" he said, feeling the blush of embarrassment creeping up his neck.

"I'm reading *Prater Violet*, too," she said.

Julian pretended he understood her. He nodded. He tried to convey a knowing smile from behind his mask.

"He lived in Santa Monica. Is that why you're reading it?"

Who the hell was Prater Violet? When did he live in Santa Monica?

"Uh-huh," he said. "Exactly."

They made a plan to walk their dogs on parallel sidewalks the next day, and as Julian hurried back to his grandmother's he googled "Prater Violet" on his phone. A novel written in 1945. Okay. About making a film with the eminent émigré Berthold Viertel. Okay, getting closer. A novel written by Christopher Isherwood, the English writer who wrote *Berlin Stories*, which was the basis of *Cabaret*. *Cabaret*! Finally: a name he knew.

Prater Violet was written by Christopher Isherwood, who had lived in Santa Monica. Christopher Isherwood who had known just the right words, just the right words he thought his grandmother had known.

"Christopher Isherwood," he said when he got inside. "Christopher Isherwood lived here."

"Well, not in this house. He lived in Pacific Palisades. Near where I grew up, across the street from Salka Viertel. In fact, he lived in the apartment over her garage for a while. Handsome, charming fellow, even with all his Buddhism or whatever it was."

"He was an exile," Julian said, hoping for some sort of confession. Confession of what, though? Quoting without attribution? "A perpetual stranger."

"And the passivism," his grandmother continued. "Well, that followed him like, like . . ." She paused. "Like fleas!" She nodded with satisfaction. "That was why he was here instead of in Europe fighting for Queen and Country. But even in America, before the U.S. began to fight, well, passivism was not popular, Julian. Everywhere he went, people would jump at the poor man, try to convince him war was necessary, at least this war against Hitler. Then they would come up with the silliest excuses for why, although this war was necessary for the soul of freedom, the United States should stay out of it. Not everyone, not the Jews or the other émigrés. But the Americans! No wonder the poor soul kept driving into the hills to consult with his maharishi fellow. Of course, all I noticed at the time was his excellent German when he chatted with my parents. Courteous young man. Very droll."

Julian sat down, closed his eyes, put his head in his hands. He wished his grandmother would shut up. The sun outside was glaring through the windows. Mamie was droning on about famous people he'd never heard of.

"You drop a lot of names, Grandma," he said.

"As long as they don't drop me!" she said cheerfully.

Julian lifted his head and stared at her, a frail carrot-topped lady. "The world is weird and twisted up and I don't recognize anyone or anything anymore," he said.

"Don't tell Agatha," Mamie said, back behind her newspaper. "She'll tell you you have dementia."

"Is that what dementia's like?"

"Julian! How the hell would I know?"

Julian got up to hang the dog's leash on the hook by the side door, which opened to a walkway running the length of the house and bordered by the neighbor's fence and a trumpet vine overflowing from the neighbor's yard. The neighbor was rarely seen. He drank, according to Mamie.

"Then again, so do we," she had added.

"I met a girl in a flowered mask with a puppy named Cindy," Julian said.

"Well, I hope you bump into Cindy and her dog again, Julian."

"Cindy was the dog."

"I prefer Cynthia. Don't you? Cynthia is a lovely name."

"So, you knew Christopher Isherwood?"

"Oh, he was always around. Not one of us, I mean not a Jewish refugee, but one of us, nevertheless. My parents bought their car from him. I think it was a Ford. Whatever it was, it stalled with great regularity."

His grandmother's family had ridden around in Christopher Isherwood's old car and he, Julian, had not known who Christopher Isherwood was.

"You should have seen my grandfather learn to drive. He made friends with a chauffeur who taught us all. Well, businessman and retired chauffeur. There's a street named after him."

"Great-great-grandpa Künstler?"

"Don't be ridiculous."

Julian considered himself educated, overeducated in some areas, yet these ragged holes appeared in his knowledge as if moths had been feasting. I am so lopsidedly ignorant, he thought. Mamie might forget things, but I don't know them to forget. Did the tattered mind of the young move right into the tattered mind of the old? Was that how it worked? Or was there some period when ignorance had been mended and forgetfulness had not yet begun unraveling the weave?

"Why all this Isherwood? Are you a fan?" Mamie was saying. "I'm sure I have the *Berlin Stories* somewhere. Go look."

Mamie's library was in her bedroom. Three walls of shelves holding battered old books, some with spines so old and dry that slivers of faded cloth hung down like rags.

"Your bookshelves look like Miss Havisham's house," he said. "I'm scared to go near them."

And I may not know Christopher Isherwood, but I know my Dickens. I've read *Great Expectations*. And seen the series. It was on Netflix.

"Dust and memories," Mamie said. "That's what a bookcase is, Julian. That's what life is when you come right down to it. Dust and memories."

"I am an exile," he said, declaiming, one hand on his heart. "A perpetual stranger."

"You know, Thomas Mann said that if you didn't quote, how could the world be written down, the world that pressed to be written down?"

Aha, Julian thought. Plagiarist Granny confesses at last. With a quote from Thomas Mann? Well played, Mamie.

"Quotation is like jazz. That's what your grandfather used to say. Or was it jazz is like quotation?"

20

"I AM BITTERLY ASHAMED THAT I AM HERE, IN SAFETY," JULIAN SAID.

"Aren't we all, dear. Julian, I'm thinking of getting a puppy for Prince Jan. After all, I have you."

And I seem to have you, Julian thought. Not a bad choice, Fate. Not bad at all. If I have to be under house arrest with anyone, I'm lucky it's her.

Mamie, his wonderful grandmother—exotic and quixotic, his mother sometimes said. And neurotic, his father would add. For Julian she had always been, instead, possibility: an extension of his family into foreign lands, an escape from the locked-in dailiness of life. Even when the stories she'd told him when he was little were about the man with the vegetable wagon who came weekly to the house in Vienna, the man Helga the cook insisted was named Herr Pferdmist, which meant Mr. Horse Manure, her stories had somehow been adventure stories.

As the days passed, Julian began to observe Mamie more closely. Sometimes he even sketched her as she walked painfully through her house, small drawings in his Moleskine of someone just recognizable as Mamie leaning on her cane, more bent over than when he'd arrived in February. He captioned them with the date.

He would watch her stop to pat her violins in their cases, as if they were the puppies she now frequently threatened to get. When she slipped a vinyl LP out of its sleeve and balanced it on her turntable, she did so with such animation that he half expected her to start spinning it back and forth, a DJ Bubby making the music new. Instead, she dropped the needle lightly into the vinyl groove, closed her eyes and listened, swaying slightly, conducting with a pencil. If there was a violin part, she fingered the notes in the air, moving her hand up and down the neck of an imaginary violin.

He loved her. Not a new feeling—he had always loved her. But he'd loved her in a rhythmic, unconscious way, each visit from his grandmother or trip to her house in Los Angeles a new revelation of love, soon forgotten, made irrelevant by distance, by time. Now he loved her consciously, consistently, daily. He loved the way she looked, somewhat the worse for wear, that bright hair dyed by Agatha every three weeks, her lipstick an optimistic pink, her silk scarves thrown around her neck with the same aplomb as in her youth, her gentle gravelly voice, her stories.

People and places surged toward each other and back again in the stories. Galicia, Vienna, Santa Monica.

Well, Santa Monica, Pacific Palisades, Brentwood, Beverly Hills—it seemed they were all one, a sunny outpost of Mitteleuropa. Men in suits and hats strolled along the Ringstrasse, men in suits and hats strolled up and down the Santa Monica promenade. Composers, directors, hangers-on, writers and wives—in the orange-perfumed California sunshine, they spoke German in all the accents of the cold, moody empire that had been.

How would he ever capture this world, this clash of histories, in a script set in the future? The future, his own to make up, seemed barren and stilted compared to this vital past.

"But that's the fun," Sophie said when he confided his plans and its obstacles to her.

"There were so many parties," Mamie told him. "So many patios and swimming pools. I went to all of them with my parents that first year, my grandfather in tow. Grandfather and I must have been a confusing pair. I mean, who was chaperoning whom? What must the Hollywood guests and hosts and maids and busboys have made of us? A dour little girl mimicking people behind their backs and an old man in a wool suit blotted with white patches of cigar ash. What a pair!

"And then there were my parents, the preternaturally cheerful émigré couple with their sketchy English. Whenever they were at a loss in their new language, they would wave me over to interpret.

"'Come, Grandfather,' I would say. 'We must Americanize for Otto and Ilse.'

"Americanizing was my special job in the family. Some children took out the garbage or dried the dishes. I Americanized. I picked up slang— *booze, dumbbell, screwy*. I noticed fashion, longer skirts, shorter skirts, pants with cuffs. I was meant to be the guide in this promised land no one had promised us and we had never asked for. But I was almost as bewildered as they were. Those parties! Sometimes they were coffee and cake and Eduard Steuermann playing Berg on the piano. Can you imagine? Chaplin was there, too. He was very good-looking, you know."

"You met Charlie Chaplin? Really?"

"A nodding acquaintance."

"Jesus."

"No, not him. Not even to nod to."

"He traveled in other circles?"

She laughed. "But it *was* heaven, Julian. Those days." Her face seemed to lift with pleasure. Her eyes, often narrow and hawklike, were wide. "Once," she said, "there was a birthday party for an old man, composer, writer, I can't recall. But I do remember the food! Coffee with mountains of whipped cream, a platter of small, square sandwiches stuffed with liverwurst and cheese, and another plate piled with pastries, and cakes—three different cakes. And that was only teatime! Then came dinner—a buffet of frankfurters and sauerkraut and potatoes and shrimp salad and rye bread and salamis. And then, of course, an apple strudel. Glorious émigré gluttony!" That orange eyebrow was, as so often, raised at him. This time defiantly. "Can you blame us?"

Sometimes there were Hollywood parties, which were not like Viennese parties at all. No liverwurst. No *schlagsahne*. But fountains spewing pink colored water, servers dressed as Greek slave girls and slave boys carrying trays of vol-au-vents; buffets beneath tents surrounded by billowy flower beds.

"It was like the circus!" Mamie said.

Once, a helicopter dropped little gifts on the guests. The guests ran to grab them, as if they were starving and the gifts were packages of emergency food.

"Fools that we were. There was war in Europe, in Britain, in the Far East, for heaven's sake. War and genocide. But we ran after tiny parachutes floating through the air carrying trinkets."

Tiny Moroccan-leather horoscope books, small baskets of fresh strawberries. And a party cracker that held a pink porcelain lady playing a piano.

"That was a promotion for Steinway."

Ilse had shaken her head in something between dismay and delight. "Hollywood."

Otto, taking in the green, velvet lawns and crudely fashioned "classical" statues, the bubbling fountains of pink and blue water, the guests squealing with excitement, said, "No." And he smiled his big enthusiastic smile and said, "America!"

"It does seem like a pretty glamorous exile," Julian said. "No wonder your father liked America."

"That was in the beginning," Mamie said. "And that was not America."

"Capitalism," Agatha said.

"Decadence! Such fun while it lasted."

21

JULIAN WATCHED MAMIE WITH MORE AND MORE INTEREST AS HER STORIES moved along. He watched her face—a smile and laugh and a grimace and frown and a smile again.

"Your expressions are so . . . expressive," he told her.

"My grandfather did not seem to care what was or was not America," she said, continuing her story, without responding. "He spoke about nothing but the Old World."

Julian sometimes thought of Mamie's face, even with all its animation, as being stately, like a stately house. Its age, its survival, its history—all bestowed importance upon its owner.

"Grandfather would speak only German, and he simply refused to make the connection between his former countrymen and the indecent war on its Jews."

Mamie Künstler had been beautiful as a young woman. Julian had seen photographs of her driving her convertible cars, one man or another in the passenger seat, or a large dog, or a different large dog beside her. Her hair, escaping from a scarf, tousled by the wind. When Julian was very young his grandmother's hair had been a deep auburn, not the bright red she adopted in later years. She is still beautiful in her ancient old age, he thought. The same serious, handsome face.

"It was as if Germanic high culture and the German language existed in some abstract sphere empty of Germanic people, free of Nazis, free even of anti-Semitism."

There were photos all over the house of Mamie playing her violin, brows furrowed, eyes closed, always looking as if she were playing something sad and significant. Julian had sensed her sadness when he was a little boy, though she never said she was sad or sighed the way his father did or complained the way his mother did. Never.

"Oh, well, that's Mamie," Roberta once said to Frank. "She is like a drill sergeant of good cheer. A cynic, too. Quite a combination. It's a wonder you got out whole."

But cynical and cheerful and powerful as Mamie always was, Julian had sensed she was sad. Now he was beginning to understand why.

"Grandfather had somehow imbibed a sweet nectar of Germanic artistic superiority and purity without ever tasting its poison. He listened to the music of German and Austrian composers only. Handel, Mozart, Schubert, Beethoven, Brahms, Wagner, Strauss, Mahler—there were so many to choose from, he said. Why bother with Debussy or Verdi? He read only in German, too—Goethe, Schiller, Hölderlin, Rilke, Musil, Zweig, Heine, Heinrich and Thomas Mann. He had brought a dozen books with him in his suitcase with only one suit. Sometimes he sat with an open book and simply stared at the Gothic print, longingly, not even turning the pages."

Mamie was born to be born in Los Angeles, she liked to say. But the world she had been really born into was a world that now existed only in Grandfather's stories.

"Grandfather's only concession to the reality of Los Angeles was in the afternoons, when no one else was around, just us two, when he would offer me a cigarette from the box on the coffee table and light it with a match from a matchbook crumpled in his vest pocket and ask me to translate the American newspaper for him. I would translate the article from English into German out loud, then read it out loud in English.

"'Husky Woman Appointed Boys Athletic Head. Helen Hengii, forty, mother of a five-year-old daughter, has accepted a post as boys' athletic supervisor at Pittsburgh's Oakmont High School. She is six feet tall and weighs a hundred and seventy-five pounds.'

"He would repeat after me in English, 'Husky Vooman, Husky Vooman,' laughing, bits of wet, chewed cigar stuck to his lower lip.

"The smell of cigar nauseated me, but I loved it, too. It was my grand-father's perfume.

"'Local supervisors impose a twenty-five-cent parking fee at Santa Monica beaches.'

"'Dirty bastards.'

The House committee investigating un-American activities asked a Republican state finance officer why he was writing to someone, who was himself accused of an anti-Semitic campaign, to ask if Secretary of State Hull's wife was "a part or full-blooded Semite."

"'Dirty bastards.'"

Hunting with bow and arrow was torture that even dictators would not resort to and should be banned.

"'Dirty, dirty bastards.'"

The Germans bombed London.

"'Dirty bastards.'" Hands over face. "'Dirty bastards, dirty bastards.'

"It was the only English he knew fluently besides Husky Vooman," Mamie said. "And luckily, he told me, the world being what it was, he would often have occasion to use it."

22

~

"You must have missed Vienna," Julian said one day. "And your old life."

"We all miss the land of our childhood. If we were happy. I was happy there. And I've been happy here. My old life, as you put it, is my whole life. Because I'm old. I miss more than you at your age can even imagine."

Julian took her hand, the right hand, not the left that had been wrapped tight, tight, and was still, unwrapped and healed, treated like an ailing baby by Agatha. The right hand, its fingers a little crooked, its blue veins meandering along like rivers, rivers seen from above or on a map. Rivers going somewhere.

"You love your parents," Mamie said. "And your sister and her family, but you're so young you're still moving away from them, as you should be. I'm so old I sometimes move back to my parents."

"When you're lost in thought?"

She nodded.

"You miss them," he said, "but there's no going back."

"Julian, my dear, we'll make an émigré of you yet."

23

MAMIE WANTED A BOTTLE OF PORT.

"Under the circumstances," she explained, "we must have port after dinner."

Julian, who had never tasted port, called the liquor store on Lincoln Boulevard, put Mamie on to discuss what kind, paid over the phone with her credit card, and drove to the store where a frazzled-looking man in a blue surgical mask handed him a brown paper bag through the car window.

"It was like a drug buy," Julian told Sophie on one of their dog walks. They were navigating the streets that ran along Venice's few remaining canals. Prince Jan seemed happy to plod along, but Cindy, who lunged repeatedly at the ducks, was on high alert.

"Sorry," Sophie said.

"Puppies," Julian said, as if he knew puppies and their energy well, as if he'd known puppies all his life.

"I've never tasted port," Sophie said. "It's something people in books drink."

"Mamie is teaching me the ways of the world. A vanished world, but so be it."

"You will be an old gentleman of the nineteenth century before you leave her house."

If I ever do leave her house, he thought, though now at least he could go to Sophie's house to sit in the yard. They retreated from the canals and headed there.

He was happy to sit in Sophie's yard, even masked and ten feet apart on the artificial turf the family had put down during the last drought. Prince Jan loved to roll on it. It worked on his coat like a brush. They watched Cindy jump on Prince Jan and Prince Jan fend her off with a heavy, world-weary paw.

"Mamie told me another Garbo story. Want to hear?"

"Do you think the stories are real?"

"Why would she tell them otherwise?"

"To tell a good story. You're a funny kind of writer not to know that, Julian."

Julian wondered whether to take offense or to feel complimented. A funny kind of a writer. At least that was a writer, right?

"Do you want to hear it?"

Sophie nodded enthusiastically. Mamie's stories fascinated her. It had become clear that her little piece of Southern California turf was full of secrets. It was like a podcast full of important cultural figures.

"So, I said, 'Grandma, did you ever see Garbo again?'"

"Was Agatha there?" Though Sophie had never met Agatha, she was often a character in the stories, Sophie's favorite.

"Agatha was there. We were drinking port, but Agatha was having tea. Agatha does not drink. There is some background to her abstinence, or that is what she often implies, but what that background is no one has ever been able to find out."

"The mysterious Agatha!"

"Mamie once said, and I quote, 'One does not really want to know the sordid details, if indeed there are any. One suspects she simply does not like the taste.'"

"Oh," Sophie said sadly. "Well, then, one is disappointed."

"But wait! There's more!" Julian said in his TV commercial voice. He pulled out his notebook, opened it with a stagey flourish, and began to recite:

❊

"Six months passed before twelve-year-old Mamie Künstler saw La Divina again. It was again on the beach. She was there with the puppy, who was obsessively chasing the waves' foam as it rolled in, then chasing it back out. In spite of the large sunglasses and the tennis visor that hid most of La Divina's face, Mamie recognized her right away, even from afar. So did a lot of others, judging from the extraordinary number of people who fluttered by in that ostentatiously casual way people do when they glimpse a movie star."

"You take awfully good notes, Julian."

"I filled in a little. Good so far, right?"

Sophie nodded and Julian resumed.

"Garbo's disguise seemed somehow to bring attention to her rather than avert it. As if she were wearing a long false red beard. Mamie said nothing, nothing at all, when she saw her. She made no move to greet her or to move closer to her. She was as starstruck as the next twelve-year-old girl. The fact that she'd met Garbo made her shyness worse: What if Greta Garbo, famous movie star, didn't remember her, what if she didn't remember giving her the puppy? It would be mortifying. It would break Mamie's heart."

"She said that?"

"Yup. Well, okay, she said she would have been heartbroken."

"Yours is better."

Did Sophie really say that? Julian heard his own heart pounding, told it to pipe down, and continued.

"Garbo was with two other women, all three chatting away, Garbo most of all. How lively and garrulous she seemed, far more relaxed than she had been at the Thanksgiving dinner. Mamie watched from the corner of her eye, careful not to seem interested, when the puppy, who had grown quite large in the last few months but had lost none of her puppy behavior, the great big, wet, sandy puppy ran toward the three ladies, and Mamie, a well-brought-up child from Vienna, called her back, instinctively, loudly—a dog must not disturb the grown-up ladies, a wet dog must not jump up on ladies! So Mamie called out: 'Garbo!'

"Because Garbo was, unsurprisingly, the puppy's name.

"'Garbo!'

"Garbo the puppy ignored her and leaped up on Garbo the lady who, once she had escaped the flopping wet paws, looked at Mamie with murder in her eyes.

"'That is her name, Fraulein,' the girl said. 'I am most sorry. It is her name.'

"'It is my name.'

"'Yes, I am knowing that.'

"'My god,' one of the women said in German. 'Speak German, child. Your English is worse than mine.'

"In German, Mamie apologized again for the dog's rambunctious behavior and unfortunate name. 'But you see, you gave the puppy to me. So, I wanted to honor you by naming the generous gift after you.'

"'Why, you must be the little Künstler child,' said Greta Garbo.

"'Little Salomea Künstler!' cried one of the ladies. "'I met you and your parents on the ship. Do you remember me?'

"'Frau Viertel, yes.' She did remember this kind woman from the ship. She shook the woman's hand and said, 'You are Salomea, too.'

"'And this is the puppy?' Greta Garbo said. 'She is quite enormous.' She patted Garbo the dog with her large, tanned hand. 'Better behaved than your dogs,' she said to Frau Viertel.

"'I must get out of the sun,' said the third lady. This one was wearing black leather breeches and a black leather blouse, and she was carrying an open white leather parasol. Mamie had never seen anything like it or her. She shifted her gaze from Garbo, now throwing the dog's ball, to this bizarre creature. But surely if you wear leather riding breeches and have a leather umbrella on the beach, she thought, you must expect stares.

"'In that getup?' Garbo said, laughing. 'Of course, you must get out of the sun. Why *are* you dressed as a chauffeur, my dear?' asked Greta Garbo. 'A chauffeur with a parasol?'

"Mamie was grateful for the outlandish outfit. It was a distraction from the beauty of Greta Garbo, there before her, beauty undeterred by her sun visor, by her hair, loose and wild and windblown. She stared at the strange lady in breeches, but she saw only Garbo.

"'And why are you dressed as a schoolboy on holiday?' asked leather lady.

"Greta Garbo looked down at her rather large feet in straw sandals. She wiggled her toes. She had on white shorts and a navy-blue jersey. 'Because,' she said in her deep, low voice, 'I *am* a schoolboy on holiday.'

"They were laughing now, waving goodbye. They continued on their stroll, some of the gawpers gawping at Mamie now, most trailing behind the three women, making zigzag detours to disguise their paths, just like the little sandpipers skittering everywhere that day.

"Mamie sat on the sand and watched them depart. She hugged her wet dog close, then she turned to the waves and watched them and the birds and the tireless puppy, who had squirmed out of her arms. She might have been there for hours. She didn't really know. She wondered where the three women were going. She wondered if they'd come back.

"When she got home and described the most beautiful woman and Salomea Viertel, who apparently had unruly dogs, and the odd woman in leather breeches, her mother and father exchanged looks and her mother said, 'How very like Berlin it is here.'

"Her grandfather, who had always disliked Berlin because it was not as refined as Vienna, said Santa Monica was nothing like Berlin. Santa Monica was no Vienna, but it was not gloomy and Prussian and the wasps-nest source of the Third Reich.

"'Hitler was born in Austria,' Mamie said.

"'That's exactly,' he said, his new English phrase, and he left the room with the loudest steps he could manage. He was not a large man, and he was not as strong as he once was, but he must have made an effort, for Mamie could still remember the sound many decades later. She could remember quite a few things. The sand had been hot even as the sun slid down. She'd put her brown socks and white tennis shoes back on before heading to the house. She'd had trouble catching the puppy to put on her leash.

"'Garbo,' she called self-consciously. 'Garbo!'

"'Who were those ladies Greta Garbo was with?' she asked her parents. 'Were they movie stars, too? The one wearing the leather clothing was *böse Augen machen*.' Side-eye, but Mamie could not think of the English. They all lapsed into German then.

"'That lady was no lady,' her father said.

"'Otto.'

"'I am speaking poetically.'

"'She is a Spanish lady,' her mother said. 'That is why she seems so strange. Mercedes d'Acosta.'

"'Like the car? So she was a chauffeur!'

"'No, not a chauffeur. A writer. A very rich and rather eccentric writer.'

"Mercedes d'Acosta was famous when Mamie was a child. Scandalously famous. She always dressed in black and white. Tallulah Bankhead called her Countess Dracula. She claimed to have seduced any woman who was anybody—Tallulah, Isadora Duncan, Eva Le Gallienne, Dietrich. She was a terrible writer. But Mamie knew none of that then.

"'The other lady was Salka Viertel,' Ilse said. 'You met her on the ship, don't you remember?'

"'She is also named Salomea.'

"'That's right. She's a screenwriter, and a close friend of your benefactress, Miss Garbo. My goodness. You have just bumped into Santa Monica royalty on the beach, little mouse.'

"'Garbo jumped on Garbo,' Mamie said.

"'Did she mind?' her mother asked.

"'Which one?'

"'Salomea,' her father said. His warning voice. His warning name.

"The conversation ended there."

Julian broke off his dramatic reading. He had done all the voices, just as his grandmother had, though not with her range and specificity, it was true. But he had done it, lost himself in telling the story of Mamie and the two Garbos.

To his surprise, he realized he was standing.

Sophie clapped, and he bowed.

"You are an amazing storyteller, Julian."

"No, I just read her story."

"Okay, well, you're an amazing reader."

And Julian left the Astroturf garden in a happier state of mind than he had known in a long time.

Mamie watched him come in the front door and saw he was smiling, his smile so big it pushed his mask up in what she thought of as happy wrinkles.

"Dogs have a good time?"

"Yes, they did."

"Did Julian have a good time?"

"Yes, I did!"

It is lovely to fall in love, Mamie thought. She had been listening to *Tristan* and reliving that day on the beach with her puppy and the three women. Telling Julian about it had brought it close. Telling him about it brought what she didn't tell him even closer.

When Garbo had looked straight at Mamie. When Mamie looked back. When the air between them disappeared. When Mamie could hear herself breathing.

The eyelashes, the long, long famous eyelashes that closed and opened. Mamie knew she was gaping like a child at the zoo.

But she hadn't felt childish. She hadn't known what she felt, only figuring that out years later.

24

The physical beauty of Venice and the moral ugliness of America were more and more difficult for Julian to reconcile. On the day George Floyd was murdered in Minneapolis by a police officer kneeling on his neck, the jacaranda trees burst into bloom, canopies of unnatural color, a spectacular purple, blossoms lush and bizarre.

Then May turned into June and helicopters rasped above the purple trees, sirens screeched from every direction. There was the pop pop pop of tear gas or pepper spray or guns—you couldn't be sure.

The closed shops on Abbot Kinney now boarded up their windows. There was a 1:00 P.M. curfew.

"The émigrés had curfews during the war," Mamie said.

As citizens of Austria, though Austria had revoked their citizenship because they were Jews, the Künstlers, like all their émigré friends in Los Angeles, were not allowed out of their house between eight at night and six in the morning. Perhaps that's why all those émigré parties took place in the afternoon, Mamie thought. How lucky we were not to be rounded up like all the Japanese families imprisoned in camps. Not that I noticed that horror then. What the hell did I notice? There must have been sailors and soldiers all over the city, but I can barely picture them. All she could remember of the curfew, hard as she tried, was playing chess with Grandfather and the night she taught the family different slang ways to say money: *dough, bread, two bits, sawbuck.*

"Curfews started at eight," Mamie told Julian. "All those violinists and playwrights—what did they think we were going to do? Put on a show?"

She laughed.

"But even we did not have to come inside on a lovely afternoon. One o'clock. Dear god."

By noon, all the dog walkers were out trying to talk their dogs into performing their bodily functions at this unaccustomed time. Julian had not seen so many people milling around since the lockdown began. It was a beautiful, crisp sunny day. Puffy white clouds softened the bright sky. People nodded, waved, smiled, shook their heads at the new life they all were leading. There was a confused atmosphere of doom and neighborly cheer.

Julian walked with Sophie, the street between them as always, their dogs disobedient each in its own way, Cindy pulling forward, Prince Jan pulling back.

They traded outraged comments, tossing them at each other across the street, louder than usual to compensate for the helicopters.

"Last night," Sophie called out, "some idiot looted T-shirts from Med Men and tried to set them on fire in our yard."

"He stole T-shirts from a weed store? Then started a fire? Genius."

"A fire in California in the summer! It's the dry season," she added politely for the New Yorker. "Wildfires."

He nodded. "Yeah. Jesus."

"Luckily, the shirts didn't burn."

"They were too stoned," he said.

Sophie laughed, then said, "Are you going to the demonstration tomorrow at the Baptist church?"

Julian shook his head. "I can't. Orders from the high command. It sucks. It really sucks."

He was furious with Jay, who had called at the first sign of any protests in Los Angeles.

"You are not a free man, my friend," his brother-in-law said. "You can't risk it, Julian."

"I am bitterly ashamed that I am here, in safety."

"You say that a lot."

"It's a quote."

"Well, you're not that safe, Julian. I hate to break it to you."

Jay was a doctor. And he was Black. Julian had to admit that, right now, even more than usual, Jay's assessment carried a lot of weight.

"That was a quote from Christopher Isherwood. The writer. He used to live here. During World War Two."

"I know who Christopher Isherwood is, Julian."

"Oh. I didn't. How can I be a writer and not know who Christopher Isherwood is?"

"Well, now you know," Jay said. "So all you have to do is write. To be a writer." He sounded tired. Of Julian.

"But you and Annabella are going to the demonstrations, right?"

"She is. But she doesn't live with an old lady. I'm working, not marching. And Julian, I strip off my hospital clothes in the garage, throw them in the washer, and shower and wear a mask inside. I have not hugged my kids in months. It's bad here. It's hell at the hospital. I don't want to expose my kids to that, I don't want to expose my wife to that."

"I'm sorry," Julian said.

"I sleep in the guest room. And your parents aren't setting foot out of their apartment, if that makes you feel any better."

"Really? How the hell did you manage that? They haven't missed a protest march in fifty years."

"I told them no, unequivocally no. They said, 'But Jay, Black Lives Matter.'" He laughed. "And I said, 'I'm glad you think so, since you have two little Black grandchildren and a Black son-in-law, but our lives will matter even if you stay inside. You want to be around for those Black grandbabies, don't you? Don't they deserve grandparents, just like white grandbabies? Their little Black lives matter too, don't they?'" He laughed again. "Sometimes I have to pull out the big guns with them. 'Grandbabies.' They liked the sound of that."

Frank and Roberta were deeply impressed by the fact that they had a Black son-in-law and Black grandchildren. It was a point of soaring liberal pride. Their blatant, fawning adoration struck Julian as a kind of inverse racism and embarrassed him terribly, and Annabella often told them to shut up when they fussed over Jay. "I'm surprised they don't touch his hair and say how delightfully springy it is," she said to Julian in the early days of their courtship. But Jay seemed to find their parents amusing and rather touching.

"You treat them like patients," Annabella once said. "Patting them on the arm, not really listening, going about your business doing what needs to be done."

Jay was offended. "I always listen to my patients. Your parents are not my patients."

"It's condescending."

. "They're my in-laws. Of course I'm condescending."

"Don't you mind having in-laws who see you as a symbol of their own virtue?"

Jay seemed to think about that, then said, "If I have to be a symbol, and in this country I so often do, then, no, I don't mind being a symbol of tolerance and decency."

"Don't you just want to be a human being?" Annabella said. They appeared to have forgotten Julian's presence, and he sat as quietly as he could.

But Jay said nothing in response, just gave his wife a dark look and left the room.

"Men," she said dismissively, and she too walked out.

Julian felt shy around Jay. He always had. His sister was five years older than he was, and Jay was five years older than Annabella. Ten years between them. Julian had still been in high school when Annabella and Jay got together in Chicago. Julian hardly ever saw them. But he heard about them constantly.

"The children made the cutest Black Lives Matter signs for their windows," his mother said on their next call. "Imagine how Annabella and Jay feel, seeing this cruelty on TV. The violence. Thinking of the futures of those little boys . . ."

Julian wanted to bang his head against the wall. Or hers. Why? What she said was true. It must be torture for his sister and Jay. Anyway, he was just like his mother, an onlooker, a concerned but clueless onlooker doing nothing. Maybe that was why he squirmed at every word about this that came out of her mouth.

"You stay home with Grandma Mamie, all right?" Jay had said to him.

"I guess, but . . ."

"No buts. I mean it."

And Julian did as he was told. He walked the dog beneath the purple jacaranda trees, which were imported from Australia, of course. Nothing in Los Angeles was authentic.

"Well, the racism," Mamie said. "That's homegrown."

So he listened to the amplified voices of men and women calling for justice and the cheers of a crowd gathered at the Baptist church in Oakwood. Oakwood, the only section of Venice where African Americans were once allowed to live, now gentrifying at speed, studded with elaborate flat-roofed modern houses. Julian could hear the voices, but he could not join the crowd. He was useless, one of those useless white people who raged uselessly on Twitter, his new hobby.

"They also serve who only stand and wait," Jay had said to him.

"You're quoting an imperialist at me to make me feel better?" At least he knew who Rudyard Kipling was.

"Milton? An imperialist?"

"Yeah, well." Julian quickly changed the subject. "My parents have started singing John Lennon songs to me. On the phone. In unison."

"At least they didn't sing 'Amazing Grace,' Julian."

In the background, Julian could hear his sister: "They wouldn't dare."

When Julian hung up, he went outside to smoke a joint. No stores were open, it was hard to find flour, there were riots and rioting police, but you could have weed delivered.

25

Of course Mamie had a story to tell during those difficult days. But this was not like Julian's parents' competitive suffering of the victims of Stalin and Hitler and, grudgingly, Mao. She was not competing with the misery of the present. She was, it seemed, reminded of the old days by these new days.

"I vividly remember the day Mr. Tabor was forced to leave the bench where he was sitting with Grandfather," she said one evening after hours of watching the news on TV.

"Who is Mr. Tabor?"

"Why, he practically founded Venice, Julian."

"I thought Abbot Kinney founded Venice. And that's why they named Abbot Kinney Boulevard after him."

"Well, right off Abbot Kinney Boulevard is a little street called Irving Tabor Court."

"Okay."

"We met him that first summer. When school was out, my grandfather and I got into the habit of walking to the beach together. Grandfather would sit on a bench while I swam or looked for shells. Or daydreamed. Grandfather made a few elderly friends on that bench, mostly other émigrés. They would talk and I would walk. I liked to watch the men on their surfboards. That was new for me. So exotic. But there were also children with their shovels and pails, and that was so familiar. Unsettling times for me—exotic, familiar. Make up your mind, America. But enjoyable, so enjoyable. I'd walk back to see if the old men had worn each other out talking about the old days and complaining about the new days. In German, of course."

"Do you still speak German? Did it stay with you?"

"God yes. And French. If I knew what the hell Agatha speaks, I could probably pick up that, too. The émigré's curse."

"Really? That's your curse? I could think of others, Mamie."

"Let's not. Let's not go there, as you people say."

Julian laughed. You people.

"It wasn't until I met Mr. Tabor that I stuck around the bench to listen. The first time we spotted him, he was sitting on the bench, a tall, thin Black man, ankles crossed, his hat pulled low over his eyes. Grandfather sat down on the bench next to him and they started talking. An old man who couldn't speak English and a Colored man not allowed on that part of the beach."

"That's what we said in 1940," Mamie said when Julian opened his mouth to interrupt. "We said 'Colored.'"

"Well, we don't say that anymore," Julian said, and he began to enlighten her. She waved a hand to silence him. "Yes, yes, I know. And that's all for the good. I was just providing a historical footnote."

"Still."

"Well, don't start sulking, Julian. The NAACP—do you know what that stands for?" she said.

"Yes, but—"

"—but it is not 1940? True. Thank god. Point taken."

"Words matter," he said.

"Yes, they do, and that was the word that we used, and that matters, too. How can you know things have changed, Julian, if you don't know how things were?"

And she continued her story:

"My grandfather sat on the bench next to Mr. Tabor, who said, 'I can't swim. Can you? Hats off to the young ones.'

"He lifted his hat to me in my bathing suit.

"'Husky vooman,' Grandfather replied, lifting his hat.

"'Irving,' the Black man answered, offering his hand. 'Irving Tabor.'

"They shook hands, then leaned back almost in unison, two old men on a bench, their hats tilted down against the sun as they watched the boys and girls running on the sand, the teenagers leaning on one elbow on their blankets, the gulls, the white swish of foam, the curling waves, the heads of swimmers.

"'Hi there, Husky,' Irving said the next day at the same bench. He walked to that bench from Venice almost every day in the summer—his 'constitutional.' He told us he lived in Venice, just south of where we lived. He'd built a whole complex for his family in the Oakwood section of Venice.

"It was just around this time that the Künstlers bought a car. And, yes, we bought the old rattletrap from Christopher Isherwood. It was more than ten years old, but it moved forward when it was supposed to and backward when it was supposed to do that. It stopped on command. It was black with four doors and looked rather like a hearse. Grandfather was delighted with this new acquisition, though he could not drive.

"'Grandfather says you live on a beach and can't swim,' I said to Mr. Tabor. 'And he has a car and can't drive. It is a parallel.'

"'Well, I do know how to drive,' Mr. Tabor said. 'That was my profession for many years. Part of it, anyway.'

"And Irving Tabor began to tell us a story, his story:

"'Years ago there was a rich white man named Abbot Kinney who decided to build a city. A crazy city that would look just like Venice, Italy. Kinney bought some land on the coast with some partners and they divided it up.

"'Kinney won the lousy parcel of land, a big marshy swamp, that's all it was—won it on a coin toss,' Mr. Tabor said.

"A coin toss! Grandfather and I looked at each other, amazed at a country where ordinary citizens behaved with the casual arrogance of aristocrats.

"'He built what he called a pleasure pier. There were all kinds of amusements. There was a theater and a dance hall. Oh, and a plunge pool, too—heated salt water. He called the city Venice of America. He wanted it to look like Venice, Italy, so he had his workmen dig canals and build gondolas for those canals.'

"We were all silent for a moment, marveling, Tabor as much as Grandfather and me.

"Then he said, 'Not much left now. Most of the canals are filled in, paved over. Plunge pool paved over, too—it's that circle, Windward Circle, by the old post office. But it was something in those days. 1905. It opened on July Fourth. Before that, when they were still working on it, one of my cousins told me about this Abbot Kinney fellow who was building this resort city and maybe we could find work. So I followed my cousin, and I got a job on the pier sweeping, handyman type of thing. And one day when I was working this white fellow with his suit and his bowler hat and his big mustache, he says, "My good man, can you drive an automobile?" And of course I said, "Yes, I certainly could." But just like you, Husky, I never had driven an automobile in my life.'

"I was trying to translate, but I realized, watching the two of them, that Grandfather understood a lot more English than he let on.

"'Canals! Gondolas!' Grandfather said in German. 'This America is full of wonders.'

"I smiled apologetically at Mr. Tabor. 'We are from Vienna in Austria. Grandfather has not yet learned so much English. You are from Venice of America?'

"'I'm from New Orleans originally. Everyone here is from somewhere else, you know.'

"Grandfather offered him a cigar and the two of them sat puffing like two exhaust pipes, then Mr. Tabor said God had been looking after him that day because Kinney's car had not yet been delivered from Detroit, which gave him time to learn to drive. He had a friend who worked at a Ford dealership who taught him, and from then on, he and Kinney were inseparable. Tabor drove him everywhere. When they got to a hotel that didn't let Blacks in, Kinney refused to stay there himself, and they both slept in the car.

"'I became what you might call an advisor. We built that business up. It was a beautiful business. Concerts and lectures, roller coasters, restaurants. People came from all around. But you know, Kinney died in 1920, and then, same year, the pier burned down. And that was it. The dream city was over. The family built the pier back up again, but it was never the same. I lost a good friend when Abbot Kinney died. So did Venice of America.'

"We three sat, silent and serious for a few minutes. Then, well, I couldn't stand it anymore, and said, 'Poor Mr. Kinney,' but what I meant was, Please keep talking.

"I had given up any idea of swimming or walking on the beach by this time. I was in, I don't know, almost a trance. It was not real, this place by the sea where an old Black man (he seemed old to me; everyone did) had once helped build a city of pleasure piers and canals, a city that another man in a bowler decided to build, as if you could just decide to build cities. Cities grew, like Vienna, slowly over centuries. They were not conceived in a man's imagination and then hammered together. Canals dug out, streets laid out, hammer, hammer, dig, dig and then a city appeared, abracadabra, just like that, fresh from the marshes, and then just as suddenly disappeared in the glow of flames.

"My grandfather was just as caught up as I was. I had not seen him this animated for years.

"'This is a fairy tale, little mouse. A fairy tale about millionaires instead of princes! America! Venice of America! In Austria, with all our history, we have no history like this!'

"Venice of America, named after the historic city in Italy, was beyond history. Even then, in 1940, it was a fantastical place, a made-up place. Oil well towers reaching up beyond little bungalows beside them. A neat wooden house and its yard, its white picket fence enclosing not a tree or a bed of flowers but a steel steeple and the stink of oil. A modest bungalow, then oil derrick; next little house, then pumping jack, and on and on. It was a crowded, noisy, dirty place."

"Weird," Julian said. "Idealism and capitalism together."

"Strange bedfellows, indeed."

"Oil and water," said Agatha.

Mamie and Julian stared at her.

"Agatha, you never cease to amaze me," Mamie said.

"Your Majesty." And Agatha bowed her ironic bow and backed out of the room.

26

When his father appeared on Julian's iPad screen, his face eager and full of love, Julian smiled, thinking he looked a little like Prince Jan waiting to be fed.

"We are both on edge," said Julian's mother, her head appearing, pushing Frank's to half screen. "The world is on fire!"

"Yes! It's a revolution!" Frank said. "A real revolution!"

"Neither of you look on edge," Mamie said. You look excited, she thought. Like you're waiting for the circus to come to town. Innocent creatures. They have no idea. "Revolutions are not always all they're cracked up to be," she said gently.

She put her reading glasses on. Frank's hair was thinning just a bit. He looked a little puffy. But there were his eyes, those same intense brown eyes, as shiny and engaging as when he was a little boy. She felt a tug, a wrenching tug, of maternal love. "Are you eating too much salt, darling?"

"We all have to be better listeners," Frank said.

"That and a nickel," Mamie said. Frank was good and decent and his dark eyes went straight to her heart, but there was no denying it, the boy could be sanctimonious. The boy! She laughed to herself.

"This country has an ugly history," Roberta said. "It's time we recognized that."

"Yes," Mamie said. "Very ugly. History so often is. Especially when it's not history but is now."

"Ha!" Frank said, sounding a bit like me, Mamie thought with some pride. "Listen to her! Right on, Mother!"

Right on, Mother. Only Frank Künstler would say such a thing, Mamie thought with delight. So 1960s yet so formal somehow, from an even earlier era.

"We are in a historic moment," Roberta said. "Finally the running dogs are on the run."

"Oh god, Mom, not the running dogs again," said Julian. Maybe that was why he had never liked dogs. "The running dogs are running? Aren't they always running? Hence 'running dogs'?"

"Don't be fresh," his mother said.

"Aren't they tired of running by now?" He imagined all the capitalist canines panting with long pink tongues hanging from their jaws, their tails drooping.

"This country," Frank murmured. "Our sad history."

Mamie thought of her own history in "this country," a place with dark, agonizing shadows in its glorious myth of itself. America had welcomed her. It had protected her. So many of her friends could not get to "this country" with its ugly past and had therefore perished in the ugly present of the camps. All countries had ugly histories, she supposed, depending on where you stood, which economic hill you looked down from, or which chilly racial cliff you clung to. But this American ugliness had gone on for so long. Had she been aware of racism and inequality when she was growing up? No, she had not. It was the air one breathed.

She thought of all the Black soldiers who came back from the war and found the same dangerous, inhospitable place they'd left, changed but unchanged for them. The "Colored beach" at Bay Street, called the Inkwell; and that Black resort area in Manhattan Beach owned by the Bruce family, which the city reclaimed through eminent domain to get the Black landowners out. The land of opportunity seized and given to someone else. The *Los Angeles Times* ran an article recently about the Bruce family. How many other families had stories like that, she wondered.

"The police are like storm troopers," Roberta said, appearing again over her husband's shoulder. She had a spreading stripe of gray roots in her hair. She, too, looked puffy.

"Are you eating too much salt, too?" Mamie said.

"Roberta, really," Frank was saying. "Stormtroopers?" He was careful not to make casual Nazi comparisons when his mother was listening. Roberta had no such scruples.

"Well, they are."

"Well," he admitted, "yeah, they really are."

"You can compare them to the Brownshirts," Mamie said. "I won't take offense. I don't own oppression. Jews don't own oppression."

Julian said, "Okay, time to go, folks."

"But I do think Trump is more like Stalin or perhaps Mao," Mamie was saying. "The affect is Hitler, but the effect is quite different. This genocide by virus, it's a different style altogether, not Germanic, although the children in cages, that was more what you're thinking, I believe."

The oppression contest was Julian's least favorite topic of family conversation, with the exception, perhaps, of the oppressor contest. Which would come soon, he could feel it rumbling, like gas bubbles in the parental stomach. Who was worse: Hitler or Stalin? Mao rarely came into it. Perhaps because Julian's parents had been 1960s radicals and Mao still had some unfortunate lingering cachet from which they could not free themselves. Julian also believed this to be a parochial and racial exclusion: only Chinese people were murdered by Mao. Hitler and Stalin had gone after Jews: now that's oppression! He once brought this up, and since then his parents had, to his horrified amusement, tried to remember to be more inclusive and incorporate Mao in any comparative dictator discussion.

"Mom, Dad, it's cocktail time. We have to stay on schedule here. Nothing ever happens anymore. This is the only thing that happens, once a day, cocktail hour."

"Hours," Mamie said. "Plural."

"Schedule very big importance for old," Agatha said, entering the living room with their drinks on the tray.

"Ah, the jingling tray," Mamie said. "Goodbye, Frank. Cheerio, Roberta.

Off duty now, children. The world will go to hell without any help from us."

Because she did not know how to use an iPad and certainly not how to disconnect from Zoom, Mamie simply turned the tablet facedown. Julian could hear his parents either saying their goodbyes or protesting. He couldn't tell which.

27

~

"They didn't see Irving Tabor for a week or so after he told them about Venice of America," Julian told Sophie. The two of them were seated in their designated chairs on the Astroturf lawn. The dogs were rolling around, growling savagely, then taking quick breaks to drink together from the water bowl. "Those two are like an old married couple."

"So what happened when they did see him again?"

"You're a good audience, Sophie."

"Is that my cue to say you are a good performer?"

Julian blushed. "Yes, please."

"Okay, you are, but what happens next?"

"They didn't see Mr. Tabor for a week or so, and they were both disappointed. But finally, on a hot afternoon, they spotted him on the bench, his hat tipped over his eyes, his arms folded across his chest.

"'He's sleeping,' Mamie's grandfather said in German. '*Er schläft.*'

"'I am not sleeping,' Mr. Tabor said.

"They really did understand each other! Perhaps it was a special old-man language, a mixture of grunts and groans and sighs and puffs of stinking cigar, a few words thrown in for good measure. Mamie didn't know. What she did know was that anytime they saw Irving Tabor on the bench, her grandfather's step lightened and out came the cigars. Sometimes her grandfather brought the cigars, sometimes Mr. Tabor did. They would bite off the ends and light the cigars, their cheeks puffing in and out like bellows. They would savor the foul smoke, then nod to each other to indicate mutual satisfaction and friendship. They were a funny pair to look at, Mr. Tabor nicely dressed and slender, her grandfather shabby and stout, one Black, one white, all their differences shrouded in tobacco smoke.

"Sometimes the two men did fall asleep, and Mamie would leave them and wander along the beach, her feet in the water, her head in the clouds—daydreaming. Walking through the foam and watching it recede, watching the pinprick holes left behind, the broken shells, the reflections on the sand smooth as glass. Walking there on the edge of the water she knew no one could hear her if she sang or talked to herself— she was protected by the loud surf. She walked sprayed with mist, feet cool, head hot—and she dreamed of riding a horse (or a bull) through the waves, of dancing with boys, of clothes, of Heinrich Heine, whom she'd just begun to read in German, of Nancy Drew, whom she'd begun to read in English. And she would make up stories, naïve stories of rescues and escapes and joyous homecomings.

"But none of her stories held up to Irving Tabor's. He told them about Venice parades with floats pulled by mules, musicians dancing behind, just like the ones in New Orleans; swirling dance contests in the dance hall on the pier; the day the suffragette came to speak at the lecture hall; the travels in the car with Abbot Kinney over every kind of terrain: the stars they saw in the desert, the snow that covered the mountains. California was its own country, Mr. Tabor said. He'd seen whaling ships in the north, and he'd seen whales raising their calves in the south.

"'But there's no place like home,' he said. 'Little Dorothy was right about that. Not that I would want to live in Kansas, mind you.'

"'Home,' Grandfather said. '*Heimat.*'

"'It never leaves us, does it? Even when we leave home.'

"Her grandfather did not say much on the hot, dusty walk back to the house, and Mamie wondered: Is this what it is to get old? To think about all that you have lost, to mourn it day in and day out, to see it in the clouds you've buried your head in?

"She struggled with thoughts of what she'd lost all the time, and just as she sometimes had trouble forgetting what she wanted to, she also had trouble remembering everything she wanted to. Which made it feel as though she'd lost what she'd lost a second time. She didn't want to lose her best friend, Frieda Baum, for instance. If she could remember every detail of her face, she thought, she could keep Frieda with her. But Frieda's face faded, and her voice faded, and she became a blurry memory among so many blurry memories. She found out later that Frieda was lost in the most profound sense, lost not just to Mamie, but also to the world. She had been taken away with her family, Mamie knew even then. But it was not until years later that she learned Frieda had died at Auschwitz. Frieda's home had rejected her, spat her into an extermination camp. So what kind of home had it been to begin with? And was Mr. Tabor right? Would this home that rejected Frieda and rejected Mamie, would it stay with Mamie forever? Or would it fade like Frieda's face?

"It was a melancholy walk back to the house that day."

Julian stopped. Had he gotten it right? He'd spent much of the night before rehearsing, practicing, trying to remember every word of his grandmother's story. It was exhausting, but it was also invigorating. And it was sad. To tell his grandmother's story was to relive it.

"Sometimes I don't know how my grandmother can bear it. Bear anything," Julian said.

"Yeah. The world is, well, it ain't pretty."

"Except for the pretty parts."

"If you can see them."

A funny little pause between them, a look. Two shrugs, one on each side of this strange divide they found themselves in.

"When I try to imagine my grandmother's life, to really understand it, it's just overwhelming. She seems like some giant heroic lady, and I feel like a pipsqueak."

"*Pipsqueak*. That's a good word. I like that word. Well, we can be pipsqueaks together, I guess. Pipsqueaks Anonymous. But your grandmother seems happy, doesn't she?" Sophie said.

"She insists on it. 'Otherwise, what's the point of me?' That's what she told me."

The dogs were done playing. They were lying in the sun. Julian closed his eyes against the glare and resumed, but this time in Mamie's voice which, after a bit of practice, he could now mimic extremely well.

❧

"When Herr Tabor, as Grandfather called him, had saved up a little money in the early days, he bought a lot in Oakwood. He built a little house for himself and his family, a shotgun house just like the houses in New Orleans. When other members of his family arrived in Venice, he built other little houses on his property, a whole complex surrounding a courtyard. He worked for Abbot Kinney as his driver and advisor for many years before Abbot Kinney died in 1920.

"'He lived in a big house at number one Grand Canal. When he died,' Mr. Tabor said, 'he left his house to me in his will.'

"Mr. Tabor told us so many stories about our new country that summer. I think it must have amused him that he, an outsider himself because of his race and originally coming from New Orleans, was the one to educate the two white Viennese greenhorns about California. But it was the story of the house that was my favorite. It took place right there, in Venice, but it seemed to me even then to be a larger story. A story fit for a fairy tale. Or a myth.

"'Now what I want you to understand is that when I inherited the house on the Grand Canal from my friend Abbot Kinney, founder of Venice, I couldn't live in it. No Coloreds allowed on the canals of Venice of America. Maybe in Venice, Italy, but not in Venice of America. So you are probably wondering what I did with my beautiful house. You are probably thinking I sold my house to someone who *could* live at One Grand Canal, to someone rich and someone white."

"'Dirty bastards,' Grandfather said, inevitably.

"'You said it, Husky. But I didn't sell my house. I still have it, and I live there with my family. How did you do that, Irving Tabor? you are asking yourselves.'

"Which, yes, we were.

"'I will now tell you.' Pause and big, mischievous smile. 'I called my brothers and I said, "The Mountain is coming to Mohammed, boys." So we cut Mr. Abbot Kinney's house, now belonging to Mr. Irving Tabor, into three pieces. Three pieces of house. And we loaded those three pieces one at a time onto a raft, and we floated each piece of house, one by one by one, on the raft, which was pulled by mules, along the Venice canals. Right past the white people in their whites-only houses. And then we loaded each piece on a truck and the mules pulled that truck through the streets of Oakwood, where they let the Black folks live, and we unloaded those three pieces of house and we put them back together and that, Husky my friend, is where I live now, in my beautiful house with my beautiful family.'

"The cheek of it! The ingenious, elegant defiance. Grandfather and Mr. Irving roared with laughter.

"I was ecstatic. This really was a fairy-tale place—fairy godfathers and wicked witchy neighbors and a magic house that swam to its happy home.

"I left them and walked and walked and wondered where Oakwood was. I knew where Venice was, way down where the beach was lined with oil wells, the pier sagging, half burned, into the sea. It was a noisy, pungent place rising in the distance. I turned back before I reached the pier.

"I ignored the tiny shorebirds that scattered in front of me. My feet were covered with tar, which would make my mother unhappy. But I was happy. As happy as a little girl pried away from a different, happy life can be. Because somewhere nearby was a house that had also been pried from its home. Rejected, torn apart, rescued, dragged, through no fault of its own, across land and water. And put back together in a new and better place.

"'Your house is just like us,' I said to Mr. Tabor when I returned to the bench.

"'My house is green. You're as red as a lobster.'

"'No, I meant—'

"'I know, I know, child. My house found a home.'

"'*Gutt!*' said Grandfather. He slapped his friend on the back.

"'*Gutt* to you, too, Husky.'

"After we got home, I realized we had not asked the address of the magic house. How would we go see it? How would we go pay our respects to a house that understood all we had been through? How would we gain its wisdom?

"We didn't see Irving Tabor for a while after that day. I wondered if Grandfather had said something while I was walking on the beach. I was always a little nervous that Grandfather would refer to Mr. Tabor as a *Schwartze*. I was never sure if that was the proper German name for people of Mr. Tabor's race—it meant black—or if it was an offensive term like Hebe or yid or kike or the other things I'd heard Jews called. But Grandfather said there was no bad blood between them, not to worry.

"Then it was autumn, though you couldn't tell by the weather, which was hotter than it had been in summer, and drier—desert dry, even in Santa Monica. School started, a major event for me—and for my wardrobe. I was lucky that autumn—my feet had grown over the summer, and because I needed new shoes anyway I was able to convince my mother to buy me the brown and white saddle shoes I had been lobbying for. We went to the shoe store and picked them out, an early present from her for my thirteenth birthday. The choice of clothing is always important for a thirteen-year-old, I suppose, but for me it felt urgent. I was not yet comfortable enough with American fashion to be confident about the length a skirt ought to be, how tight or loose a sweater should be, what kind of collar I needed in order to look like the other girls at my school, but I felt I had to blend in. How nice it would have been to have a uniform, as we did at my school in Vienna.

"Grandfather and I went on our walks later in the day now, after I got home from anxious days of scouting my fellow students' costumes and slang and demeanor. The walks were a balm, a step back in time to a world where I knew what I was about. The dog pranced happily beside us, we spoke German, we laughed at Austrian jokes, we sang Austrian songs (all of this softly: in America German had become the language of traitors and spies). I heard stories of all the relatives from several generations back and how they ruined their or someone else's life. Grandfather carried his large black umbrella open to protect us from the sun. We were not inconspicuous, and at first I worried about bumping into a schoolmate. But soon I forgot to worry and simply enjoyed the walks and the beach and the dog and the nostalgia. I even let Grandfather hold my hand.

"When Mr. Tabor had not appeared on the bench for weeks, Grandfather said that Tabor was a man of business, that he ran a large, successful janitorial firm. None of us, he said, has the time to sit around on a bench and swap tales like old, retired men, and he shot me a look that suggested I not point out the obvious.

"Then, like the tide, Mr. Tabor reappeared. He had been busy, yes, business was good. But sometimes on his afternoon constitutional he just did not make it as far north as the bench Grandfather liked, he said. There was a section of beach farther south in Santa Monica where Black people gathered. My parents later told me it was called Inkwell Beach and was an example of American segregation, something they as left-leaning, socialist-leaning Europeans, as Jews discriminated against in the severest ways in Austria, found horrifying. But at the time it did not occur to me that Mr. Tabor limited himself to that beach because he had been turned back by police. I assumed he wanted to sit on a bench there to talk to his old friends, which was often true, and sometimes ventured north to talk to his new friends, Grandfather and me. How much we miss when we are looking around us, how much we see when we look back. Even small things. I remember those saddle shoes, every scuff and scrape. It was important not to have clean saddle shoes, so decreed the feet of every girl I knew at school. My parents tried to make me polish the white parts. They were unsuccessful. Small things. And big things. I vividly remember the day Mr. Tabor was forced to leave the bench where he sat with Grandfather. I try not to think about it, as I try not to think about so many things. It was a painful, haunting day. I try not to think about it, I rarely speak of it, but it happened, and I was there, and it stays with me.

"Grandfather tried to intervene with the policeman, who looked simultaneously healthy and unhealthy with that particularly beefy American complexion. But Grandfather spoke, naturally, in German. German did not go over well with the police officer. He threatened to arrest us all. He called us all the demeaning names he could think of. On the subject of Jews and Negroes, the words came readily to him. Mr. Tabor tipped his hat at Grandfather. Grandfather tipped his hat at Mr. Tabor. Tabor walked one way, we walked the other.

"It's still difficult for me to explain my feelings that day. There was rage, but there was also embarrassment, embarrassment on behalf of Mr. Tabor, embarrassment on behalf of Grandfather and me, embarrassment for the stupidity and spiteful malevolence of that policeman slapping his nightstick in his hand and calling us foul names, for the beach divided up like feudal states, for America, for Austria, for Germany, for Europe, for humankind as a whole. I did not understand America's original sin, I knew very little and thought even less about segregation. I was a thirteen-year-old Jewish girl happy to be alive. But the incident was too reminiscent of Vienna, the insult to Mr. Tabor and my grandfather too acute for even me to miss. And there was fear. The threat of a man in uniform. I wish that awful day turned me into a precocious civil rights activist. But all it did was frighten me and embarrass me and envelop me in loneliness.

"'Even here, in your paradise,' Grandfather said as we walked home. He spat on the street, something I had never seen him do. He opened his umbrella, though there was neither rain nor sun, just blank colorless skies. 'You never know,' he said, and raised it above our heads.

"After that day, Grandfather and I tried walking farther south on the beach, hoping we'd see Mr. Tabor, and we did, a few times. They shook hands, exchanged cigars, tipped hats. But there were no more stories. The only stories that would have been possible after that day would be angry stories, bitter stories, on both sides. Neither Grandfather nor Mr. Tabor was inclined to offer those tales to the other. Out of respect, I imagine. Or humiliation. At any rate, the spell had been broken. Their shared story was over.

"It wasn't until years and years later that I finally saw the magical house that had ridden on barges and a mule-drawn carriage. By then the last remnants of the amusement park were gone. Most of the canals had been filled in. The Venice pier was just a pier to walk out on to fish. A street had been named after Abbot Kinney. A smaller street had been named after Irving Tabor. Memorials. Everything gone but the names.

"But there, on the corner of Santa Clara and Sixth, there was the house. Not a name, not a memorial, but a living, breathing house, a beautiful green house in its serene totality. The house that came apart and came together again. The house that sailed, broken and rejected, until it found its home."

⁂

THE day after Mamie told him this story, Julian decided to take Prince Jan on a search for the Kinney-Tabor house, the house that had sailed in three pieces to its new home. A one-story bungalow, soft green, a bright white picket fence, a peaceful-looking house nestled into its trees. The house that Abbot Kinney built and Irving Tabor rebuilt.

Julian stood looking at it for a long time. The house that had found a home, that's what Mamie had said. He thought of all the people who had found a home within that house: Abbot Kinney, Irving Tabor, generations of Tabor's descendants. Julian had grown up in an apartment in a building on Manhattan's Upper West Side, and he still viewed houses as somewhat exotic. The houses in Venice were so close together the streets might almost have been horizontal apartment buildings. No elevator man to let you in when you forgot your key or to let you ride up and down when you were in a bad mood and too little to go outside on your own. But here in Venice the little houses were pretty and proud and independent, each with its own bit of grass or gravel. Brave little houses. Especially this one. The same family still owned the green house, Irving Tabor's family.

Very softly, Julian said, "Goodbye, Brave Green House," smiled at his silliness, and walked thoughtfully home.

"Did you knock on the door?" Mamie asked when he got back.

"Grandma! There's a pandemic. You can't go knocking on people's doors."

"What a shame."

"Did you ever knock on the door?" he asked. "Did you go in? See who lived there? Introduce yourself? Tell them you knew Irving Tabor when you were a little girl?"

"Certainly not."

"How come?"

"Respect, Julian."

"I'm just asking."

"No, dear, I mean respect for Mr. Tabor's house. It has gone through so much. It doesn't want a visit from me to bring up old, painful memories."

"That's adorable," said the same person who had moments before bidden the brave green house goodbye.

Part Three

28

ONE HOT, SUNNY SUMMER DAY, MAMIE SAT HER GRANDSON DOWN IN HER armchair, a big comfortable thing covered in heavy worn fabric that once had been, at a guess, blue.

"My listening chair."

It reposed in pride—pride of place, yes, but also pride of geometric space, the apex of a triangle, the other two points being the large old-fashioned loudspeakers encased in wood, each one about three feet high.

"You are now in the sweet spot, Julian."

No one but Mamie sat in her listening chair. The dingy-blue sweet spot was reserved for her. Sharing her throne was out of character, she knew, and Julian squirmed there a bit apprehensively, as she had intended.

"I am honored," he said. "I think."

"Yes, you *are* honored, Julian. Whatever you think, dear."

There was often music playing in the house. Classical music, mostly, and the occasional bit of jazz. Julian barely noticed it. When his grandmother settled into her listening chair, he went out for a walk with the dog or retreated to his room. She had never invited him to join her.

"You know," she said, "it was Tchaikovsky who started World War Two."

"Not a Tchaikovsky fan, then?"

"On the contrary. But one day in December in 1941, my mother was driving us along the Pacific. PCH was called Roosevelt Highway back then. Those were the days when people 'went for a drive' for pleasure, can you imagine? My parents liked to take the car for a spin while the Sunday Philharmonic concert was being broadcast from Carnegie Hall. And there we were in the old rattletrap admiring the waves and breathing in the sea breeze and listening to Arthur Rubinstein play the Tchaikovsky Piano Concerto no. 1, when . . ."

Julian waited in suspense. These narrative pauses were often followed by "all of sudden" or "from out of the blue" and then, boom, Ernst Lubitsch might appear at his own beach front door or Johnny Weissmuller with a plate of sandwiches at a party.

"Like a bolt from the blue . . ."

"Like a bolt from the blue," he said to encourage her along.

"The announcer broke in!"

"And? And?"

"Pearl Harbor, Julian."

"Pearl Harbor. Jesus."

"During the first movement!"

Now she went bustling over to her collection of LPs.

Sitting in the exalted blue music chair, Julian watched her and remembered holding her violin when he was about five. Mamie had asked him if he wanted to learn to play.

"It has all the notes, you know. Not like that piano your mother keeps in the living room for decoration. The violin has all the notes in all the world."

He could still remember the smell of the bow, like pine trees. But the strings of the violin hurt his fingertips. And when Mamie played for the family, which she did fairly often when he was so young, he found the music dull and impenetrable.

"We can get a violin to fit you," Mamie said. "A half size, I think."

"No, thank you," he'd said politely. "I have a new iPod!"

Mamie had never mentioned music to him again.

Until now.

She shuffled over to her turntable and gently slipped a vinyl record from its case. She doted on her records. They were so handsome, she said—black and shiny as Tyrone Power's hair. The weight, the balance, the spirals of energy, the miracle contained in each groove.

"Vinyl is very hip, you know," Julian said.

She said, "Progress is circular." Then, addressing the record in her hand, "Just like you, my darling."

She placed the record on the turntable. Thank you, she said silently to her twisted, arthritic fingers. We cannot play ourselves, but we can play what others play.

"We are ready," she said, still looking at her hands. "Are you ready, Julian?"

"For?"

"The soundtrack to my next story."

"I'm all ears," he said.

"Ah, would that, would that . . ."

And the needle dropped on the record.

When the piece finished, about thirty minutes later, Mamie said, "Lovely, isn't it?"

Julian nodded. It was lovely. Dramatic. Lyrical. He had trouble placing classical music in time, but he could tell it was not Mozart, which was where he always started—he could usually determine whether music was before Mozart or after Mozart. He could not always get much more accurate than that. This was definitely after Mozart. Way after.

"Lovely," he said, unwilling to commit himself any further and risk his grandmother's scorn.

"Now let me give you some context, Julian. My father was a composer. He was well regarded in Vienna and in all the music circles of Europe at the time. A conventional composer in the tradition of the late Romantics, and his work was considered a bit dowdy, even before we left Vienna. But he was popular enough to have landed an excellent teaching position at the conservatory there."

"Did your father write the piece we just listened to?" Julian said. "I didn't know anything of his had been recorded."

"No, no, no." She banged her cane with her usual fierceness and, as always when she banged it on the rug in the living room, it made no sound. Even on the flagstone outside it was muted by its rubber tip. Julian thought she would do better with a big bell. Or a trumpet. "Listen, please," she said. "And stop interrupting. I'm old, Julian. How would you feel if I died before I finished telling you my stories? You must not interrupt."

"Wow. Low blows, Grandma."

"Thank you. I have had many years of practice."

She proceeded to talk not about the music they had just listened to or its composer. She spoke instead about her father. Julian knew very little about his great-grandfather. Otto Künstler was rarely spoken of and Julian had often wondered why. But now Mamie had launched into a story about him.

Otto came to America full of hope and expectations, she said, but soon found there was little demand for his services as a composer. It was true he had not been a highly successful composer in Vienna, but he had been a serious one who taught other serious composers, some of whom would go on to become quite famous themselves. But in Los Angeles, no one who needed lessons had ever heard of him. Those who had heard of him were far beyond anything he could teach them. He was just another émigré with bad English scrambling for pupils. And so he taught little American girls and boys to play scales and arpeggios. Otto Künstler, who had studied with Zemlinsky, now taught Cheryl Gold and Peter Blakely and MaryAnne Church and Bobbie Schwartz to play "In the Hall of the Mountain King" and Bach's Prelude in C Major.

"That's so sad," Julian said. "It must have been incredibly frustrating, too."

"Yet he was lucky, and he knew it."

"Which made it worse?"

Mamie said, Yes. She did not elaborate.

Julian waited, but still no more information about her father. He tried a different approach.

"What did he look like?" he asked.

"Handsome. A big shock of hair that fell in his face when he played the piano. Serious. Long serious face. Huge smile."

Julian remembered now. He'd seen a few pictures when, as a little boy, he'd rummaged through a box of stuff Mamie kept in a closet: a thin, hand-some man bent over a sheet of music, holding a pencil, frowning; the same man grinning in funny baggy shorts and short-sleeved shirt and sandals and dark socks holding up a little girl in Vienna. His hair in both pictures was thick, long, and swooping over one eye—it was Romantic hair.

He had pulled that box out of Mamie's closet, a big round hat box full of treasures. A pencil case with a picture of Felix the Cat playing the violin, a small stuffed toy dog with one ear, and so many photos. The man with the shock of dark hair, a woman in an old-fashioned dress, a little boy (lots and lots of the little boy) who looked like Julian but wasn't Julian, a tiny handmade notebook. He sat on the floor with the pictures and trea-sures spread out around him. He'd been so little. Four? His grandmother came in and gasped. And then he held up a photo of a beautiful young woman laughing and Mamie snatched it from his hand. He remembered the movement, the swiftness, the arc. He could not remember anything after that. Had she been angry? Had she laughed? Had he dreamed the whole episode?

"Did you have a—"

But Mamie was well into her story now, which seemed to be about what a lousy music student she, the daughter of a composer, turned out to be. As a very young child she would demand to know where the sound came from. Little felt hammers? Why? How? Who decided which ham-mer hit which string and who decided which sound a hammer and its string were supposed to make? And why did one hammer on one string make that sound while another hammer on another string made a differ-ent sound, and who decided? Who said middle C had to sound like that? Who said that particular sound was middle C? Who decided where the middle was? The middle of what?

"Who decides? The emperor?"

That made her father laugh, which enraged her.

Who made up the scale? she demanded.

"Mozart," her grandfather said.

"Pythagoras," her father said.

"Pythagoras was not Austrian."

"No, Father, he wasn't."

"So, then, Mozart. Bach would also be a correct answer."

At which point Mamie had come out with what she considered her deepest question of all: Whoever it was who did make up the scale, how did they decide? Who said a scale had to have those notes? And why? Why, why, why?

Her father expounded on the phenomenon of vibrations for years after that, ringing a bell for Mamie, tapping a triangle, beating a drum, showing her illustrations of the ear and all its parts, but by the time they reached California, he had given up trying to explain the physics of sound to his child.

"How many times can a man scream 'vibrations' to his daughter?" Mamie asked Julian. "Quite a few, it turns out. But eventually the 'whys' won, and I stopped being pushed onto that piano bench."

Julian, who had never wondered what or why a scale was, was suddenly full of curiosity. He tried to remember his high school physics class. All he could recall was a textbook illustration of a rock on a . . . shit! What was it called? His brain reached and grabbed and . . . he could not find the word. Maybe all this wine every day was a bad idea. Maybe he was the one approaching dementia. It certainly wasn't his grandmother. She always knew the right words.

"Grandma!" he said. "Word retrieval emergency! The thing kids sit on, the board, and one side goes up and the other goes down and . . ."

"Teeter-totter."

"No, it starts with an *s* maybe . . ."

"Teeter-totter," she said, following up with the definitive though muted slam of her cane on the rug: discussion over.

Julian googled teeter-totter on his phone anyway.

"Seesaw!" he said.

But Mamie was already talking about the Sunday afternoon gatherings in the Los Angeles of her youth and paid no attention to him.

She and her grandfather were sipping very good, strong coffee, she said. Topped with whipped cream. They were sitting on a wrought iron bench—she could remember the diamond pattern it left on her thighs—when her father walked up with a man dressed in tennis whites.

"Little girls should not drink a coffee," her father said in strained English.

"I am not a little girl," Mamie answered in perfect English. "I am thirteen." They had been in the country for a little over a year and she was feeling more comfortable with clothes, with English, even with her schoolmates. They went for ice cream after school together, the girls sitting at one booth, the boys at another, giggling. Mamie did not like the word *giggle* and she felt silly engaging in the activity of giggling. But she had convinced herself it was an American custom, and in the interest of assimilation she allowed herself to join in. Once she'd given in the first time, she found it easier and easier to giggle.

"It sounds like you're talking about weed, Grandma."

"Weed. You'd think you children invented the stuff. Your condescension is misguided, dear. The point is I giggled in front of this distinguished man. Then I pointed out to my father that if I'd been a boy and my family were proper Jews I would have had a bar mitzvah and been proclaimed a man."

She had learned about bar mitzvahs from her new friends at school. She had been invited to several, baffling affairs at a temple and a party with dancing afterward.

"You are certainly not a man," her father said.

This in German.

She'd been tempted to giggle again, but something about the man in tennis whites kept her quiet. He was bald, a feature she always noticed because of that big, romantic sweep of her father's hair, of which she was very proud. This man had no hair on the top of his head or in front, just on the sides and back, a semicircle. He was an ordinary-looking man, except he wasn't. Maybe it was his eyes.

"He had the only eyes I have ever seen that could legitimately be called burning," Mamie said.

He had a deep suntan.

"Brown as a nut as people used to say. And a nose, an aggressive but pleasant big nose. And big ears.

"'I have not had the honor of knowing you personally until this moment,' he said in English, and he leaned in to a little bow. His smile told me he was teasing, but no one had ever addressed me so formally, with so much respect, even teasing respect—certainly not an adult, not a man, and not in the United States, the land of casual hi-theres and wide, meaningless smiles.

"'How do you do,' I answered, also in English, tempted to curtsy, though not tempted enough. This was America, after all.

"'It is my conviction that people know who is one of them and who is not,' he continued. Who ees vun uff zem.

"I am vun uff you! I wanted to say. Whoever 'you' might be!

"'Yes,' I said instead, as solemnly as I could.

"'Your esteemed father reports that you wish to emancipate dissonance.'"

His courtesy filled Mamie with nostalgia for Vienna. And she was drawn to his sympathetic big ears—Oh, she did not want to disappoint him. But emancipate dissonance?

Was it a technical tennis term? He looked so nice in his pressed, creased white flannel pants and white polo shirt. Mamie had never played tennis.

Dissonance was a musical term, she knew that from her aborted piano lessons. Dissonance was something that occurred when you did what you were told not to do, when you played a note not sanctioned by the scale, or worse when you played two notes together that the scale did not allow to fraternize.

"So, did I want to emancipate dissonance?" she asked Julian. "You bet I did!"

She had never considered it before, but yes! Emancipation was necessary. It was urgent. Poor, struggling dissonance, trapped and voiceless in its incomprehensible octave. This would be like freeing the lions at the zoo.

"You question the conventions and seek meaning in something greater, isn't that so?" the man said.

"Doesn't everyone?"

"Ah!" her father cried. "She never disappoints."

"Your father tells me you question the scale."

"I have tried to explain the physics of sound, you know," Otto said. He tapped his ear. "It's all here, Mamie."

"No," said the man in white. He tapped his heart. "It is all here." He paused, smiled, and tapped his forehead. "And here."

Her father said, "In that particular head, yes."

Mamie had never seen her father so deferential. This made the man even more interesting. She wanted to be deferential, too. She stood up, offered her hand, and said, "I am Salomea Künstler, known as Mamie."

Then, before he could introduce himself back to her, she said, "Who created the scale? Don't say 'God,' please. Sir."

"God? But we will talk of God and creation both," the man said. "If you will allow?" And again, the mischievous smile, the piercing eyes. "If you wish to understand the nature of creation, you must ask yourself this question: Was there light before God said, 'Let there be light'? Of course not! How can you create light if light already exists?"

Mamie was mesmerized. This distinguished man had become almost merry, dancing from foot to foot. "You cannot! You cannot!" he cried.

Then, still dancing with excitement, he said, "But if there was never any light before God said 'Let there be light,' then how did God know what light was?"

He stared at her. He clapped his hands together.

"*That* is creation," he said.

❧

"So you see," Mamie told Julian, "I was smitten, I was a disciple from the moment I met him. How could I not have been?"

❧

THE man spoke more and more quickly. "There was not yet light! There had never been light! Never! Only God's omniscience could embrace a vision of it and only his omnipotence could call it forth."

He paused to make sure Mamie was following him.

Mamie thought, What if there is no God? Then what? But she said nothing. Because if there really was no light and God did say "Let there be light" and then there was light, well, then, yes, logically it was God who created light.

"We poor human beings," he said, smiling gently, "when we refer to one of the better minds among us as a creator, we should never forget what a creator really is."

"A god?" Mamie asked.

Her grandfather gave a muffled snort behind her. The man in white looked pleased.

"A creator has a vision of something that has not existed before his vision," he said. "And a creator has the power to bring his vision to life."

"Are you a creator?" she asked. He did not look like a god, that was for sure. She tried unsuccessfully to imagine him with his big ears and nose, his bronze bald head, dressed in his white flannel pants and short-sleeved knit shirt, whisking Europa above the waves.

"A brilliant composer," her father broke in. "The creator not only of new and startling and original music, but of a whole new method of composing."

"Have you invented new scales, too?" Mamie asked. "Oh, I hope so. And keys. Keys are quite oppressive. Why should it be the key of C? Why can't you play an F in the key of C major? And the piano, too, you know, is oppressive. It misses all the notes in between the notes."

Her father said, "Salomea. Your manners." But he was beaming.

The man gave a shout of laughter and said, "Mees Künstler, vee stand alone against a verld of enemies. Do you play tennis? No? I vill teach you."

29

JULIAN COULD REMEMBER SO MANY TIMES WATCHING HIS GRANDMOTHER BEAT his father at tennis. Frank loved tennis and played every Saturday at the public courts in Riverside Park, even in the winter, but Mamie put his game to shame. She was a fantastic player, even in her early eighties, before serious arthritis set in. She had been a tennis fanatic in her younger years. Whoever taught her to play, Julian thought, taught her to play fiercely, fearlessly, and to win. Julian opened his laptop and googled "tennis composer Los Angeles."

Gershwin! George Gershwin! There was a black-and-white photograph for sale on eBay showing Gershwin in his tennis whites on his tennis court. Maybe Julian could buy it for Mamie as a surprise. Four hundred and thirty-seven dollars and fifty cents? No, Julian could not buy it for Mamie as a surprise. He gazed sadly at the photograph, then thought: that fifty cents. Why?

He read a little more about Gershwin in Los Angeles. He lived across the street from Shirley Temple! Maybe Mamie knew Shirley Temple! Julian's mother loved Shirley Temple and made Julian and his sister watch black-and-white movies of her tap-dancing and smiling and pouting and cheering up various old codgers. Where was Shirley Temple when you needed her? Julian thought. But wait, this Wikipedia entry said Gershwin died in 1937. Grandma Mamie did not get to the United States until 1939.

Drat, Julian thought. *Drat*? He had been out of the real world too long. The real world that was so unreal.

"Grandma, who was the composer who taught you to play such good tennis?" he said at breakfast the next morning. "It wasn't Gershwin. He died before you got here."

"Gershwin? Whatever gave you that idea?"

"Tennis."

Mamie smashed the yolk of her poached egg, and they both watched it ooze slowly over her toast. "Such a pretty sight. But then it coagulates and loses its charm. Like all of us."

"Was he famous?"

"Ha! Not as famous as he thought he should be."

Julian groaned. What a horrible tease his grandmother was. She was enjoying this, he could tell. She did not have enough stimulation. Neither did he. And here they were, facing each other over the kitchen table, Mamie tormenting Julian out of boredom, Julian burning with curiosity out of boredom.

"Come on, Grandma, what's the big mystery?"

"There is no mystery. He's just a character in a story. Call him what you like."

"I thought you didn't like secrets."

"I like privacy, Julian. Quite a different thing."

"Well, okay, but if you didn't sleep with him, I don't see what the big deal is. You didn't sleep with him, did you?"

"Julian! Certainly not! I was just a child. He was an old man. I'm surprised at you for even suggesting such thing. It's indecent."

He carried their coffees out to the garden and they took to their respective lounge chairs and stretched out beneath the whir of hummingbirds and the insistent declarations of crows. They waited out the day as it crawled forward from lunch to tea, and then, at long last, cocktails.

"Now, don't get me wrong, Julian, he *was* important," Mamie said, martini in hand. "Perhaps the most important composer of his time. Yes, arguably the most important. Not like my poor father. My father was competent, I think you would say. A terrible indictment. A competent composer. It amazes me that he was so cheerful for so long."

"What was his name?"

"Otto. Otto Künstler."

"No, the important composer who taught you to play tennis."

"Oh, you mean L.A.'s one and only Arnold?"

"Arnold *Schwarzenegger*? He's not a composer. You *know* him?"

"Really, Julian. Arnold Schoenberg."

Julian almost blurted out: Who is he, again? He stopped himself just in time. Perhaps Arnold Schoenberg was related to Christopher Isherwood. By marriage. Or related to Julian's ignorance. By blood. No, he remembered now: Schoenberg had a Saint Bernard dog.

"Interesting," he said.

"Sometimes I think you are having me on, Julian."

"Well, Arnold Schwarzenegger *is* Austrian."

"And I didn't sleep with him either."

His grandmother's martini glass shimmered in the afternoon sun. Martinis were so beautiful. So clear. So pure. The glass was bright with icy condensation. The olives idled, lucid and green. Mamie brought the glass to her glaring-pink lipsticked lips and sipped, leaving a perfect pink print behind.

"I wish I liked martinis," he said.

But his grandmother seemed not to hear. "My father was a kind man at heart," she was saying. "But he wasn't happy. He tried to be. He felt he ought to be. He was grateful, you see, to be alive. But when we left Vienna, he left something behind. I mean, he left everything behind, but you understand what I mean. Eventually, gratitude turned to guilt."

"Yes," he said. He understood guilt.

His grandmother had slipped off into one of her reveries, and Julian thought it was time to refill his glass of whiskey. "And by refill, I mean fill, to the top, barkeep," he said softly. He went to the kitchen and got some ice, one, two, three cubes.

"Are even numbers of ice cubes bad luck, like olives?" he said when he returned.

"At this moment in history? Probably."

Agatha rang the dinner bell and helped Grandma Mamie toddle to the table.

"Sit next to me, Agatha," he said.

She glared at him. She said, "You are drunken."

"Hard times," Mamie said. "Hard times."

"All times hard," said Agatha.

⁂

THE next Google reference after Gershwin was, indeed, Arnold Schoenberg. Grandma's tennis teacher. Schoenberg looked like everyone's Jewish uncle. He had changed his name from Schönberg to Schoenberg, losing the umlaut as a protest against the Nazis. Julian wondered if he should change his name from Künstler to Koenstler.

Schoenberg, the father of atonal music. Forget the octave. Forget minor keys and major keys. Compose music using all twelve notes. Twelve half tones, all inclusive, sharps and flats welcome, white keys and black keys. The composer would decide on a series of twelve notes, then arrange them as desired into a tone row. All twelve notes must be used, and no note could be repeated until all the notes in the tone row of twelve had been used, but go ahead, turn the series upside down. Or inside out.

Julian understood this was radical and groundbreaking even if he did not really understand the theory. But the point of all this revolutionary innovation? The emancipation of the dissonance!

"It means two notes, or more, played together, are left longing for some sort of resolution," Mamie said. "Bach did it, Mozart did it. When they were reaching for a sound not sanctioned by the key of the composition. For a little flavor, for interest, for depth. Liszt, Satie, Strauss—they all embraced dissonance when they needed it. Stravinsky, Ives . . ."

But there was no formal recognition of its importance, of its necessity as music moved into new sounds and onto new pathways. That's what Schoenberg wanted to do—to give dissonance the respect it deserved. So he gave it its own method.

"He wanted freedom from tradition, but not chaos. He found a way to free dissonance, to allow it to blossom, on its own terms, by giving it rules," Mamie said. "His rules, of course. He was a revolutionary, but a conservative revolutionary. He did not approve of chaos. And chaos was what he saw coming. Long before most people did. In music. In Germany, too."

"I've never listened to any Schoenberg."

"Yes, you have. I played a piece for you yesterday."

"But that was not dissonant. Was it?"

No, that was not dissonant, Mamie told him. She led him back to the listening chair. Then, with a sprightly step and a face of almost spiteful glee, Mamie slipped a record onto the turntable and said, "This is dissonance, dear."

Forty minutes later, Julian said, "Aha."

"It is an acquired taste," she replied.

"Like martinis."

"Now when Irving Thalberg heard the first piece I played you on the radio, he got Schoenberg to come to his office. A big deal: big honor to meet Thalberg in Thalberg's mind; big honor to Thalberg in Schoenberg's mind. So Thalberg compliments Schoenberg on his 'Enchanted Night,' his 'lovely' composition, and Schoenberg, being Schoenberg, says, 'I do not write lovely music.' Wonderful. Perfect. I wish I'd been there."

"But the music is lovely."

"Yes. It was composed before the twelve tones came and bewitched him. You know, there was a riot in the concert hall when his Second String Quartet was first performed. An actual riot!" she said. "Booing and hissing. People rushing for the exits. Mahler was there. He told someone to stop hissing, and the man said, 'I hiss at you, too.' Oh, to have been alive in Vienna then."

After playing the Second String Quartet, Mamie played another that sounded, to Julian, like Looney Tunes cartoon music.

"Bingo. John Adams noticed that, too—Schoenberg's influence on Hollywood."

"President John Adams?"

Mamie did not reply. Her eyes were closed again, her fingers plucking imaginary strings, sweeping an imaginary bow.

Peace on earth, some hanging gardens, foliage and a heart—Mamie whispered the titles with such soft reverence that Julian would catch only a word, sometimes two. Pianos, strings, a cappella voices, hundreds together.

Mamie chuckled at what she said was a satire. "Perfect, perfect," she said.

And then: "Nobody really took to this, his Kol Nidre."

It blasted from the speakers, harsh though not particularly atonal.

"He wanted to strip away Bruch's sentimentality."

"Well, he succeeded there," Julian said.

"Not even the rabbi who commissioned it liked it. It's *my* least favorite. Why mess with perfection?"

The music played on. Julian sat on the sofa as if in a trance. Maybe it was a trance. Maybe Mamie had hypnotized him, forcing him to listen to a composer whose music was weird, almost creepy, but also fascinating.

She played a piece with just a few instruments and a singer sort of chanting.

"He told Thalberg that this was the way he'd score *The Good Earth*. In that style. And that he, not the director, would have to be in charge of all dialogue and the actors."

Mamie began to chant in the same way as the singer: "All the dialogue chaaanted in this pecoooliar waay. And he asked for double the feeee! He carried an umbreeellaaa to the meeting with Thaaalberg and would not let anyone take it from him because he did nooot wanttt to forget it."

An alarmed Agatha rushed into the living room.

"I'm fine," Mamie said in her normal voice. "But can you imagine *Sprechtstimme* in *The Good Earth*? Paul Muni *sprechstimming*?"

"No," Agatha said with dignity and went back to her room.

"Those were wonderful days in their way, Julian. The émigré artists suffered, yes, but they *were* artists, and they filled Los Angeles. There was no culture here—no high culture—but émigré culture. And no money but Hollywood money. But *The Good Earth*? Oh, that is one soundtrack I would love to hear. Of course, even the twelve-tone stuff sounds tame now. And 'lovely'! Time, Julian. Time does that."

Julian thought Time was slowed down enough by the lockdown. It did not need this exciting, often beautiful, sometimes monotonous, frequently jarring music to be playing all day to emphasize the absence of real life.

But the more he listened, the more interested he became, the more moved, charmed, excited by the music, just as Mamie had predicted he would.

Later: "Notice how he cannot resist harmony."

They were listening to the Piano Concerto, op. 42.

"Listen, Julian. Do you hear how harmony calls to him, like the Sirens calling to Odysseus?"

But it had been a long day of listening. A little Schoenberg would have gone a long way, he thought.

Mamie said: "Nothing stays revolutionary, that is my point, Julian. Age and time and familiarity appropriate everything new."

"Is that so terrible? At least there aren't riots at Schoenberg concerts anymore."

"Comfort is complacency, Julian. You are definitely not a proper modernist. But why should you be? Modernism's old hat, isn't it? Even postmodernism is old hat. What comes after postmodernism? Don't know. I lost track after that. Just as well."

Mamie gestured for him to vacate the listening chair for the couch, settled herself in the blue armchair, and said: "I am bossy, and you are acquiescent. But you have a spark, Julian. Fan the spark! Fan the spark!" She waved her hands, as if she were encouraging a campfire. "I'm down to embers myself."

"No you're—"

"Embers keep you warm. I worked hard for my embers. I relish them."

"Did you like being a studio musician?"

"Studio musicians made good money. I was pretty good, too. I couldn't play in the L.A. Philharmonic or anything like that—no women there. But we had chamber groups. And I could play fiddle like a hillbilly, too. You know how many women were studio musicians then?"

Julian shook his head.

Mamie pointed to herself. "You're looking at her." She held out her gnarled fingers. "We had fun while it lasted, didn't we?" she asked her left hand.

"Oh, yes, by all means get out your little notebook," she told Julian then. She watched him writing. Why, he's left-handed, she thought. And I never noticed! No wonder he didn't want to play the violin when I shoved it in his grubby little child paws.

"I had beautiful handwriting when I was a child," she said. "It's shaky now, like me. But it suffices. Like me!"

30

WHY AM I TELLING JULIAN MY STORIES? MAMIE WONDERED. AND MAKING HIM listen to Schoenberg? It's child abuse. Sometimes as she spoke about her life and the lives of those she'd grown up with, she even wondered what a story was. It had a beginning, a middle, an end, isn't that what they said? Was that all it was, simple as that? But as with middle C, she wondered how one knew where the middle was located. Who, she quoted her younger self to herself, decided?

Knowing she was near the end of her run, she thought it should be possible to look back and search for the middle of her story. But each time she did, the middle seemed to shift. The numerical middle, forty-six and a half, was indistinguishable from forty-six or forty-five or -eight or -nine and on and on. Perhaps life did not have definite middles. Just beginnings and ends and . . . everything in between?

But stories were not life. Stories were different.

Or were they?

Her stories began before she was born, but they would end when she did.

Or would they?

Was that why she was telling stories? Immortality? Immortality in the mind and heart of a sweet, immature fellow who wrote her stories down? But whose immortality? Schoenberg's? Garbo's? They had their own immortalities. Irving Tabor had his. Her parents, though. And Grandfather. And Al. That was a pleasant thought, keeping them alive for another generation.

But were any of her stories really hers? Once she told the tale to Julian, did it not become Julian's story? And those told to her by Grandfather or her mother or father? Did they become Mamie's with the telling? A transmission. Like genes. And like genes they mutated. She had probably changed all of them, misremembering the way memory does. Stories recorded not history but what had settled, like tea leaves, in her mind. She was reading tea leaves, then. A fanciful occupation.

"Agatha," she called. "Do we have any loose tea?"

"Bags, You Highness."

"Well, never mind then. Never mind."

"Quoth the raven," Agatha said.

"Agatha, you have just confirmed my theory of historical literary transmission."

Agatha's confident twist on Edgar Allan Poe made her think of the great émigré controversy that grew from Thomas Mann's *Dr. Faustus.* Mann's hero was a composer named Adrian Leverkühn, who made a pact with the devil. In return for his soul, already tortured, he would be given years of radical musical insight and success. And syphilis, of course.

But Leverkühn's musical brilliance and innovation did not originate in his creator's mind. On the contrary, the brilliant and innovative Thomas Mann mined the insights of Arnold Schoenberg, a living, nonfictional, brilliant and innovative composer, a friend who had no idea his singular and momentous contribution to the historical progress of musical composition was to be purloined, bestowed by Mann on a fictional syphilitic composer in cahoots with the devil.

But, oh, do not mess with Arnold, Mamie thought. A man who felt his invisibility in Los Angeles as a seeping wound. *Die Wunde.* Like Amfortas, like Tristan. He had been banned in Berlin and Vienna and wherever Hitler had his way; he was ignored in the United States. Was his creation now to be absorbed and lost to his legacy forever by Thomas Mann's mad and scrofulous Leverkühn?

"*Die Wunde. Wo?*" Isolde sings to Tristan.

Where? There, there in the heart of Arnold Schoenberg.

Oh, but don't mess with Mann, either. Celebrated Thomas Mann. He, too, had his theory. He could attribute the creation of the twelve-tone method to his own creation because of his theory. Mosaic and pastiche, the use of quotation without quotation marks, superior to independent invention, because all life was a cultural product taking a form of mythic clichés. And he was Thomas Mann, not invisible at all. He was the face and the voice of anti-Nazi Germans. In Los Angeles, in the United States, in the world, he was revered. He was brilliant and he was recognized for his brilliance.

"You know, Julian, Schoenberg and Mann had a feud, a terrible, painful feud."

"About what?"

"Today you would call it intellectual property. Then, we thought Mann a coldhearted self-centered artist and Schoenberg a hotheaded self-centered artist."

"Did they fight a duel?"

"In the cultural magazines and journals, and in the hearts of their immigrant countrymen, yes."

⁂

"I do not have syphilis!" Schoenberg shouted, running through the Brentwood Country Mart.

Alma Mahler—was she bored that day?—had alerted Schoenberg to Leverkühn's claim to the twelve-tone row—the fictional composer's theft, as Schoenberg saw it. And the theft was beautifully written and thought out, too, thanks to the help of Theodor Adorno. Theodor W. Adorno, philosopher and sociologist. Exiled with the rest of them in Los Angeles. The 'W.' stood for Wiesengrund, his Jewish father's surname. Theodor chose to use Adorno, his mother's maiden name. To Schoenberg, the man who had given up his umlaut, Adorno remained Wiesengrund. Until the *Doctor Faustus* affair. Then Adorno became simply "the traitor." Mann himself? He became "the pirate."

Mamie was there that day with her mother, there at the Brentwood

Country Mart as Schoenberg flew past them in the aisle of lettuces and beetroot, a bald, red-faced arrow aimed at Marta Feuchtwanger as she innocently picked through the day's produce.

"Lies, Frau Marta! Lies! You know I have never had syphilis!"

Mamie could not bring herself to tell Julian this part of the story. Just an anecdote, anyway, in lots of books about the period, why should she embarrass the old man, even if he was long dead? As for Thomas Mann, his "thefts" were the stories he heard, the world as he saw it, handed down to him, or across to him, for him to pick up and make his own. Quotation without quotation marks—what else is there, really? Words are used over and over again. Like musical notes. And how beautifully Mann used his. And everyone else's.

She certainly did not want to color Julian's reading of *The Magic Mountain*, which he had recently picked up. She wanted Julian to imbibe everything—port! Schoenberg! Mann! Mamie Künstler's misshapen memories! The endless virus had closed him off from his world, the real world, the present-day world that ought to be out there. Mamie wanted to open a new world for him, though this new world was so old it was almost forgotten.

Is that why I am telling him my stories? To "broaden his horizons"?

"Julian, let me tell you about the time I first saw Thomas Mann."

"Did you call him Tom? Yes, I'd love to hear about you meeting Thomas Mann. You know I would!"

"It's another party story. This time, a birthday party for Heinrich Mann, the older brother. Poor Heinrich. Revered in Germany; revered in the émigré community. Some people thought he was a better writer than Thomas. But he did not have the happiest life in Los Angeles. He was married to a much younger woman named Nelly. People said she'd been a barmaid in Munich. He adored her. But she drank and eventually killed herself. It was tragic. He was broke, too. He had a job for a year at the studio like my mother, but that ended. His books were obviously not being sold in Germany or Austria, and they never really took off in the United States."

"He wrote *The Blue Angel*, right? I mean, it was based on his book."

"You *have* been watching TCM! Heinrich was still worshipped among the German speakers in L.A. So, when Salka Viertel threw a seventy-fifth birthday party for him, *tout émigré* L.A. wanted to be there. It was a pretty exclusive guest list, though. The Künstlers didn't quite make it on, and we weren't the only ones. But it was just too big an event for the rest of the community to ignore. The greatest minds of Europe would gather in a house in Pacific Palisades! People were so excited that they were volunteering to help in the kitchen just to catch a glimpse of all the eminent men and women gathered in one place.

"Of course, my father would not dream of going anywhere unless formally invited. It would be beneath his dignity."

It seemed that with each passing day more and more of life in America was beneath the dignity of Otto Künstler. As his skin got thinner and thinner, Ilse made sure to be at his side more than ever, reassuring him, bringing coffee or tea or vodka on a tray to the piano where he always sat either playing in a frenzied, unmodulated way or just staring at the wall. Ilse hovered over him. It was because she understood his unhappiness so well that she was so worried. She tried to protect him, but a cup of tea or a glass of schnapps does not protect a man from himself. And even in her attempts to care for him, she had to be discreet, hoping he would not notice.

"And, oh, Julian, when he did notice, it was awful," Mamie said. "He would become so angry, but so silent. Boiling, a slow, silent boil. It was frightening. The stillness, the fury. My mother left him alone in the house only when she had to."

A birthday party for Heinrich Mann, another man to whom the New World had shut itself off, had almost as little appeal for Ilse as for Otto, so they did not grace the Viertels' kitchen that day.

"Grandfather and I were less sensitive than my father and less responsible than my mother, so of course we were dying to go. A real event! A privilege, in fact. Great fun, we were sure. And we were right on all counts."

The lesser Germanophones were happily crowded in the Viertels' kitchen, squeezing together in the doorway to the dining room, getting in the way of the cook and the real servers, in order to get a glimpse of the historic gathering. The two great men were surrounded by other great men—the novelist Alfred Neumann; Franz Werfel and the oddly magnificent Alma Mahler Werfel; Alfred Polgar, the columnist and theater critic, whom the Künstlers knew slightly from MGM where he, like Ilse, had landed as a writer; the novelist and playwright Lion Feuchtwanger and his wife, Marta, neighbors they had met several times; Alfred Doeblin, author of *Berlin Alexanderplatz*, which Mamie had just started reading; Walter Mehring, Dadaist cabaret poet whom Mamie had never seen before and thought was magnificently handsome with his long, aristocratic nose and large sad eyes; Herbert Marcuse, the philosopher, even more famous in the next generation than he was then and who, like Mehring, had come all the way from New York for this dinner; Bruno Frank and his wife, Liesl, who were founders of the organization that had brought the Künstlers and so many others out of Europe into Los Angeles—the list went on and on. To seat so many, the Ping-Pong table had been brought in and dressed in a stiff, ironed tablecloth.

There, gathered and waiting for their roast beef, was the world of Mamie's grandfather. Not the Viennese world he had lived in day-to-day running his store and eating his meals, but the greater world of his imagination and his soul, the real world he would have said, a world of generations of German language and literature and music, the world of Germanic culture, a world he still believed in.

"Though I doubt many of the men and women sitting at that table still believed in that world," Mamie said. "They knew they were extinct even as they toasted their continued existence."

And the toasts! First, while the roast beef was overcooking and the cook was in despair, Thomas Mann pulled from his pocket a thick bundle of paper from which he read a long, long tribute to his brother. The kitchen was steaming hot, and when he finished at last, there was a quiet but audible sigh of relief from us in the cheap seats. The dinner guests looked hungrily past one another toward the kitchen from which wafted the smell of a feast.

But then, before anyone could rush out with a serving platter, Heinrich stood up. He reached in his jacket, extracted an equally thick wad of paper, and began his own orotund appreciation of his younger brother.

"And the roast beef overcooked?" Julian laughed. The idea of the hungry intellectuals at the table, the other intellectuals in the boiling hot kitchen—it was wonderful. What a scene. How could he put it into *Émigrés in Space*? He couldn't wait to tell Sophie.

"You know, Mamie . . ."

Julian had begun calling her Mamie. She liked it. "Grandma" had begun to sound both childish and insufficient for the relationship that had crept up on them.

"You know, Mamie, your stories are extremely entertaining."

Ah, she thought. Perhaps that's the reason I tell him stories. That, right there. Legacy? Shmegacy. Entertainment! Was it the opiate of the masses like religion? Or was it subversive: a glimpse of joy? Joy was always subversive. So, was narrative comfort a bourgeois soporific or was it as radical as hope?

31

~

On the way to Sophie's house for their daily canine playdate, Julian called Eli.

"I'm getting fat," Eli said. He was eating chips all day while studying, eating his mother's comfort food at night, and eating the rewards of her new hobby: baking cookies and cakes and pies.

"She goes online and scrolls through the *New York Times* recipe app like she's on Twitter. She's obsessed. She talks about the different people who contribute recipes as if she knows them personally. 'Ali said this, Ali said that. Melissa was amazing today. And Pierre! Well, you can always count on Pierre.' It's an obsession. It's not healthy. Oh, and she's still washing the fruit and cereal boxes. And she puts cheese on everything. I used to like cheese. I hate cheese now. It's disgusting. It droops when you heat it. It drools. Everything is disgusting. Except the chocolate cheesecake she made yesterday. That was pretty good."

"I met a girl," Julian said.

"That's so enterprising. Your FedEx driver?"

"My neighbor. We sit outside in masks and watch our dogs play. And we talk. A lot. The rest of the time my grandmother plays records of Schoenberg music and tells me stories about Greta Garbo."

"What is the cheese consumption factor out there, Julian? Heavy like here?"

"It's really sunny."

"Fuck you."

"Thank you for moving out of the apartment. You made all this happen."

"Fuck you, Julian."

"Well, gotta go. I have reached the gate of my mysterious masked lady."

"And another fuck you, old pal."

❧

THE dogs rolled in the green faux lawn. Cindy squeaked, Prince Jan grunted, Julian gazed at Sophie and wondered as always what the rest of her looked like.

"If they ever develop a vaccine, will you lower your mask?"

"Hold your breath," she said.

"You mean like don't hold my breath? You'll wear that thing forever?"

"No, really, hold your breath."

He did and slowly, with the languorous timing of a stripper, Sophie detached one elastic from one ear, the other elastic from the other ear. She batted her eyelashes at him, then slowly, slowly lowered the mask as if it were a veil, an exotic veil.

Aroused in spite of his amusement, Julian held his breath with difficulty. She was standing now, swinging her mask suggestively, and Julian saw her face and it was a beautiful face and he pointed desperately at his own mask to indicate he could no longer hold his breath and she quickly replaced her mask and he exhaled, and they laughed and laughed and Julian thought, I am in love.

"Now you," she said.

Julian felt shy, as though he were stripping naked before her, but he detached his mask, with less drama and artistry, and when he replaced it, she said, "You will do. You will do nicely, Julian Künstler," and they stared at each other for another hour or so as the dogs played in the green turf.

32

MAMIE COULD NOT STOP THINKING ABOUT ARNOLD SCHOENBERG. WHAT A strange obsession to come upon her so late in life. Then again, she could not stop thinking of the past in general. She could picture her mother, driving off to work in their jalopy, a wave and a smile. "Off to the salt mines," she would say, a phrase she'd picked up at the studio.

Sometimes Ilse brought Mamie with her to the flimsy bungalow office at the studio. Mamie helped her with English. Ilse Künstler could not pronounce "th" and was never able to, it turned out, her whole life long. Her vocabulary was limited, too. Of course, some of the writers spoke no English at all. They sat with their doors open like cows in a shed, heads hanging, milked for their stories, stories that nobody really wanted, historical stories of kings and queens, war stories, romances, musicals, most of the stories to be dragged hopefully through meetings then unceremoniously consigned to dustbins that might legitimately be called dustbins of history. But at a time when history, their history, was worse than the contents of any dustbin, they knew they were lucky to be there, which made them grateful and sad.

There was a lot of real dust in those offices, too. Dust and drink. And the Middle Europeans miserable in the knowledge that they were lucky to be safe in their stalls, that their fellow European writers were in prison or dead or worse, worse being the part they could not bring themselves to think about, though they could not help thinking about it. Every one of them had heard the rumors of the camps.

Ilse was sometimes so frustrated by the uselessness of her work, a worthless trinket dangling in the shadow of European horror, that she threatened to quit. The threat was voiced to her family. Thankfully it never went further.

"I am doing nothing," she would say. "I'm worth nothing. Yet I get paid to do nothing."

"If you quit you will be paid nothing to do nothing," Mamie pointed out.

And her mother covered her face with her hands, then returned to her scenario for a film about a rebellion against tyranny masquerading as a film about a prince who married beneath him.

So the past was not always so comfortable, Mamie thought.

"The past," she said to Julian, "is almost as confusing as the present."

Agatha swanned past them, pocketbook swinging, on her way to the kitchen, where the table was covered with postcards to be sent out to encourage people to vote.

"I lick stamps now," Agatha said. "I am concerned citizen."

"I didn't know you were a citizen at all," Mamie called after her.

"Citizen of world," Agatha called back.

"What world?" Mamie mumbled. "Mars?"

"What is it with you two?" Julian said. "You're like an old married couple. Like Cindy and Prince Jan."

"We are old, it's true. But Agatha is not my type, dear," Mamie said. "Prince Jan is very handsome, though, aren't you, you gorgeous creature?"

The dog looked up, eyes sad and hopeful as always.

Julian wondered what Mamie's human type could be. He looked around at the various photos of his father as a child, of Mamie in an earlier convertible, an earlier Saint Bernard beside her in the passenger seat, its ears flying in the wind. Or one of her boyfriends, the dog relegated to the backseat. There was no picture of her husband, Al. There were a half-dozen photographs of famous conductors and musicians signed to Mamie. There was no picture of Schoenberg, though. No picture of Garbo.

"Have you had a lot of boyfriends?"

"More than my fair share."

But that was all he could get out of her. Funny what she told him about and what she didn't.

"You think about your childhood a lot, don't you?" he asked.

Mamie was sitting in her listening chair though there was no music playing. She was reading the *New York Times* using both her reading glasses and a magnifying glass. From behind the paper, she said, "I think it's a sign of age."

Agatha the Deaf called out from the kitchen, "Senilitous."

"Speak for yourself," Mamie called back.

Julian played the scene out for Sophie later.

33

"THE SCALE IS THE NATURAL ARRANGEMENT OF BEAUTIFUL SOUND," OTTO Künstler said.

Mamie could hear his voice still—the soft, forced gentleness, the impatience underneath, the pride in his own words beneath that, and then, at the very lowest level, confusion that he had to spell this out to his own daughter.

"The scale is the natural arrangement of beautiful sound."

"How? Why? Who decides?"

Over and over her father's explanations and her questions, a circle of resentment that rolled like a wheel until one of them broke loose and gave up.

"Look," her father said, lifting the piano's lid. "Look at the strings."

"I know, I know, but . . ."

"Each string is a certain length, a different length. Each one vibrates differently when plucked, in a harpsichord, or hit with these little hammers in the piano."

"Father, you've shown me this before."

"But you don't see it yet. Just look. And listen."

His voice was as even and as layered with different meanings, its own vibrations, in Los Angeles as it was in Vienna.

"One presses the keys, which make these little hammers hit a string. Each string is exactly the right length to release its own perfect sound.

When the correct keys are pressed at the same time, they produce a beautiful, harmonious sound. It is very simple, little Mamie mouse."

But what of all the sounds in between the sounds made by the black keys and the white keys? little Mamie mouse wondered. The sounds she heard when a violinist would tune his instrument? Weren't those sounds musical sounds, too? What about Benny Goodman's clarinet when it stretched between sounds on the radio as she and Grandfather listened and smoked cigarettes? But, for once, she said nothing.

Her father looked at her hopefully. Maybe this time she would give in. Maybe he had gotten through. It was so very simple. She was so very stubborn. He played middle C, then a chord, and gave an encouraging smile.

But alas:

"The piano is not very nice," she said with the same old determination.

"Dear god."

"It is cruel to all the sounds that stray from its rules. All the sounds that are different."

"The rules are based on nature. They are natural laws," Otto said. "There must be rules. That is all there is to it. You are provoking me, Salomea."

"I don't want to play the piano. I'm sorry. The piano is a dictator. I'm sorry, but I think the piano is cruel to all the other notes and I feel sorry for them. The piano is like Hitler."

This was when he raised his hand to smack her but quickly lowered it, ashamed of his impulse but equally ashamed of his daughter.

"Hitler!" he cried, as if in pain, his face twisted and white. "How dare you! A child who knows nothing, a child who has been rescued from the Nazis through the intervention of so many musicians, a child so ignorant and safe and indulged. Never speak like that again in this house."

Mamie stared at his hand, at his face, at his anger. She began to cry.

"Never! Do you hear me?"

He slammed the fallboard down.

"You are old enough to know better."

He slid off the piano bench and looked down at her.

He said, "I am ashamed."

And he left her to tremble in disgrace.

<hr />

"I had gone too far," Mamie said to Julian. "Not only too far, I had gone too far in such an ugly, evil direction. The worst possible, most painful, truly disgusting direction. What possessed me to invoke Hitler, that obscenity? Anger, yes. Frustration at not being able to love what my father loved, yes, that too. And . . ."

"And?"

"And I knew what would hurt him. Children instinctively do."

Julian thought back to his argument with his parents before he came to live with his grandmother. He'd always known what would enrage them, it was true.

"What I did not know," Mamie said, "was how *much* it would hurt him. I should have. It's obvious now. But that skill does not come as easily to a child as the simpler ability to cause pain."

"Did he ever hit you? Or spank you?"

"Oh no. He was a mild man usually. My mother took a hairbrush to me now and then. It was the style in those days."

"How about Al?"

"Al?"

She laughed.

"Al wasn't home long enough to take a swat at anybody. Not me, not your father. He wasn't home long enough for me to take a swing at him, more's the pity. Moving target, that Al."

<hr />

THE next time Julian called home he asked his father about Al Smith.

"Has it occurred to you that this might be a painful topic for your father?" his mother asked.

And Julian, who liked to think of himself as a sensitive person, certainly more sensitive than his mother and father, realized that it had not occurred to him.

"Sorry, Dad. I was curious, you know, being out here with Mamie. Sorry."

"Oh, don't mind your mother. My father is not a mystery, Julian, just a blur. I barely remember him, that's how young I was when he left. He was a trumpet player. Mamie says he was a mediocre jazz trumpet player, for what that's worth. You know her. Competitive does not even begin to describe Salomea Künstler. Can you imagine two musicians in one house? After Al left, my mother was lucky enough and talented enough and ballsy enough to find plenty of work—I mean she worked hard, sawing away at that violin—and she used her maiden name for work and then gave her name to me to keep it alive, and we are all Künstlers now. He died when I was ten. I've told you all this, haven't I?"

"I guess so."

"It's a gaping wound," his mother said.

"Pay no attention to your mother, Julian."

"Okay."

Why, Julian wondered, did they always have to be on the phone together? He could picture them, his mother on the landline extension in the kitchen, his father in the bedroom. Why did they even have a landline?

"It's terrible to grow up without a father, Julian," his mother said. "Always remember that."

"Okay."

"It wasn't so bad. My mother took up enough room for two fathers."

"Okay."

Julian was sorry he'd asked. He did not want to hear about his father's sadness or anyone's sadness. There was sadness everywhere. The world was a gaping wound. That was enough.

"Well, I'm lucky I have you," he said dutifully. And he was, he knew he was, so he was glad he said it, although it was difficult forming the words and spitting them out. Sentimentality hovered over his parents like a fluffy cloud. They seemed to worship it. And coax it out of others.

"A loving family," his father said. "That's what matters in life."

A loving family was what mattered in life, but was it necessary to declare it so frequently? Then Julian reminded himself: truth is never pretty. And this was a truth: a loving family did matter in life.

Then: Oh, wait, my father grew up without a father. That's why he says that so often. Again, he was almost stupefied by his own insensitivity.

"Yes, yes," he said. "So true, Dad."

He could feel both his parents not only smile but visibly relax the way the dog did when he was given cookies.

"I miss you so much," he said, realizing that he did.

Then they talked about the grandchildren and Julian gave a reassuring account of Mamie.

"Hey, Dad, why, when Mamie says 'son of a bitch,' does she put on a thick German accent?"

"Tradition," his father said.

His mother began singing "Tradition" from *Fiddler on the Roof*, and Julian, who missed them both so much, hung up, relieved that he was three thousand miles away.

34

NOW THAT MAMIE HAD LEARNED THAT SOME THINGS WERE NOT JOKES, EVER, no matter how cleverly you used them, she was gradually able to go back to teasing her father and evoking the fond, irritated cry of "Salomea, you are provoking me." For his part, he gave up trying to teach her to play the piano.

"He was so horrified about what I'd said about the piano that he never wanted to see me near one again. And now he could dump me onto my new friend and brilliant teacher, Arnold Schoenberg. Schoenberg was not teaching me piano or anything to do with music, though. He taught me to play tennis."

Schoenberg loved tennis. He played with Gershwin, Charlie Chaplin, Henry Cowell—any friend who was willing. He played when he was ill, and he was often ill, suffering from severe asthma. And when he couldn't get to a tennis court, he played Ping-Pong at home.

"Technique and tradition in order to transcend technique and tradition—yes, his students learned that. We learned to look at what we were doing, look at what others had done, look at what could be done, and maybe we would see what had not yet been done."

His composition students who came to him to learn about new music were made to compose endless variations of old forms instead.

"John Cage was his student. Surely you've heard of John Cage, Julian."

"Sort of."

She pointed at his phone, and he dutifully googled and read.

"Chance, huh?"

"Cage could only take so much Schoenberg Germanic pedagogy. He left the classes after a few years. But listen to his early works and you'll hear the influence."

"So, Mamie, you know I'm not planning to be a musician or a composer, right?"

"You plan to be a civilized adult, I suppose."

"Well, yes, but . . ."

"You will listen to John Cage, and that will nudge you on your way."

"But . . ."

"Schoenberg wrote a textbook you might want to dip into. The *Theory of Harmony.*"

"Oy."

"In it he celebrates making mistakes. That should appeal to you."

Julian looked so hurt that Mamie said, "Mistakes are how we learn. Schoenberg teased his students all the time. But I am not Schoenberg. And so it is I who have made a mistake. Forgive me, Julian. You are very patient, an open vessel. I should not fill you up, then kick you over!"

Julian wandered over to the wall of LPs, all arranged alphabetically. He found the John Cage section, ran his fingers across the edges of the album covers. Chance. He would listen. Chance sounded restful. Better than Fate.

Mamie was already back to Schoenberg. "He was a gifted, sensitive, demanding pedagogue," she was saying. "That was what anyone who studied with him discovered. His dedication was so great that it resembled joy. But he did understand the value of making mistakes, Julian. Yes, he would smack his children's hands when they made a mistake at the roulette game he had created. And he was merciless to his composition students who screwed up. 'Presto con fuoco! Fuoco means fire! Call the fire engines at once!' he told a student who played her piece too placidly. 'Your harmony is like Woostie!' he once yelled. That was his word for Worcestershire sauce. 'Put it on beefsteak! Or you can put it on angel food cake, too, but this would not be so good, I don't think!'"

Sounds like a real peach, Julian thought.

"But then you take a look at *Theory of Harmony*, and the entire pedagogy is based on the idea that mistakes lead to progress: that all of Western music was a kind of wonderful preliminary mistake, one you must master, leading to twelve-tone composition."

An arrogant peach.

"But you liked him?" he said. Though Schoenberg sounded monstrous. Terrifying. More like Mamie than she would perhaps care to admit.

"All his students loved him. He was a miracle. We worshipped him. He was so funny, too! And so sweet with his little children."

"Did he give them music lessons? Like your father?"

"Of course not. He made them toys. He was an inventor, Julian. My father was a practitioner."

One of Schoenberg's sons, Ronny, became a champion tennis player some years later, but not because his father taught him.

"It must have been like me and my father," Mamie said. "Too close, too much emotion."

Schoenberg did go to every one of Ronny's matches, however. And he developed a way of scoring that recorded not only every point, but every mistake.

"Every move, really. He believed in progress, you see. That is why he taught. And at the same time, he wanted everyone to be an autodidact, even those he taught."

There was no perfect shot in tennis—you always fell short. But tennis, like music, was an attempt to take your own abstract, theoretical idea of what a perfect shot was and make it real. How could you know how to play well until you knew the physical and theoretical requirements of the game? Until you tried, and failed, to bring them to life?

When Mamie would apologize for missing a shot, her tennis maestro would say, "Such nonsense. Now, you hit ball like so, I return ball like so, you do not have anticipation of ball. I could have hit ball like so, yes? Or like so. All are possibilities for anticipations, I think. So! Again!"

And the ball would fly toward her, and she would hit it, or she would miss it and he would hit it again and again, here then there, cheerful and serious.

"I am not ordinary teacher," he said. "Perhaps you already realize this."

After playing, they would sit on the grass with lemonade.

"So, we agree, correct explanation is goal of all inquiry, yes?" the composer would ask.

"Yes," said the pupil.

"But, you see, most explanations are not correct explanation, most explanations are wrong," he said. "Like your swing."

"Oh dear."

"But even if explanation usually turns to be wrong, like your swing, we do not have to allow pleasure in searching for explanation be spoiled! We will not allow pleasure be spoiled," he said, smiling broadly.

And they did not. The pleasure—the soft exclamation of the gut strings receiving the clay-stained ball, the twang as the ball was launched back in the air, the soft scratch of the clay court beneath the soles of Mamie's tennis shoes, the ball shooting past her racket and bouncing behind her back then lying still in the sun; the sun itself, the sweat on the nape of her neck; the switch from running, to stopping, to turning, to running again—the pleasure in searching for a beautiful swing, an unstoppable serve, in just getting the ball over the net, that pleasure was what the game was about, what all games were about.

"Schoenberg taught me that," Mamie said.

35

PLEASURE. IT CAME IN SUCH UNEXPECTED WAYS, MAMIE THOUGHT. LIKE sorrow.

"In 1947, both pleasure and misery came looking for me," she told Julian.

"You were twenty?"

She nodded. "First," she said, "my sweet lumbering dog died. We buried her beneath the orange tree."

The hole they'd dug was so big, Mamie remembered. The dog was wrapped in a clean white sheet. Her tail, so rich and feathery, stuck out from one end of the big bundle. Mamie had cried when the pellets of soil landed on the tail, the brown and white tail that had greeted her every day for eight years.

"There were good things, too. Wonderful things. Important things. The war was over! That was the main thing. And more immediate things, like Grandfather. He still creaked along. With that knit shawl around his shoulders. He reminded me more and more of a grandma in a storybook. The one who tried to eat Little Red Riding Hood. So cranky. My mother was still working, miraculously. She had achieved far more success than she'd ever expected. Meaning, she had not been fired. Her original contract, the one that had gotten us out of Austria, was for only one year. Somehow, she'd been able to stretch it out with various ideas and projects. None of which was ever made, of course.

"But my father, Julian. My father. Despondent by then, truly despondent: the smiling man, so optimistic about coming to a new country, was destroyed by the news of what had happened to those who stayed behind. He went through the motions, teaching and even performing in small venues, meaning the living rooms of members of the German colony. He celebrated with us when we heard the war was over. But the war would never be over for him. His escape from annihilation was a source of shame. No one could argue him out of this. He became querulous and petulant. He snapped at his little students and pulled their ears. He barely spoke to his father ("The old fool"), spoke no German at all to anyone on loudly stated principle ("The language of swine!"), but found my thoroughly American affect even more offensive ("Do you think you can hide behind your American slang?") and persecuted my mother with demands and complaints followed by haughty lectures.

"One does not wander without punishment under the palms. Berthold Viertel said that. My father repeated it often."

She looked out the window. The skies were gray, a glaring gray. No rain, though. The drought was bad this year. The flowers in front, the nasturtiums, were long gone. Prince Jan's napping corner was a dry, dusty hollow.

Julian waited patiently. Mamie drifted away more often these days. The older the Mamie of the stories got, the longer the present-day Mamie took to talk about her.

"Maybe it's too close, too intimate," Sophie said when he told her.

"But it was, like, seventy-five years ago."

"She was our age, Julian."

⁂

"I was twenty years old." Mamie resumed her tale at last. "I'd just met Al. I was in my second year at UCLA, but I was still living at home."

"That doesn't sound like fun."

"No. And UCLA was a pretty poky little school then, Julian. Did you know there was no music department? It was part of the education department! And Schoenberg was there. UCLA had Arnold Schoenberg on the faculty. They paid him badly, too. Fools. I took his beginning composition class. That's where I met Al."

Mamie had not meant to talk about Al. But here she was. Here you are, Al. You bastard, you charmer. We did have fun, didn't we?

"There were clubs in those days, nightclubs—"

"We have clubs."

"Not like these. Central Avenue. The Dunbar Hotel, Club Alabam—those were the big ones. And Jack's Basket Room—that's where I went with your grandfather. Oh, he wasn't playing there, he was never good enough to jam with those musicians. Dexter Gordon? Charlie Parker? No, Al came to listen, just like me. But he did look sharp that night, and he could play, he could definitely play. I met him in Composition 101 with Professor Arnold Schoenberg. Well, that sealed the deal for me. A jazz trumpet player who studied with Schoenberg? I was swept off my feet."

And now she was back to Schoenberg. She hadn't meant to talk about him today either. But how could she resist? Being in his class was somewhere between fighting a lion in the Colosseum and ecstatic spiritual tripping.

"He could be cruel, sardonic, and terribly funny."

"Al?"

"Well, yes, but now I'm talking about Schoenberg. Schoenberg teaching the unqualified nitwits who took his class with no idea who he was. And, of course, there was a coterie of devotees who worshipped him. That was the story of his life, actually."

"Which were you?"

She laughed. "One of my compositions was so bad he said, 'It turns me the stomach over.'" She laughed again. "One boy was playing his piece on the piano, a rather rollicking composition, and Schoenberg began to gallop up and down the room waving one arm like a cowboy with a lasso yelling, 'Hi yo Silver!'

"It was excruciating, to be his student, and exhilarating. And there were the clubs and concerts of new music every Sunday at Evenings on the Roof. Fifty cents a ticket. The sign said: THE CONCERTS ARE FOR THE

PLEASURE OF THE PERFORMERS AND WILL BE PLAYED REGARDLESS OF AN AUDI-
ENCE. Oh, it was a glorious time."

"Except for living home?"

"You're projecting, I see. But yes, my dear boy, yes. Still speaking German to my dear grandfather, still translating the news. I didn't have too
much time for beach walks during the school year, and he was far too
weak, but I still listened to the radio with him. When I wasn't watching
my father's enraged face, trying to protect my mother from his rants. Or
watching my mother fade, on purpose I think, hiding, shrinking behind
acquiescence. I did not seem to be able to help her, though I tried. I
cooked with her, went to stores with her, convinced her to spruce up the
house, to buy material for new curtains and helped her sew them, made
her dance with me to the music on the radio. She did as she was told, but
there was no joy left. My father began shutting himself up in the small
attic room, which provided a bit of relief. It had a view of the Pacific,
though we knew he was interested in neither views nor the Pacific Ocean.

"I tried to comfort all of them, but at the same time I was exhausted and
young and wanted to live in my new, young country, not in the horror of a
lost world. The truth of what we now call the Holocaust was still so difficult
to absorb. No one wanted to believe the truth, though no one doubted it.

"And into the world of family sorrrow, here comes Greta Garbo, barefoot on the beach in shorts and long tanned legs. I am standing in the wet
sand at low tide, thinking of my poor canine Garbo and how she loved
to rest her heated bulk on just this kind of smooth, cool, wet sand. And
here comes Greta Garbo.

"Pleasure comes to you in unexpected ways. That's how pleasure
works.

"And there she is. I have not seen her since Garbo the dog jumped on
her, when I called out her name, so many years ago.

"She stands beside me and says, 'You are the one with the dog.' She
remembers me. She recognizes me.

"'The dog is dead,' I say. 'Like the seagull.'

"She is confused, takes a step back, looks me over. 'Ah,' she says. 'Yes,
I remember. Chekhov is a bore.'

"And we begin to walk north, away from the little house where my sad father and brave mother and increasingly confused grandfather live.

"She complains about a writer who has criticized her in print.

"'He will certainly be immortal for as long as he lives,' she says. 'That is a quote from Heine,' she adds.

"She was completely uneducated, you know. Left school in eighth grade, I believe. For the stage. She hadn't made a movie in years. She never made another film, actually. She was forty-two. But still, people followed her, stared at her."

"Was she still beautiful?"

Mamie laughed. "You have no idea, Julian. No idea."

When he related all this to Sophie, she was uncharacteristically quiet.

"What?"

"I don't know. I feel like I'm eavesdropping."

He thought about that. "Am I betraying a confidence? I thought you like to hear the stories."

"I do. Even the eavesdropping ones. Especially the eavesdropping ones. What does that say about me?"

"You're human? You're curious? You're a gossip-mongering vulgarian?"

Sophie nodded. "All that. You may continue."

Julian told her how Mamie talked about the way Greta Garbo walked. Not in the mincing movie star fashion of so many of the great beauties then and now. No, she strode.

"Good word," Sophie said. "*Strode*."

Garbo's pace was quick and sure. She had long strides. That walk was meant to take her away from people, help her escape. But it had the opposite effect. Her fast, long gait instead drew the attention of the people she wanted to avoid. Mamie knew a lot about escape. She longed to share this knowledge with her friend. To explain the benefits of camouflage. But the one time she worked up the courage to bring the subject up, Garbo looked at her with pity, as if she were a mouse giving advice to a cheetah.

"A mouse is gray and can hide in the dust," Mamie said to Julian. "A cheetah leaps through the trees in dappled sunlight, runs across the savanna in the bright sun, runs through the night hidden by darkness.

You cannot convince a cheetah of anything, I learned. Then again, why would you want to?"

Mamie Künstler and Greta Garbo began to take walks together frequently.

"And when Garbo called my grandmother," Julian told Sophie, "she used a pseudonym. I mean she really was kind of paranoid, I think. She used the same pseudonym as Queen Victoria! Mrs. Brown."

Mamie's parents knew exactly who she was when she called. Her voice was not something she could hide under a sun hat. They were touched by her attention to their daughter. Greta Garbo was famously lonely, famously seeking solitude, yet she sought the company of Mamie Künstler, an eccentric movie star finding quiet companionship with an eccentric twenty-year-old.

They walked, walked and walked and walked. They climbed through barbed wire fences in the mountains, got lost in the woods, dove into the waves on the beach. They talked about nothing in particular. Garbo was exuberant and funny and waved her arms and joked about her big feet. She did handstands and climbed trees like a happy child. Only when they approached civilization again did she become dour, almost sullen. She pulled her hat lower. Or her scarf closer over her hair. Her walk became faster and furtive at the same time.

Again, Mamie thought of telling her that she only attracted attention by this behavior. That it marked her. But she realized that Garbo was already marked, that she was in fact a mark. That she was La Divina, a goddess, but she could not disguise herself as a bull or a swan or a shower of gold.

"Sometimes she would take me for a drive," Mamie told Julian. "Terrifying! She drove incredibly fast, and she ran every stoplight."

They drove to the mountains to walk. They drove to the desert. They drove to her house to sit by the pool. She once saw Cecil Beaton arrive as she was leaving.

"Oh, he was the photographer in *The Crown*," Sophie said. She was an avid Royals watcher, sympathetic to Harry but sad for the queen. "The old guy. Not the photographer married to Princess Margaret," she added, in case Julian had not seen *The Crown*.

"Yeah, and he was queer, too. And madly in love with Garbo. I looked him up."

Then he told her about the day Mamie and Garbo went ice-skating. Garbo would often pick Mamie up without saying where they were going. But one day she phoned and said to wear a sweater: they were going ice-skating.

"I had been a competent skater as a child," Mamie told Julian. "Little Viennese girls generally were—and though I was not brilliant and twirling, neither did I clump along with bent ankles clutching a chair like some of my friends. I loved the cold air and the scraping sounds and the movement, the quickness, the propulsion. But I was confused: 'Where have you found a frozen lake in this city?'

"'In Westwood Village!'

"'Ice-skating in summer?' my mother said.

"'This America,' said Grandfather. 'No seasons. And no sense.'

"'It is a marvel,' my mother said.

"'A marvel? Perhaps,' said my father. 'But to what end?'

"The skating rink was called Tropical Ice. Isn't that marvelous? It still makes me laugh. Tropical Ice. I was so happy. We laughed and chatted as she sped along San Vicente Boulevard. I was going skating with La Divina, though La Divina looked anything but divine that day. She was in what she thought was full camouflage. A lumberjack cap, with flaps tied together beneath her chin. How many heavy sweaters? Two? Three? Heavy trousers tucked into heavy socks. And sunglasses of course.

"Not a trace of her beauty, just a bulky balloon sliding across the ice.

"I started to laugh. I couldn't help it, and I couldn't stop. Then other skaters caught a glimpse, and they began to laugh, too. Well! That was the end of the skating. Poor Greta. She thought they were laughing at Greta Garbo. But they were laughing at the Michelin Man.

"I was young enough to be angry, my day of skating ruined, and we drove away, though not west toward the beach, where I lived, but to Beverly Hills, in silence.

"'Those people have spoiled our day,' she said at last. 'No skating. So. We will sunbathe and drink vodka instead.'

"I was twenty, not old enough to drink vodka.

"'And I don't like vodka, so it's just as well.'

"'Gin, then.'

"I shook my head.

"'Well, then, we will drink lemonade.'

"She drove to her house on Amalfi Drive and marched out to the swimming pool. She stripped her skating clothes off, sweater by sweater by sweater, stepped out of the bulky pants, and naked as a goddess, she dove in."

That was what Mamie told Julian. She told him Garbo was devoted to skinny-dipping. What she didn't say was: There *are* seasons in Los Angeles, Grandfather. And that summer was my season of Garbo. One short summer in the lingering shadow of war and deprivation and genocide.

Passion comes upon you when it comes upon you, Mamie thought. There is no training for it, no protection against it. Passion is a terrible thing, a thing not to be missed, a headlong thing.

Part Four

36

〜

AUTUMN IN LOS ANGELES WAS A SURPRISE TO JULIAN. HE HAD NOT EXPECTED trees to lose their leaves here, but so many did. He certainly did not expect the air to get hotter and hotter, but it did. Mamie's garden seemed to shrink, parched and dusty, swathed in dead, brown sycamore leaves the size of fedoras that drifted over from a neighbor's tree. The smell of wildfires was often in the air; a hazy, brown ribbon across the sky. The presidential election seemed to hang in the sky, too, full of foreboding, which seemed to have seeped beneath one's skin, and promise and hope, too, which one tried to feel strong enough to believe.

"But one is hampered," Mamie said.

The virus deaths and hospitalizations had risen sharply in Los Angeles.

"We are a hot spot now," she said. "That used to mean something quite different. Even the clichés are changing."

On September thirteenth, Agatha made a cake, a dense one-layer chocolate cake that was Mamie's favorite.

"Happy birthday, old friend," she said.

She'd made hot chocolate with whipped cream and apple strudel for breakfast, too.

Mamie was delighted. And moved. How long had Agatha lived in the guesthouse? If I am ninety-four, she thought, then she has been here for thirty years. Agatha had packed her belongings in two suitcases, then walked out of her old life into Mamie's. The friends they'd made in the neighborhood they'd made together. I suppose Julian is right—we are like an old married couple. She wondered if people thought they really were a couple. That made her smile. It was impossible for her to imagine Agatha as having a physical relationship with anyone but the pocketbook on her wrist. There had been that husband, though, she reminded herself. Agatha never spoke about him. She never told him where she'd gone when she moved out. Even now, decades later, she feared meeting him in the grocery store or the hardware store. Mamie had driven past Agatha's former house a few times. A family, a young man and young wife and two small children, was living there. Agatha was not reassured, but it seemed that just as Agatha had made herself disappear from his life, her husband had vanished from hers. Maybe he was dead. Maybe Agatha murdered him, Mamie thought. Probably not: Agatha told her that she still carried pepper spray with her at all times. Mamie suspected that was the principal cargo of the pocketbook.

"Agatha," she said when she saw the cake, "you have outdone yourself. You have made your old friend very happy."

"You give me home when home I need. I give you cake. We even," Agatha said. Then she smiled, something Julian had never seen before, and said, "Never can be even. I know." A pause for the punch line: "My cake too good."

Frank and Roberta were beamed in on Julian's laptop, then Annabella, Jay, and their two little boys.

Frank and Roberta had sent a leather-bound photo album.

"You can illustrate your stories," Frank said when Mamie unwrapped it.

"Make sure to label the photos, Mamie," said Roberta.

"So you'll know who's who when I'm dead? Yes, all right."

"Happy birthday dear Mamie Mom Grandma!" they sang. "Happy birthday to you!"

Mamie did not blow out the candles. "Airborne," Jay reminded everyone. "The virus is airborne."

The two little boys became hysterical at the idea that they would never again be able to blow out their birthday candles.

"You'll each have your own cake in your own room, how about that?" Mamie said. "Then blow as much as you want."

"Daddy?"

"Daddy?"

They were pulling on their masked father's sleeve.

"Yes, yes, okay, okay. Jesus lord."

"Don't say Jesus Lord! We're Jewish!" the boys cried. "Grandma Roberta said."

Roberta: "It's matrilinear. I didn't make the rules."

Mamie waved and closed the lid of the computer, as Julian had taught her to do.

Julian's present was a pack of playing cards designed by Arnold Schoenberg.

It was Arnold Schoenberg's birthday, too, she reminded him. "But I'm sure he doesn't expect a gift."

Julian and Agatha followed Mamie into her bedroom, where she dug around in her closet to find a box of old pictures to put into the album.

"There," she said, pointing to a high shelf loaded with sweaters. "The box is back there somewhere."

Julian began to push the sweaters aside but was pushed aside himself by Agatha.

"I make pile," she said. "Neat fold."

When she had slowly removed each sweater and refolded it and laid it on top of the dresser, making a colorful pile, she allowed Julian to remove a large hatbox.

"Women used to wear hats," Mamie said. "Extraordinary. But we did."

They trooped back to the kitchen and sat at the table, the hatbox in the middle like a big, round casserole.

"We will fill the album with memories," she said. "And label them!"

"If you remember memories," Agatha said.

But Mamie had already lifted the lid of the hatbox and reached inside.

"Quite a jumble," she said.

She pulled out a photo of Julian's father as a boy holding a baseball bat. Then came a handful of photos of Al playing his horn.

"He has one of those jazz beards!" Julian said.

"A goatee, Julian." Though she liked "jazz beard" better, she admitted to herself.

Then more of Frank, a few of Mamie on the beach as a young woman, some buildings in Paris and Rome and London. Some from Japan. And then a snapshot taken at a lake. Leaning on a large boulder was a woman in shorts and a short-sleeved shirt, barefoot, her head thrown back in laughter.

"Is that Garbo?" Julian said.

※

"But Mamie shoved that picture in her pocket so fast I barely saw it," Julian told Sophie. "She said, 'We are done for today.' I asked if it was Garbo and she said she was tired and closed the hatbox, and that was that."

"You think there's a story behind it? I mean, what lake? What were they doing at a lake?"

"It was a big lake, that's all I could see. With mountains around it."

"A picnic?"

Julian shrugged. "She's so secretive sometimes."

"Yeah, but she's dead."

"Not Greta Garbo. My grandmother."

Sophie said, "I was making a joke."

They were walking to the beach, trying to get there in time for the sunset. The dogs were with them.

"Any more stories?" Sophie said.

"Oh yeah. More tennis with Schoenberg. He made her a little notebook to track all her mistakes, all her moves really, in his special code. Bits of different paper, like scrap paper, neatly laced up with string as a binding. Can you believe this important man bothered to do that? He liked to make things and invent things, Mamie said."

"Well, yeah, he invented atonal music, basically."

"And toys for his kids and board games. Four-person chess, things like that."

"You know," Julian said a minute later, "I am so sick of this." He knew Sophie would know what he meant because he said it so often and she said it so often, too.

"It's like waiting for that sex-filled wedding night, except we're waiting for a vaccine," she said, "so we can hold hands!"

"Ahem."

"And all that."

They sat on the beach and watched the sky turn beautiful garish colors. Gulls flew overhead. Surfers in wet suits lay on their boards waiting for waves.

"I miss you," Julian said. He stood up and yelled at the waves, "I miss her!" He turned back to Sophie. "I miss you. I really miss you, Sophie."

Sophie stood up and held out her hand and they walked, hand not in hand, almost six feet apart, along the water's edge. The sun dropped beneath the horizon and the sky, so bright and rich and crazy, was suddenly the color of lead.

Frustration. Anticipation. A new kind of exile, he thought. Then he looked at Sophie silhouetted against the darkening silver sky.

Could be worse, he thought.

"Any more about the Garbo picture?" she asked later as they neared her house. "The lake, the mountains?"

"Not a word."

37

Mamie touched the photo of Greta Garbo in her pocket. Garbo standing by a boulder that stood by a lake at the foot of a mountain, broad open laughing mouth, closed eyes. She took it out of her pocket without looking at it and slipped it under her pillow.

I'm not hiding it, she told herself. Just placing it. Where no one will see it.

That was a trip she would never forget.

Julian had asked her if she ever wanted to travel again. At her age! What a question. But even when she was younger, for years now, she had avoided travel. She had traveled too far and at too young an age. Why on earth would she leave her little plot of earth now? Her orange tree? Her home? We must cultivate our garden, Voltaire said. We must do our work for as long as we can. We must do what we can, though it may not be much. She had worked and she had done what she could in the world outside, and if it had not been much, it was all she had to give. Now was the time to garden in her own garden. Here she hurt no one, and she was content. And she could cultivate Julian! That made her laugh.

When she'd arrived in California, Mamie thought all of America was her garden, a new, infinite garden. She had started her new, voluntary travels in California. She hadn't gone as far as Irving Tabor had, perhaps. She had not seen whaling ships in San Francisco. But she had seen whales calving in Baja. Then she and Al had gone to Chicago, New York, New Orleans, Paris, London, Prague. Then Japan. Later, after Al took off, she'd played in Berlin and Munich. Never Vienna, though. Vienna was a memory of promenades and cake. And of terror. Vienna must not be disturbed. Or resurrected.

Mamie climbed into bed beside Prince Jan, who had already fallen asleep. With his snores as a soothing background, she pulled the photo from beneath her pillow. She remembered taking it, standing with her back to the cabin on a tiny island in a pure blue lake. The lake spread before her, the mountains enclosing them, enclosing her and the woman she loved.

A tiny island in a lake in the Sierra Nevada mountains. In the backseat of a big car, she'd had no idea where they were going, the chauffeur driving them north, and farther north: so far north they would have been in Finland if they had started from Vienna, yet still they were in California. She was heartily eating a chicken sandwich, her second on the long trip, her lap covered with crumbs. Beside her, Greta Garbo.

"Now, my greedy little curly-headed shepherd boy," Garbo said, wiping crumbs off Mamie's lap, "stop chewing and look out the window." And there below them was a lake between two mountain peaks. And there in the middle of the lake was a little island. And there on the little island was the little cabin.

The chauffeur loaded their bags and baskets and boxes of food and drink into a rowboat and Garbo took the oars and off they went to the island, owned by a friend who had given her the keys to his cabin.

"This is our lake," she said, "and that is our cabin!"

Mamie had been in a daze of happiness. The trip itself was a surprise, the destination a secret. All she'd been told was that she was to bring a swimsuit and sturdy shoes. Hours and hours passed in the car, and Garbo would tell her only that it was a secret, a secret surprise. Garbo loved secrets. She was notorious for making the most mundane event or outing a secret. But this secret was far from mundane.

Garbo rowed and Mamie watched her arms, smooth and strong, the muscles tightening and loosening, the oars dipping with a splash and lifting out of the flat, shining water. The light was low and pink, the late sun glowing on the water. Garbo had her chin tilted up. For once there was no hat, no scarf to disguise her. Her chin, her jawline, her ears, the nose, the forehead, the long, absurdly long eyelashes—they belonged on a big screen, a silver screen; they belonged on a movie star. But they are here, Mamie thought. With me. And we are alone.

"We are alone," Garbo said. "Which means we are free."

Mamie's parents thought she was with a school friend, three weeks in the mountains with her family. Ilse and Otto were not suspicious of her friendship with Garbo as much as they were confused. The actress was more than twenty years older than Mamie; she was not, in their brief encounters with her, a particularly interesting person, her main topics of conversation being her peculiar diet and various spiritualist fads she serially embraced. They did not understand their daughter's interest in Garbo, except perhaps as crazed movie fan. Far more puzzling for them was Garbo's interest in Mamie.

"They're all narcissists, of course," Otto said. "They like a young, undiscerning audience. Schoenberg's the same."

Ilse was less sure, but Mamie had never seemed happier, and Ilse pushed whatever decadent Weimar thoughts she had out of her mind.

"When I telephone and say 'Meet Beiler,'" Garbo said, "that means meet me at Union Station the next day for our holiday."

It was not just Mamie and Mamie's parents who couldn't know where they were going. It was the world. Garbo was obsessed with being followed. Was that why she ran every stop light when she drove?

"I will go back to Sweden," she said on that trip. She was tired of Hollywood, tired of the people. She would go home. Then: "I'm sorry, my curly-headed shepherd boy." Because she knew for Mamie there was no Sweden, no home, to go back to.

"You are a fellow émigré," Mamie said, "however many times you threaten to return to the country of your birth."

In today's world we would be judged in a different spirit, Mamie thought, putting the photograph in the drawer of her bedside table. Different, yes, though equally harsh. Judgments would rain down upon us as they would have then, just different judgments. Two women running off together in those days? A scandal to those who understood women.

Now? It would be the disparity of ages, the disparity in power. She, older and famous, would be seen as having all the power. And I, just twenty, an innocent, an exploited innocent.

Of course, it was the opposite. She knew that even then. Her youth was what she had to offer, and she was burning to offer it up, as burning as any Greek burning a sacrificial lamb for their gods and goddesses. Her youth was what drew Garbo to her and what held Garbo to her, she knew that and reveled in it. That was her power. It was ravishing, if ravishing were an active verb.

The power of Greta Garbo, still the most famous movie star in the world—well, that was something else. Her fame was so immense, so overwhelming, it seemed to weigh her down, almost to disfigure her, if that were possible for someone so beautiful. But, yes, certainly her fame was also a source of power, great humming power that seemed to engulf her and emanate from her at the same time, a sublime, ethereal heaviness; you could almost hear it, you could almost see it, uplifting and oppressive, both at once. That power roared so loud and so forcefully that Mamie was able to hear it as if it were her own.

A victim? Mamie thought with a smile. I think not.

She had been infused with that power and took it as her due. She knew she was young, she saw it all as an adventure, and she knew she would move on from it, that she would have to. This was Greta Garbo! Twice her age! A woman who belonged to the world. A woman who would grow tired of her despite her youth. A woman she would grow tired of despite her beauty.

Was that cold of me? No, it was young of me.

Garbo was terrified of so many things Mamie never even thought about. Cancer was one. Her sister had died of cancer, and that haunted her. Failure was another: every success meant a higher standard, a standard she never felt she met. *Ninotchka*, for example. An almost perfect film that brought her career springing back to life. But it was a disappointment to her; it filled her with dismay. Why? Who knows.

"I am a rather sad, tired boy," she often said.

She was filled with cold, northern gloom. She was sunny and light.

During those weeks on their little island, she seemed to shed her fame, her expectations, the expectations of others, her fears and disappointments, her gloom, just the way she shed her clothes that first night. For three weeks, she climbed the rocks and cliffs barefoot, the wind blowing her hair, looking like some sort of goddess. Not Norse—nothing like Wagner's hefty ladies. No: Greek. Slender, browned by the sun. When she dove into the lake, she gave a cry of delight at the cold water and reemerged with droplets of lake water glistening on her long eyelashes. Those famous eyelashes. And Mamie watched, heart pounding.

The absurdity of their situation enveloped them with its need for seclusion and secrecy. It brought them closer, made every moment urgent. Only the necessity of two people, of themselves, was real, two bodies beneath the sun and the moon and caressed by the chilled night air. Every cliché of romance, every movie angle, every breathless overwrought thought, was there for them.

Mamie could still hear her heart pounding, all these years later. The blood still pumped and sounded in her ears. Oh, yes, now it would be sexual harassment or grooming or some such thing. But then? Oh, it was love.

They arrived at the creaky wooden dock, tied up the boat, unloaded their provisions, and Garbo tore off her clothes and stood, rosy in the setting sun, then dove into the water. Mamie followed, rather stunned, though it was not the first time, by Garbo's nakedness, then by her own, then by the icy water. They swam until they couldn't stand the cold, then lay on the dock in the disappearing sunlight. When the stars appeared, they dove back in, and they lay on their backs in the cold water, looking up at the cold sky, and floated for what seemed like hours. Garbo took Mamie's hand and they lay there on the quiet deep black water beneath the quiet deep black sky, not speaking, just listening to the sounds of the night. The lapping of the water on the shore. Rustling in the trees. And their own breathing.

Mamie had never been as happy as that night. Unless it was the next night and the night after that and all the nights of their stay. She knew they must have eaten, because she could not recall being hungry. She knew they must have lit the stove, because she did not remember being cold. All she did remember was Garbo, her hand in Mamie's in the water, her face in Mamie's hands, that face against Mamie's face, that deep voice in her ears.

"I have been a bad, bad boy," Garbo said one night.

"What have you done now?"

"I have made you happy. I have let you make me happy. But now we must go back. There is no happiness there."

Mamie laughed at her and kissed and stroked her hair. But, of course, Greta Garbo knew Greta Garbo, and she was right.

There was no happiness "there" for the two of them. She made sure of that. She left Los Angeles. She did not answer Mamie's letters or phone calls. They never saw each other again.

She was such a private person because she feared being swallowed up, Mamie thought now. By her fans, yes, but even by her friends. Even I was a threat, wasn't I?

She later learned this was common Garbo behavior—even with those to whom she was closest, even more so with them. Mamie was unhappy at first. She hoped she would bump into her on the beach or at a party. Mamie drove by her house once, hoping for just a glimpse. But her life soon went off in another direction. She did not forget about Greta Garbo and the lake and the time they spent together when they fell in love. How could she? But she did not mourn her. She had learned so early in life to lose what she loved.

I met you, Al, that autumn, remember? What good timing. And what good times! You knew nothing of this, did you? Did you ever guess? No, you were too busy running around. With me!

She'd be furious that I am telling you now, dead as you are. Don't say a word, old friend.

Yes, she's a dead duck, too, I know; but from the grave, she is shunning me at this very moment, refusing to answer my letters or phone calls.

Even when we are dead, we seem to mind our secrets being told. If we are Greta Garbo! But I am not. I am Mamie Künstler, and I'm alive.

38

⁓

RECKLESSNESS IN IMAGINATION, PRECISION IN ACTION—THAT WAS WHAT Schoenberg had taught Mamie. The game of tennis mattered to him not only as a test of skill or a competition (and he was famously competitive), but also as something complicated, elusive, and beautiful one could try to understand. It was a lesson for life, she realized soon enough. Such a pity she could never fully master the lesson. She did learn the game of tennis, though.

"She moves like a gazelle," her grandfather would say when he watched her play. "A Viennese gazelle."

"One day," she told Julian, "I was sitting on the grass after a game, filling in the little notebook, using the notations Schoenberg had invented and taught me. He pulled up a lawn chair and sat beside me."

Remembering that day, an important day for her, she could recall the smell of the grass, just mown, a dry California smell like hay. She was leaning against a large eucalyptus tree, its bark soft as cork.

Schoenberg was thoughtful, plucking at the strings of his racket.

"Look," she said, showing him the notebook. "My backhand is so much better."

Her parents had arranged real lessons from a USC college student so as not to burden the great man, and Mamie was able to play a respectable game against him now.

Schoenberg glanced at the notebook and nodded vaguely. He was thinking about something important, obviously. Perhaps it was a new piece he was working on. "It is not correct," he said suddenly. "It is not correct to say 'to land on water' for a seaplane that comes down on water." Brow furrowed. "No. Land is land, water is water. Two different things."

He looked at her expectantly.

"Land is land, water is water," she agreed.

"But people say in English: 'landing on water.' No! You land on land. A seaplane—it should be said 'watering on water.'"

He often came up with esoteric problems no one else had noticed because they were not problems at all and attempted to solve them.

"Violin," he said when she did not respond. "I think so. Yes."

"And that," she told Julian, "is how I began the violin. The violin!"

She turned to look fondly, reverently Julian thought, at the cases of violins against the wall.

"An instrument capable of every sound and every sound in between every sound. From the moment I slid a finger along the dark and moody G string, the D, the A, the high, eerie E string, the Western scale no longer seemed to imprison sounds. Just to isolate and celebrate them! A compromise, as Schoenberg explained it—a temporary truce. The natural laws my father sought to teach me were not natural laws at all. They sprang from the struggle of craftsmen, that is musicians, to shape their material, which is music."

"I wonder what you would have done if you hadn't started playing."

Mamie looked startled. "The violin was my fate."

"Hey, you're the one who turned me on to John Cage. Chance might have made you, I don't know, a nurse?"

Mamie's eyes widened in horror. "A nurse? Me? A nurse?" Then she began to laugh. From the next room Agatha's laugh joined hers. "A nurse, Agatha! Me!"

※

THAT night, Mamie lay in bed beside Prince Jan. He snored gently, murmuring and twitching now and then as he dreamed. But Mamie was far away, remembering when music had come to her.

"Every living thing has within it that which changes, develops, and destroys it," Schoenberg once said to her. Or had he written it? "The way life and death are both equally present in the embryo. What lies between is time."

She knew she was close to the end of her parenthetical time. And that's what life was for all of us, even the great Arnold Schoenberg: parenthetical time. But what a lot could happen within those parentheses. Change, development, destruction. Life and death. And music.

A nurse! she thought just as she was drifting off to sleep. And she laughed and her laugh turned into a snore, counterpoint to the dog beside her.

39

Once Mamie understood that musical scales were a compromise rather than an absolute truth, she began to enjoy them. There were so many: Japanese, Indian, African—a revelation. If she did not yet understand the emancipation of the dissonance, she sensed that she herself had been emancipated.

Those were exciting days, Mamie thought. She lay in bed, unable to sleep. Outside, a helicopter circled. They were back. Stupid waste. Even she knew the police could use drones bought at Best Buy if they needed a bird's-eye view.

Probably chasing some drug-addled homeless person in the name of law and order. Even before the pandemic, Venice had called its siren song to the fringes of society. Like me, Mamie thought. Now that even the awful shelters offered no refuge because of Covid, so many homeless people had migrated to Venice, like snowbirds, to the beach. So many. Refugees in their own city.

"Take a hike," she said to the helicopter.

Law and order. That old canard. A little law, high up the political food chain, would be nice in this day and age, but order? Well, we hold on to that fantasy for as long as we can.

The world has rules and form and basic sense, she reassured herself. But, at night, the reality of the world seems to take over.

"Yes, I know there are rules," she said out loud to Prince Jan, as if the sleeping dog had challenged her. "Physics and geometry and biology and chemistry make that very clear. All those rules that let each living thing send messages to veins, beating hearts, the sap in the trees, the green of a leaf, the dance of a bee, the trajectory of a bomb. The rules that govern how we are born from our mother's womb and how and when we die and the rules of life no longer apply, and what's left of us is buried and subject to a new set of rules, the rules of worms and decay."

That's enough, Salomea, she told herself in her father's voice.

She stroked Prince Jan's silky ear. That was part of the world, too, wasn't it? A dog, an ear as big as a flag, the comfort of a fellow being.

"If I don't stop stroking your ear it will get dog-eared," she said aloud.

But even with all the ears of all the Saint Bernards in the universe, there was still a problem that all the rules and scientific discoveries of newer and newer rules could not solve.

Not even the rules of dissonance.

⁂

It was not until long after her lessons from Arnold Schoenberg that Mamie was able to face real dissonance. The dissonance of chaos. The dissonance of the random nature of life.

"My father killed himself," she told Julian the next morning. She blurted it out. At breakfast of all places. Over the scrambled eggs. She did not know why. Because she loved Julian? Because she knew Julian loved her? Because their relationship had meaning and her father's death had none? "My mother found him hanging in the garage beside Christopher Isherwood's car. She died a few months later."

Julian stared. "Jesus."

"Those were dark days. Thank god my grandfather was already gone."

Julian reached for her hands and held them in his.

Loss, which Otto had so heroically faced at first, had soured to a sense of abandonment. Both his old country and his new country had abandoned him. The new country is bright, but my future is dark: that's what he began to say.

"He'd tried to join the U.S. Army, did you know that?"

"No. I didn't."

"But he was too old, and his lungs were terrible from his chain-smoking. So he smoked more and taught children who had no interest in music. He seemed to fade behind the cigarette smoke as time went on."

Only death is not random, she thought. It is ordained from the time we are born. But not when or where or how. Not hanging beside Christopher Isherwood's Ford.

"I'm so sorry," Julian said. "I never knew any of this."

"Dark times."

He saw she was crying, something he'd never seen before, and gently handed her a paper napkin.

"Pay no attention," she said.

"That's what Dad always says about sad things that happened to him."

"Does he? I taught him well."

Or not, she thought. Pushing away sorrow? Well, it had its place. But poor Frank, my little Franz. Still . . .

"*What* sad things?" she added, her voice hard. "He had a *lovely* childhood."

"His father, I guess. Leaving? Dying?"

"Oh, him."

"Oh, him? Come on, Grandma."

"Well, yes. That was hard."

"But Dad came out okay."

She smiled, proudly. "Yes, he did."

"And you did okay."

"Yes, I did."

He waited. "And . . ." he prompted.

Mamie looked at him, sweet and eager and comforting her like an adult. And, like a child, waiting . . .

"And you came out okay!" she said.

"Yes, I did," he said.

"Don't burden your father with this, please."

"Why? Doesn't he know? How can he not know?"

"Why!" she said. "You need to ask? Oh, I don't know, I know he knows. But we never talk about it. Out of respect."

Julian wondered, knowing the two of them, if with their silence Mamie was protecting Frank or if Frank was protecting Mamie.

"And it's too sad," he said.

"And it's too sad."

Oh, how she loved him, half man, half boy.

"I could not have handled the last year without you," she said. "Poor Julian. Exiled just like an exile."

"Exiled in paradise, you mean."

"Hardly." But if this was not paradise, what was? A roof over your head, a chicken in the pot, a grandson to talk to, Agatha her best friend and dogsbody, Prince Jan and his comforting dog's body, an orange tree outside.

"Blue skies," Julian was saying, "white clouds, fruit trees bulging with pomegranates and figs—biblical fruits! Perfect for paradise. Soft breezes. Orange blossoms. The ocean over one shoulder, mountains over the other. And thou," he added.

"Paradise for dead," Agatha said, noiselessly appearing to clear the dishes.

"I do not believe in life after death," Mamie said. "I sometimes have trouble believing in life before death: it is all so improbable."

40

THAT AFTERNOON, THEY LISTENED TO SCHOENBERG'S SUITE FOR STRING Orchestra ("In the Old Style"), a piece he wrote in 1934 when he'd just come to Los Angeles, his first composition written in L.A.

"Listen to this, Mamie." Julian had looked up the *New York Times* review on his phone. "'Only one thing could be more fantastical than the thought of Arnold Schönberg in Hollywood, and that one thing has happened. Since arriving there about a year ago Schönberg has composed in a melodic manner and in recognizable keys. That is what Hollywood has done to Schönberg. We may now expect atonal fugues by Shirley Temple.'"

"Did you know Shirley Temple lived on the same street? A tour bus would come along pointing out her house. They never pointed out Schoenberg's."

"That review calls him Schönberg with an umlaut, by the way."

"Disrespect comes in many flavors."

As they listened to the Gavotte, Mamie could almost see Schoenberg strolling jubilantly toward the tennis courts, dancing from foot to foot as he explained creation. Jaunty old man. How she loved him. Bronzed and smiling. What a teacher he was.

"We will dance to Schoenberg now, Julian," she said. "You didn't know you could dance to Schoenberg, did you?"

She put her hands on his arms. Small steps, no more than sprightly scuffs.

"Dancing," she said. A gigue, she thought. A jig. The jig is not yet up.

"I'm certain this piece is about Los Angeles, Julian. Ah, here is the soaring, triumphant part."

Schoenberg told the world he'd written the suite as a didactic exercise for student orchestras to play.

"But the student orchestras couldn't play it! It was too difficult!"

Too difficult and so full of melody and harmony. The call of the tonal. Of course it was about Los Angeles. He'd just arrived in the city that sprawled beside the sea under the generous sun. He'd arrived.

"But he hadn't arrived, had he?" Mamie said.

"You're a little out of breath. Maybe you should sit down again."

"He had merely escaped."

Julian helped her back to her chair.

"I remember his household in Brentwood," Mamie said. "Small children—his daughter and the two little boys—and his young wife holding it all together."

"Are you okay? Do you want some water?"

"The piano and sofa in the living room." Mamie's eyes closed. "A smaller piano in a smaller room with all his books, his paintings on the wall. He was a talented painter. Most of them were self-portraits, naturally. And the Ping-Pong table in the backyard. I longed to be a part of that household. Schoenberg telling the children long stories. A princess who gets hit by a tennis ball!"

Julian went to the kitchen and filled a glass with water.

"Grandma," he said, "drink this. Or maybe, like, a cookie? Maybe it's blood sugar. Mom gets low blood sugar."

"My father never told me stories," Mamie was saying. "He even began to hate the stories Grandfather told me. He said they were false. He said the Old World no longer existed, so it must never have existed."

She took the glass of water and drank some. "Water's for washing," she said, grimacing.

"I'm not giving you gin. You're acting too weird."

She sat up straighter. "Am I? Oh dear. Don't tell Agatha."

"I won't tell anyone if you'll just sit for a minute. You're out of breath."

"I wonder why I remember Schoenberg's room off his music room where he tinkered and puttered and invented. And the chess set he invented. For four players. And the track he made for the children's bicycles. It had an electric traffic light."

"You have a good memory, that's why."

"I do, that's true. But I am starting to have blanks. Sometimes I can't remember yesterday. Don't tell Agatha."

"It's only natural."

"Nature," she said. "It's a wonder Nature doesn't just wipe us all off the face of the earth after what we've done to her."

"Well, she's doing a pretty good job lately."

Mamie thought of Schoenberg, an old man with young children, fierce, renegade composer, telling the children stories as they ate their lunch. He cut the peanut butter and jelly sandwiches into postage-stamp-size pieces. If they stopped eating, he stopped the story. He was a Scheherazade of lunch.

"Agatha!"

"Your Mighty Highness."

"I'd like a peanut butter and jelly sandwich, please, Agatha."

Agatha widened her eyes in theatrical dismay. Mamie had never liked peanut butter. She had never understood the American passion for it.

"Cut up in little pieces," Mamie added. "Like postage stamps."

41

Every evening, Julian went to the mailbox to collect the flyers and catalogs and bills and the occasional letter. The mail never came in the morning, always around five o'clock. Gathering up the mail from the mailbox just outside the white picket fence was a task he enjoyed: it felt old-fashioned, as if he were in a small town. The short walk to the gate, the dented metal mailbox with its red metal flag, lowering the flap, pulling snail mail from a dark, dusty interior still hot from the day's sun—he could have been in an old TV show. He should be whistling.

He checked for any bills. He'd been unable to convince Mamie to have them paid directly from her bank account or to get billed online. But he had at least been able to take over the organizing, record keeping, and check writing himself. Electricity bill, gas bill, car insurance, three offers of better car insurance, a catalog from the Vermont Country Store, and . . .

"Agatha!" He ran into the house. "Agatha, you got a letter." It was the first letter for Agatha since he had arrived a year ago. "Here! Look!" He thrust the envelope at her. "Mrs. Agatha Jones."

She backed up as if it were a knife or a poisonous snake.

"No me." She shook her head vehemently. "No for me. No, no."

Mamie was in the garden, but she heard them and hurried, as much as she could hurry, into the kitchen. Agatha was pale. She had backed herself against the refrigerator and was shooing Julian away with one hand, the other over her eyes, as if he were a bear about to pounce.

"Give it to me, dear," Mamie said.

"Here, here," Julian said. "Agatha, I'm really sorry I scared you, but it's just a letter and I didn't open it or anything. It's addressed to Mrs. Agatha Jones, so I thought . . ."

"We'll clear this up," Mamie said. "I'm sure it's a simple mistake."

But there was no mistake. A long official envelope. Addressed to Mrs. Agatha Jones.

Julian didn't know Agatha was married. He didn't even know she had a last name. She was Agatha, pure and simple, the way Diana was Diana or Hillary was Hillary. Like Beyoncé.

"Agatha, dear, sit down. Julian, make her a cup of tea. Then we will open the letter. Together. No need to worry, Agatha. We are here. We will always take care of you no matter what is in the letter. Isn't that right, Julian?"

"Absolutely," Julian said. He could not imagine what threat the letter could contain for an elderly dogsbody, but he would stand by her. "But, you know, it's only a letter. How bad could it be? Probably from Motor Vehicles."

"Quiet," Mamie said. Agatha's mail, the essentials like Medicare and Social Security and the DMV, went to a post office box under her maiden name. Nothing came to Mamie's house. Nothing was under her married name. Agatha was as anonymous as she could make herself.

Julian poured them each a cup of tea. "Milk, two sugars for Agatha, lemon, no sugar for Mamie, milk no sugar for me."

Agatha, despite her agitation, patted his hand in approval. "You take my job yet."

"Drink your tea," Mamie ordered. "Both of you."

"I no get mail. Why I get mail?"

Mamie slit the envelope with a knife. She unfolded a typed letter.

"It says an investment bank has been trying to locate you. And if you don't claim your property it will go to the state's unclaimed property department. Here." She handed it to Agatha. "A scam? Probably a scam. They prey on us, these dirty crooks."

"It might not be a scam," Julian said. "My mother did one of those online searches once. She found out a bank owed her one dollar and forty-six cents."

"A trick," Agatha said. "He find me."

"Who?"

"Never you mind," Mamie said. "Her abusive husband."

"You call bank, please?" Agatha asked Mamie.

Julian had never seen Agatha look helpless like this. It was unnerving. He made her another cup of tea. "Cinnamon toast?" he asked. What abusive husband? He buttered the piece of toast, sprinkled cinnamon and sugar on it, and absentmindedly ate it himself. "Don't worry, Agatha," he said. "Please don't worry."

The next morning Mamie called the number listed in the letter. To her amusement, Julian supervised.

"Scam artists prey on old people," he said. "You said so yourself."

"Stop hovering." She elbowed him back.

The call was answered by the usual recording. Press one if this, two if that.

"Scam," Julian said.

Mamie pressed what she hoped was the appropriate number and left a long detailed message that ended with: "I expect a timely callback. I may be old, but I am not a fool."

Julian looked up the fund, and to his surprise there was a fund of that name, a legitimate investment fund. With a long history. "The fund looks like it's legit, Mamie. But I still say it's a scam. To take money from old people."

"Stop saying *old*, Julian. It's a kind of showing off."

"I just want to protect you and Agatha."

Mamie thought about that as she watched Julian that afternoon. He followed Agatha around as surreptitiously as he could. He opened doors for her. He grabbed plates from the shelf before she could. He turned the faucet on, dived beneath the sink for the dishwashing soap (pod, no powder!), and tried to help her pull on her pink rubber gloves. In other words, he thoroughly annoyed her. But even as she scolded him and told him to "Go! You like shadow. I trip on my shadow!" she patted his hand gratefully. "He mean well," she said to Mamie. "He oaf, but he mean well."

Mamie said, "He does mean well, the oaf, and I take full responsibility for this ethical and social progress." And he's fallen in love, too, she added to herself. So my hopes and my efforts at spiritual awakening were not misplaced. Well done, Mamie. Well done, old girl.

42

THE JASMINE AND THE VACCINE APPEARED NOW, ALMOST ON THE SAME DAY. Mamie and Agatha were excited and happy to take time out from their efforts to get in touch with a live person at the investment bank, and Mamie called to get them appointments at the hospital in Santa Monica. Julian drove them to Saint John's hospital in an optimistic mood. It was a miracle, he said. A miracle, Mamie agreed. A red letters day, said Agatha.

"What lovely people," they said when it was all over. "What kind and lovely people."

"Too bad you young," Agatha said to Julian. "You miss out."

"Good you young," Agatha said the next day when she and Mamie felt achy and tired, side effects of the vaccine.

Julian helped settle them in the living room and brought them juice and scrambled eggs.

"Fresh squeezed," he said. "I pick, I squeeze, you drink."

"I would like Prince Jan Saint Bernard," Mamie said.

"He's right here." Julian pointed to the dog, lying beside her. Maybe she was losing her marbles after all. Was that one of the temporary side effects of the vaccine?

"The book, Julian. That book taught me much of my English and even more about the habits of the American family. If the American family happens to be unconsciously but outrageously wealthy."

She told him what shelf it was on. South wall. Third shelf from the bottom. Eight volumes in. Blue cloth binding.

"I found it!" Julian said, relieved that she had not lost her powers of reason, even temporarily. "Right where you said, Mamie. Well done."

She gave him a look. "I am enduring the side effects of a medical miracle, not slipping into dementia."

"Right," Julian said. "Of course." He opened the book. "Whoa."

There inside the faded blue book was an inscription in faded blue ink: "To you, your new home and the many California adventures to come, G.G."

He read it out loud.

"Many adventures, indeed," Mamie said.

"So that's really her. G.G."

"Well, it ain't Gravel Gertie," Mamie said.

The novel began in Switzerland. Puppies romped and frolicked in a monastery cellar among their elders, strong brave dogs who rescued travelers in the Great St. Bernard Pass. Prince Jan and his brother Rollo, big paws, floppy ears, soft coats, dark intelligent eyes. Their mother told them stories of their heroic father, who died saving four travelers. The puppies pressed against her at night and listened to her breathing. They were happy and eager to start their lives digging unconscious humans from the cold white drifts of avalanches.

"This is the happy part," Mamie said. "Before the poor innocent creature's exile to California."

"He doesn't like California at all?"

"Oh, yes. He has some wonderful times and meets some lovely people. But he's been bred to save lives in the snow. And how do you save a life in a land without snow?"

"How *do* you save a life in a land without snow?" Julian asked Mamie's dog.

Prince Jan Saint Bernard opened his doleful dog eyes.

"He no speak English," Agatha said.

Mamie thought, He speaks it about as well as you do. But all she said was, "It's four o'clock. These existential questions will have to wait."

And Julian went in to prepare the jingling tray.

43

"YOU TOOK CARE OF THEM?" ANNABELLA ASKED. "YOU?"

"Well, someone had to."

"You cooked? You can't cook."

"Agatha yelled instructions into the kitchen. I can now cook. She's giving me lessons, too."

"Would you like a job in Chicago as a nanny? Low pay, long hours?"

"I'm glad Jay got vaccinated. You must be so relieved."

And Annabella, curt, superior older sister Annabella, whose watchword had been, for as long as Julian could remember, "Snap out of it," that same Annabella began to cry.

"I was so scared he would die," she said.

Then she snapped out of it.

※

FRANK and Roberta were able to be vaccinated a month later.

"This is the best news," Julian said. "I was so worried about you two."

"What a terrible time, when children have to worry about their parents," Frank said to Roberta that night.

"But, Frank, you worry about your mother all the time."

"But she's old."

They looked at each other.

"Oh dear," Roberta said.

"You'll never be old, Roberta. You're younger than springtime."

"Have you ever thought how old springtime really is? There has been springtime since the world began. Well, we're not as old as your mother, anyway."

"Not yet," Frank said. And, he thought happily, we will never be able to catch up. He said so to Roberta.

"No, not as long as she is alive."

Roberta often said blunt, insensitive things. They bounced off his consciousness, harmless, hardly noticed. He liked her sharp-tongued manner, truth be told. She was vinegary, he sometimes thought. And he loved vinegar. But he heard this comment loud and clear; it did not strike him as vinegary. It just struck him. It reminded him that his mother would, without a doubt, die. She would die someday sooner rather than later. He knew this. It was obvious. But he never thought about it. His mother was not just a force of nature; for him, she was Nature itself. Nature, like springtime, had been around since the world began. Certainly since his world began.

"I've known her my entire life," he said. He sat on the edge of the bed and put his head in his hands. What would be left to know if she were no longer here?

Roberta wanted to say, Obviously you've known her your whole life. She's your mother, she gave birth to you. But Roberta knew when to stop. She knew when Frank could levitate above her words, looking down with tolerant amusement; but she also knew when her words landed a punch. She sat beside him and put her arms around him. "Yes, you have," she said gently. "All your life. And she's not done with you yet."

They decided that night to go to Los Angeles. It was Frank who decided, really. Uncharacteristically determined, unwavering. He began checking flights on his phone.

"We're both vaccinated. My mother and Agatha are vaccinated. What's stopping us? I want to see my mother before she dies."

"She'll outlive us all, Frank."

"Then I want to see her before *I* die."

HER hair still mustard yellow, making her advice over Zoom less impressive than she thought, Annabella addressed her parents. "If either of you gets sick and dies I will kill you."

"You'll have to wait until *you* get vaccinated for that," Roberta said.

"Don't be smug, Mommy."

At the word *Mommy*, Roberta almost wept. "I wish we were coming to Chicago to see you and the little boys." But Chicago in February? Maybe not such a good idea. "In the spring," she said. "When everything has calmed down for everyone."

Jay said, "*Keinehora.*"

Roberta knew not to express her delight at hearing Jay speak Yiddish. She did not want a lecture from Annabella or, worse, a disgusted condescending look that often preceded a cluck of dismissal and an end to a call. But delighted she was. Although she noticed that Jay had not looked delighted or relieved or hopeful at all. He'd looked somber.

"*Keinehora,*" she repeated, feeling slightly less optimistic about the virus's imminent demise.

"They're like two Jewish mothers," she said when they'd hung up.

Not like my Jewish mother, Frank thought. And he remembered speeding off with her in one of her long line of convertible sports cars, sitting on her lap and steering as she kissed the back of his head and sang "Minnie the Moocher" in his ear. How old was he? Five?

"'Minnie the Moocher'?" Roberta said. She loved it when Frank sang. He was more musical than he would admit. "I haven't heard that in ages."

"She was a low down hoochie coocher," Frank sang.

44

THERE WAS ONE SMALL PATCH OF GRASS IN MAMIE'S GARDEN, A NARROW TRI-angle of green, and her grandson was stretched out on it, practically spooning with the dog. She watched him for a minute, a young man who wanted to protect her and Agatha. Clumsily, perhaps, but earnestly. Time will tell, she'd thought when he first arrived. Well, time had told, and she liked its tale.

She let her head fall against the back of the chaise and looked up at the sky. The sky that lived above them every day watching their struggles and follies. She waved to the sky. "Hey, good lookin'."

"Did you know Dad is a bird-watcher now?" Julian said. "Since the pandemic. That I'd like to see."

"You'll soon have your chance," Mamie said.

"Dad quiet long enough to notice a bird? He probably lectures them on their water consumption and ecological footprint. Oh man, the minute they come, all the questions will start. *What are your plans, Julian? When will you move on, Julian? What's the next step? Where are you headed?*"

Mamie dreaded the questions, too. More, she dreaded the answers.

"That was a damn good imitation," she said. He had alternated between his mother's and his father's voice.

"I learned from the best."

JULIAN picked up his parents at the airport.

"Aren't you jaunty," Roberta said, watching him from the backseat. What a good driver he was. She hated driving. It had been years since she'd been behind the wheel of a car. Look how he changes lanes!

"That's quite a beard," Frank said.

Mamie was waiting for them, sitting on the perilous blue swing on the porch. She tried to remember exactly when Julian had arrived, when Agatha had pulled open the sticky door and Julian had swept in and lifted them into the air. Was it just a year ago? A bit more.

Agatha had made an orange cake for Frank and Roberta. "Vegan. No cheats," she said.

"Oh, we eat dairy now. And eggs. Enough is enough with the vegan," Roberta said.

Agatha narrowed her eyes. "Today you eat vegan cake. No cheats."

Ah, dear Mother, Julian thought, I think you may have met your match.

"So, Julian," Roberta said after dinner and two sizable pieces of no-cheats cake, "you have so many stories now."

"Mamie's stories? They're really interesting."

Mamie then told them about a visit Schoenberg made to the house of Alma Mahler and Franz Werfel.

"'Marie!' Alma called to her maid. 'Bring in Beethoven's hair!'"

Schoenberg opened a wooden box, and there was a lock of brown hair, a gift to Mahler from the Vienna Philharmonic when he left to come to New York.

Julian said, "You didn't give me anyone's hair when I left New York to come to Mamie's."

Roberta could not get used to Julian calling her mother-in-law Mamie. It sounded so familiar, disrespectful. She said so.

"You're just jealous," Mamie said.

"Don't you dare call me Roberta, Julian."

"Call me anything, just don't call me late for dinner," Frank said.

Roberta looked at him, shook her head fondly, and continued: "Annabella said they were wonderful stories and that you were working them up into a screenplay."

"They are wonderful stories, that's for sure."

"You know, Eli is back at his parents'. All his classes are virtual now. But his mother told me he's eating them out of house and home."

"He's developed an unnatural relationship to cheese."

Roberta hesitated. It had been so long since she and Julian had been together. She was having trouble reading him. "She thinks it might be a good idea if he moved out of their apartment. She thinks it might not be emotionally healthy for him there. She thinks that really he should get an apartment of his own. Of course, he would need a roommate."

She waited for the recriminations. Why didn't Eli just stay in our old apartment, the idiot? Why didn't I? If you hadn't made me give it up, Mom, we could still be living there. We'll never find anything that cheap. You realize we are back to square one? You'll have to help me with the rent, obviously . . .

Julian said, "Yeah, he would, I guess." Then he turned to his father. "Hey, Dad, you started bird-watching?"

Frank barely heard him. He was watching his mother, who was watching Julian. Like a hawk. How apt that phrase was. He'd seen so many hawks in Central Park. And owls! He found the owls so moving. And when they spun their heads around? Magic. Though there'd been tragedy, too.

"Barry died," he said.

Confused looks from his nearest and dearest.

"Barry! You know, the barred owl in Central Park. She got hit by a maintenance vehicle. But now they say she'd probably already eaten a poisoned rat."

"Frank, are you drunk?" his wife said.

"She was a Twitter celebrity. There was a memorial service in the park. You know, there's a snowy owl in Brooklyn," he added. "And a bald eagle. I can't wait until it's okay to take the subway so I can see them."

"Not to go to the office, or to court, not to go to a museum, not to go to a concert. To go see a bird." Roberta shook her head. "It's all he cares about now. I send him out to the park once, just once, to get him out of the house, to get a little peace for myself, for him to get some air, and this is what happens. Frank! We are talking about your *son*."

Frank turned his attention to his son. "Have you ever seen an owl?"

"Only on Twitter."

⁂

JULIAN gave his parents his bed and slept on the couch in the living room.

"He didn't seem too eager to get a place with Eli," Roberta said to Frank. "You don't think they've had a falling-out, do you?"

"Maybe he wants to stay here."

"Don't be ridiculous."

Though she had to admit the guesthouse was comfortable and sparkled with almost ostentatious cleanliness. "Agatha must have given it a good scouring before we came."

"Julian told me he cleaned up for us. He gives Agatha a hand. At least that's what he said."

They looked at each other in disbelief, then laughed at the absurdity of Julian scrubbing the guesthouse.

"But that Agatha—she does do an amazing job. She puts up with your mother day in and day out. Keeps the house from completely falling down around their ears."

"She's a treasure," Frank said. "Isn't that the proper bourgeois term for good help?"

Roberta glared at him. "Have I ever called Agatha 'the help'? She's part of the family. Obviously. And your mother looks damn good, so I would say she is a caring and competent member of the family, too, who has everything under control. Thank god things can get back to normal, now that they're vaccinated. It must have been tough for Julian being cooped up here, of all places. But Agatha can handle things from now on."

"Good cake, too," Frank said.

He loved his wife and he loved his mother. It was true that he preferred to keep them separated, and he'd worried about this trip, but if dinner was any indication, all would be well. Dinner had been blessedly peaceful. Beautiful, too—outside in the garden, cool winter air, stars above.

"And good wine," he added.

"Julian drinking port after dinner. Wasn't that adorable? I hope we'll be able to get him a ticket on the same flight."

Frank said nothing. There was a mockingbird singing outside, which lulled him to sleep.

45

MAMIE WAS ON THE PHONE AGAIN, FIRST THING IN THE MORNING, STILL TRY-
ing to track down the scam artists who were hoping to prey on Agatha.
She wanted to take care of it before her son and daughter-in-law got wind
of what was happening and put their lawyerly two cents in. And before
Julian could stand over her shoulder making her nervous. When she did
get through this time to an actual human being, she was so surprised
she almost couldn't speak. But he sounded nice enough. Not at all like a
scammer, though what did a scammer sound like?

"I am Mrs. Agatha Jones," she said. "I have received a curious letter in
the mail."

She read him the reference number.

"This is an IRA account from 1980," the scammer said.

"Is this legit?"

"It is your husband's IRA account. You are the beneficiary."

"Beneficiary?"

"Well, yes, after his death we did try to locate you. It's taken us years."

His death? His death!

"So how much is there? A dollar forty-six?"

"A little more than that, Mrs. Jones."

46

"AGATHA, SIT DOWN," MAMIE SAID WHEN THEY HAD GATHERED FOR BREAK-fast. "Julian can make the eggs, can't you, Julian?"

Julian, happy to avoid questions from his parents, shot out of his chair and began cracking eggs into the pan.

"Now, Agatha, I have some news."

"About letter?"

"About letter."

"I must go back to violent husband?"

"No. No. Violent husband died twenty years ago. You were not con-tacted because no one could find you."

"What is all this about?" Roberta said. "What letter? What husband? You have a husband?"

"No anymore," Agatha said.

"And he seems to have left you quite a bit of money. One hundred ninety-eight thousand dollars, in fact."

Stunned silence all around.

"From out of blue?" Agatha finally said.

"From out of blue."

Julian went to Lincoln Wines and bought a bottle of Veuve Clicquot with his grandmother's credit card. They raised their glasses to Agatha, the Heiress! She demurely sipped her tea, acknowledging their toast with a nod and a small smile.

"From out of blue," she murmured. "From out of blue."

"So what will you do with your windfall?" Frank asked.

It was not enough money to buy a house in Los Angeles. But she could take a trip. A lot of trips! A cruise, maybe.

"Germs."

"You could go to Europe," Roberta suggested. "You could stay in such wonderful hotels."

Agatha shook her head. "Germs."

"Buy a car? Or two?"

"No license."

"A racehorse!" Julian said.

"Germs."

Mamie had been uncharacteristically quiet. Now she said, "What then, old friend?"

Agatha seemed to steel herself.

Oh dear god, Mamie thought. She's going to quit. Become a nun. Or a missionary or a surfer who follows the sun, though she hates the sun. She burns so easily. Maybe she will move back to whatever country she had come from? A country in Eastern Europe? Where one could buy a house for a pittance and live on beets and the interest from the rest of the money. Mamie tapped her cane in her impatience and her fear.

"Out with it."

Traitor! she added silently.

"Aye aye, Your Highness," Agatha said. She sipped her tea.

"Well?"

Agatha took a deep breath. She put her teacup down. She clutched her pocketbook with both hands. "So," she said. Then she smiled, an enormous, radiant smile. "I give myself a raise."

Mamie was so relieved she stretched her cane toward Agatha and gave her a poke.

"Well then," she said sternly. "A modest one, I hope."

47

Sophie was introduced to Julian's parents on a walk to the beach. Her hair was up in a ponytail. Roberta watched it swing as the children, as she thought of them, walked in front of her and Frank. She was a pretty girl, as much as one could see. Both she and Julian were still masked. Roberta felt almost guilty sauntering along with nothing covering her face. Guilty and exposed.

"She seems lovely," she said.

"Charming. Smart. And a knockout, too."

"Frank."

"Sexist?"

"Old-fogey-creepist."

Julian and Sophie were too far ahead for Roberta to hear what they were talking about. They were certainly talking, though. Sophie never seemed to stop.

"Chatty," she said.

"He is!" Frank said. "Nice to see."

I meant her, Roberta thought. But it was true: Julian was joining in, talking, laughing, sometimes even turning back to his parents and pointing out his new local landmarks. Crazy spec houses so big they barely fit onto their little lots. Asking five million, eight million, in Venice! The canals, so clean since the lockdown, look, you can see the bottom! Notice how light out it is? A week ago it would have been dark by now. Can you believe the trees are blossoming? In February?

He seemed so at ease, so . . . at home, she thought.

"Frank."

But Frank had his binoculars to his eyes, examining a bird in a tree. "Butterbutt," he said.

"Frank."

He lowered what he'd begun to call his bins. How she hated bird-watching language. It was like a cult.

"What?"

"Frank, doesn't Julian seem comfortable? As if he'd lived here all his life?"

Frank was writing his sighting down in his notebook. "Yes," he said.

"I don't get it."

Frank looked at her now. Roberta didn't get it? He didn't like that.

"Oh, don't look so worried," Roberta said. "Look! The Pacific!"

She took his arm and they strolled to the water's edge. The dogs, unleashed, wrestled for a minute then lay down, panting. The waves were loud and they could not hear what Julian and Sophie were saying.

"Probably about us," Roberta said.

Frank put his arm around her. "Probably."

48

⌒

THEY STAYED FOR THREE NIGHTS.

"Julian, you've been so responsible," they told him.

"You've really grown up," they said.

"We can see that."

"We are so proud of you."

"You helped your grandmother get back on her feet like a real mensch."

"And at the same time you've been working on your script."

"Really buckling down and working!"

"Yes, okay, it's true we had some worries about your writing career . . ."

"But you have proved us wrong."

"We are so impressed."

And then they offered to help him get an apartment with Eli.

"You are taking your writing seriously, we can see that."

"Your notebook!" Roberta said. "You take it out all the time just like your father takes out his birding notebook."

"We both have Moleskines," Frank said proudly.

Julian was loading their bags into the little trunk. "It's good you packed light," he said.

"So. Now that you're pursuing your dream of being a writer in a real way . . ."

"We feel we can subsidize you for a bit longer. Think of it as a grant."

Julian slammed the trunk shut and turned to face them. His parents, who loved him and respected him and wanted him back in the fold. "You guys," he said. "You're too good."

"Well, after all," Roberta added, "we've saved so much money never going to restaurants in this pandemic."

Julian could not hug them, Jay's orders, so he put his fist to his heart, banged it against his chest a few times. "This is so generous," Julian said. "Really generous of you."

"We might still be able to get you a ticket on our flight home," Frank said, pulling out his phone.

Julian banged his fist against his heart again. One more couldn't hurt, could it? Or was it a bit extra? Okay, Julian. Speak. Woof woof, he thought. Shut up, Julian. And speak for real.

"Oh, hey," he said. He looked down. He couldn't help it. The sidewalk bulged with a tree's roots beneath it. "Thank you, Mom. Thank you, Dad. Thank you both. You're amazing. You're awesome, both of you."

He could almost hear them smiling. But still he looked down. He'd have to be extra careful when he went out to walk with Mamie. The side-walk had actually split like tectonic plates.

"Yeah, so, but I'm not going back to the city. I want to stay here. I want to live here."

Roberta tried not to look disappointed. Or surprised. Though who cared what she looked like, what expressions passed across her face? Not Julian. He was staring at the ground. As well he should be. Not going back? Living here in this soulless suburb? As he himself had described it. Staying on in this shabby, though charming, little house with two batty old ladies?

"I thought you understood that," he was saying. "You know, because . . ."

"Because you didn't want to upset us by telling us," Frank said. "Cow-ardly perhaps, but you were protecting us."

"Well, I don't know if I'd put it like that." Julian shifted his feet the way people do, people who say Well I don't know if I'd put it like that. Then he looked up at them. "Okay, yeah," he said. "I was afraid to tell you. I was protecting myself, I guess. Not you."

It's as if he were George Washington and admitted he was the one who cut down the cherry tree, Roberta thought. I cannot tell a lie. She wondered if that old shibboleth was still taught in school. Unlikely. And just as well.

"You're sure this is what you want to do?" she asked Julian.

"Yeah. I've thought about it a lot."

"The girl?" she said, hating herself even as she said the words.

"Sophie? Yeah, partly. But I like it here, Mom."

Of course it was she and Frank who had sent him here in the first place, who wanted him to be independent from them. But there's independence and there's independence! And she missed him, oh she missed him terribly. Bringing his dirty laundry up to their apartment. Mooching the odd roll of paper towel and bottle of cabernet sauvignon on his way home.

"Well, then of course you should stay," she said.

"You know, Mamie and Agatha still need me here," Julian said. "For driving."

"That's true," Frank said.

"And light bulb changing," he added a little desperately.

"So no plane ticket," Frank said. He put his phone back in his pocket.

Julian felt just as terrible as he'd known he would. Of course they hadn't already understood: he hadn't told them. But it was so obvious to him that he wasn't returning to New York. How could they not have realized he lived here now?

"I can still stay in the guesthouse," he said. "Just the way you planned. A perfect plan, right?"

"It really is a perfect plan," Roberta said.

But she said it so quietly.

"I'm sorry. I should have discussed it with you."

"We're discussing it now," Frank said. He was back to his jovial voice. "Wait! Did you hear that? It's a white-throated sparrow, I think."

Roberta put her hand on Julian's arm, then pulled him in for a hug, her N95'd face in his chest. "Fuck this fucking virus," he heard her mumble into his sweatshirt.

"Okay, okay," she said, backing away to a proper, safe distance.

"Mom, I'll miss you. And Dad. But I'll visit soon."

"Visit in the spring," Frank said. "Warbler migration."

"Anyway, the guesthouse is the perfect base for me. In my new pursuit."

"Your screenplay!" his mother said. "Much better to be out here for movie projects. We should have thought of that, Frank."

"Yup. L.A. has to open up sometime," Frank said. "And you'll be ready."

"Julian, we're proud of you whatever coast you write on."

"Well, actually—"

Frank said, "You've worked for so many years for this."

"No, wait. No." He held up his hand like a traffic cop. "I don't want to be a writer anymore."

Silence. A dramatic pause, Julian thought, not sure if he was pleased with his delivery or appalled at their faces, both of which expressed some emotion somewhere between confusion and fury. He waited a beat, then delivered his line perfectly:

"I want to be an actor!"

※

"WELL, that didn't go quite as well as I hoped," he said to Sophie later that day.

"You didn't really expect them to applaud you for leaving one impossible profession for another even less possible profession, did you?"

"No. But I didn't expect icy silence for the entire drive to the airport."

"Julian!" She kicked a pebble across the street at him. "For a boy who lives in his imagination, your imagination is very . . ."

She was clearly searching for the right words. Julian hoped it would not be *small* or *pathetic*, the two that came to his mind.

"Self-contained!" she said at last.

"Mamie," Julian said when he got home. "Sophie said my imagination is self-contained. What do you think?"

"Ah, but what is the self, Julian, dear?" she said. "Let me know when you find it."

"Shell?" Agatha asked, coming in with a basket of laundry. "I find in jeans. In pocket." She handed Julian a sand dollar, completely intact, that he'd picked up on the beach.

They had their cocktails in the garden under the stars. Agatha allowed Julian to carry in the tray. He had chilled the glasses, placed three olives in each. The teapot was Mamie's best, the teacup and saucer from the same set. He poured Agatha her tea, then after some showy shaking, he poured the martinis, one for Mamie and one for himself. It was an acquired taste he had acquired, first because the drink was so beautiful, now because he liked it. Like atonal music, he thought. Like Los Angeles, the soulless suburb city. Like dogs, even this one sprawled beneath the orange tree, one paw twitching. Was Prince Jan Saint Bernard lying there dreaming, like his fictional predecessor, of rescuing people from the snow?

"Thank you for accepting me into the Colony," Julian said.

Mamie lifted her glass, Agatha her cup.

They did not go inside to watch the news that night. It was too sweet a night. Julian gave a brief performance of his breakup with Juliet and bowed as they clapped.

"She had your number," Mamie said.

"But you so good boy," Agatha said. "You deserve umbrella. Many umbrella. When it rain, boy needs umbrella."

Mamie thought of her grandfather and his big black umbrella, of the long walks in the sunshine beneath its shade. "There are umbrellas and there are umbrellas," she said. No one responded. Perhaps they hadn't heard, which was probably just as well.

"Did I ever tell you the story about Sam Behrman?" Mamie said. "A brilliant New York writer lured out here by filthy lucre? He was adapting a script from a novel in which the main character dies in the middle of the story. 'The novelist might have gone for all that death,' the producer told Sam. 'But out here we don't care for it.'"

Out here. Julian liked the sound of that. Out here we don't care for it. Then he thought of Mamie's words: "Ah, but what is the self, Julian? Let me know when you find it." He pulled the shell out of his pocket, the perfectly round sand dollar with its five lacy leaves engraved on it. He'd found it on the beach and planned to wash it and give it to Sophie. A thin thread of sand came out of the tiny hole in the bottom, and he wiped it off his shirt. The word *self* was spoken and Agatha heard the word *shell*. Maybe she had it right. Did it matter, really, what the self was any more than what the shell was?

After dinner, Julian fell asleep on the couch and Agatha and Mamie dozed in their chairs. Then Mamie started awake.

"Agatha," she whispered. "Agatha, where's your pocketbook?" She pointed at Agatha's unencumbered wrists.

Agatha shrugged. "Mace past expiration date."

"That really is what you kept there? All this time?"

"I am practical person. Now I am free person."

Mamie had never thought of the pocketbooks as manacles. If only Agatha had worn one on each wrist she might have caught on.

"Do you think the queen carries Mace in her pocketbook?" she asked.

"I hope."

She and Agatha watched Julian breathe. He snored softly, rhythmically. They watched him as if he were a movie. They watched him for a long time.

Mamie said, "That beard. It reminds me of my grandfather. It just does."

Thank god Julian does not smoke cigars, she thought later as she and Prince Jan climbed into bed. Prince Jan's head hit the pillow with a thud. You may not know how to save a life in a land without snow, she told him, but why should you? That is for the scientists and their vaccines. And she fell asleep trying to remember the name of Schoenberg's Saint Bernard.

That night, asleep on the couch, Julian dreamed that he wandered without punishment under the palms. The air was sweet. The sand was soft and cool beneath his feet. The waves were loud, and a gentle fog rolled in and enveloped him. Mamie was somewhere nearby. He could hear her.

Joyously, his grandmother was calling out into the mist. He could hear her voice.

"Bring in Beethoven's hair!" she called. "Bring in Beethoven's hair!"

Acknowledgments

IN THIS BOOK ABOUT MEMORIES AND STORIES, I HAVE OFTEN TURNED TO THE memories and stories of others. I hope the novel reveals the depth of my admiration, gratitude, and awe for those who, having lived through such dark times, shared their words and music and ideas. These memoirs and letters and diaries in particular were an inspiration for Mamie's fictional life:

Minima Moralia by Theodor Adorno; *It Was All Quite Different* by Vicki Baum; *People in a Diary* by S. N. Behrman; *The Memoirs of Elias Canetti* by Elias Canetti; *Here Lies the Heart* by Mercedes de Acosta; *Diaries Volume One: 1939–1960* by Christopher Isherwood; *Dear Los Angeles: The City in Diaries and Letters, 1542 to 2018* edited by David Kipen; *The Story of a Novel* by Thomas Mann; *Schoenberg Remembered* by Dika Newlin; *The Vienna Paradox* by Marjorie Perloff; *The Doctor Faustus Dossier* edited by E. Randol Schoenberg; *The Kindness of Strangers* by Salka Viertel; *The Vienna I Knew* by Joseph Wechsberg; and *The World of Yesterday* by Stefan Zweig.

For reading and reading and reading with ever fresh eyes, thank you, Janet. Thanks also to Adam Gopnik, saving me from compositional disaster since 1993. For allowing me to sit in on her Zoom twelve-tone composition classes, thank you, Judith Berkson. All misperceptions, needless to say, are mine. And always a thank you to Molly Friedrich and Lucy Carson for keeping the band together. Finally, thank you Sarah Crichton. That shadow following you around is me.

About the Author

Cathleen Schine is the author of *The Grammarians*, *The Three Weissmanns of Westport*, and *The Love Letter*, among other novels. She has contributed to the *New Yorker*, the *New York Review of Books*, the *New York Times Magazine*, and the *New York Times Book Review*. She lives in Los Angeles.